DANICA FLYNN

Against The
BOARDS

AGAINST THE BOARDS
A PHILADELPHIA BULLDOGS BOOK

DANICA FLYNN

Against The Boards

Copyright © 2021 Danica Flynn
This is a work of fiction. Names, characters, businesses, places, events, and incidents are either products of the author's imagination or used in a fictitious manner. Any resemblance to actual persons, living or dead, or actual events is purely coincidental.
All rights reserved.

ebook ISBN: 978-1-7342012-8-4
Print ISBN: 978-1-7342012-9-1

Cover Photography: FotoAndalucia / Shutterstock
Cover Design: Emily's World Of Design
Editor: Charlie Knight

Content Note: This book deals with some mentions of biphobia from a previous partner and parents.

For all my bi babies, out or not, you matter.

PLAYLIST

"Roxanne" By The Police
"Cold Hard Bitch" By Jet
"King of Brooklyn" By Devil Doll
"Sweater Weather" By The Neighborhood
"Truth Hurts" By Lizzo
"Elevator Love Letter" By Stars
"I Was A Fool" By Tegan And Sara
"Dope on a Rope" By The Growlers
"The Suburbs" By Arcade Fire
"Howling For You" By The Black Keys
"Take me To Church" By Hozier
"Are You Gonna Be My Girl" By Jet
"Amber" By 311
"Kiss This" By The Struts
"She's Kerosene" By The Interrupters

CHAPTER ONE

ROXANNE

"So, when can you start?"

I stared at the blonde woman in front of me in disbelief. I thought the interview was going well but not *that* well.

"Whenever you need me," I said with a smile.

When I saw the posting for the sales manager position with the Philadelphia Bulldogs, I applied on a whim. I never thought they would call me back or offer it to me on the spot. I needed to get out of St. Catharines and would have taken any job. Literally any job if it meant working for an NHL team. Even if it meant leaving Canada.

Quinn smiled at me. "I'm gonna be honest: I need the position filled ASAP. Can you start tomorrow?"

"Tomorrow?" I choked out.

"Do you need to give notice to your current employer?"

I shook my head.

After my messy break-up, I had been so gutted that I ended up quitting my job. Not the best plan when your ex-girlfriend kicked you out after you caught *her* cheating on you. Jobless and technically homeless, I had nothing holding me back from moving to a different country.

Quinn flipped through the paperwork on her desk. "Shit, you're Canadian, right?"

"Oh, I don't have to wait for a visa. I have dual citizenship."

"Oh, perfect, because I'd rather not wait. We're not in the playoffs again this year, but there's a lot of prep work for next season."

I stared at the Bulldogs' calendar on the wall behind Quinn, and dread spread through me. This month's photo depicted right-winger Tristan "TJ" Desjardins lobbing the puck into the back of the net. Kinda weird to be staring into the face of your twin brother during a job interview. Although, it might have explained why I applied for the job to begin with.

"There's something I should tell you first," I admitted, and I pointed to the calendar behind her. "That's my brother."

She stared at the photo of my brother on her wall and then looked at me curiously for a second. "Huh. Now that you mention it, I can see the resemblance."

"We're twins. Is that gonna be a conflict of interest?"

She tipped back her head and laughed.

I raised an eyebrow in confusion.

"Sorry. The GM's my husband, so it's funny you asked that. As long as we keep things professional, I don't foresee it being an issue."

A lot of NHL teams had fraternization policies, so it was interesting that the Bulldogs didn't have one. The OHL team I worked for back home in Canada had a strict policy. Not that it ever mattered to me. I hadn't been single. Or into douchey hockey players who reminded me too much of my brother.

"Can you start tomorrow?" she asked again.

"Absolutely."

"Perfect!"

She went over the information I needed for tomorrow and then walked me out of the office. She shook my hand in the hall. "I can't wait for you to get started."

"You don't even have to wait a full twenty-four hours," I said with a grin.

She waved goodbye to me, and then I walked outside. Once there, I finally took a breath.

Holy shit. I got a job with an actual NHL team!

Anxiety coursed through me when I realized I needed to find a place to live.

I pulled out my phone and hit the only number I had on speed dial. I pressed my phone to my ear while I paced in the parking lot and waited for Tristan to answer. While everyone else referred to my brother by his hockey nickname, our family still called him Tristan. Like how he was the only person I tolerated calling me Roxie.

"Yo, what up, slut?" Tristan teased in greeting.

"Hoe!" I teased back.

Your brother calling you a slut might offend other women, but Tristan and I had always teased each other this way. It was kind of our thing, and I knew he didn't mean it.

"What's up?" he asked again.

I sighed. "Theoretically, if I needed to move to Philly, where would be the best place to move to?"

"What?"

I dug my headphones out of my purse and popped them into my ears. I opened the web browser on my phone and scrolled through apartment listings. "Is Kensington a good area? Or Northern Liberties?"

"Wait, time-out. What do you mean theoretically?"

Maybe it was a twin thing, but I could practically see his brow furrowing at my question. "Okay, not theoretically. I'm moving to Philly."

"Okay..." He trailed off. "Okay, cool. Come down after I get back from The World Hockey Championship. We'll go tou—"

"No, Tristan, I need to move today. ASAP."

"Is this because you're homeless?"

I squeezed my eyes shut and swore under my breath.

My brother and I told each other everything. Although he knew about my break-up, I had conveniently left out the part about Lisa kicking me out of the apartment. I had a pretty good idea who told him, considering I had been sleeping in her guest room for the last two weeks.

"Nat told you?"

"I called her."

Shit, that wasn't good.

Tristan had dated my friend Natalie in high school, but she had been cruel to him. So cruel that I thought she was the reason he never let himself get close to anyone. I didn't think they were on speaking terms. If Tristan called her because he knew I was keeping something from him, that meant my life had spiraled more out of control than I realized.

"I'm worried about you," my brother said in a small voice.

"I'm fine! I just got a brand new job, and I'm gonna start a new life in Philly. So get used to seeing me a lot more."

"Where are you?"

"Broad Street."

"What's the job?" he asked in a huff.

"Sales Manager with the Bulldogs."

"Stay there. I'm coming to get you."

He didn't even say goodbye before he promptly hung up. Typical TJ Desjardins! Shoot the puck first and pray to the hockey gods it went into the back of the net.

I scrolled through apartment listings while I waited for my brother and tried to figure out my next step. The rumble of an engine ten minutes later made me look up. I rolled my eyes when I saw the sleek black Maserati idling in front of me. Tristan rolled the window down and grinned at me from the driver's side. I rolled my eyes at his backward baseball cap. Was it the law for hockey players to wear those?

"Get in!" he yelled.

I sighed and got into the passenger seat.

He pulled out of the parking lot and sped off. "Is this because of your break-up?"

I scowled at him. "She broke my heart."

"I'm sorry," he muttered. He squinted at me, assessing my appearance for the first time since I got into his car. "Hey! You changed your hair. You look better with dark hair. Blonde was gross on you."

"Thank you?"

I had been a little lost after my break-up, so Nat convinced me a change in my look would make me feel better. It had, and as much as I hated to admit it, I did look better with darker hair.

Tristan smirked. "It was a compliment."

I punched him in the arm. "Don't be a jerk."

"You want to talk about it?" he asked.

Tristan didn't like to talk about feelings. The fact he asked meant he knew how much I was hurting. I sometimes wondered if my brother had any feelings at all. Like, maybe

I had absorbed them all in the womb. It would explain why I was such an emotional wreck for most of my life.

"I needed to get out of St. Catharines," I admitted.

"But all the way to the States?"

"I have no one in Canada."

"You still have—"

"No. They made it very clear they want nothing to do with me."

"Roxie, that's not true. They'll come around," he reassured me. He parked his car in the garage of his condo building. "Mom just doesn't understand bisexuality."

"Yeah, well, what about Dad?"

Tristan sighed. "I don't know."

"It hurts," I muttered.

When I came out to my family, Tristan had the best reaction. He shrugged and asked if I wanted another beer. Mom said, "Bisexuality isn't real," and that I needed to "choose a side." What hurt more than her biphobia, though, was my dad's silence. That was four years ago. I came out to them during my third year at university, and when they didn't accept me, I never went home again. Occasionally they called me, but I had nothing to say to them, and I let their calls go unanswered.

Tristan squeezed my hand. "I know."

I sighed and tried not to think about it. "So you never answered my question. Where's a good area to move to?"

"Okay, here's the plan. You stay in my room while I'm overseas, and we can look together when I get back, or Kat can help you."

I raised an eyebrow. "Who's Kat?"

He barked out a laugh. "The GM's assistant. Also my goaltender's mom, so she's off-limits."

"Really?"

He suddenly looked very solemn. "I'd never break the code."

I rolled my eyes. Hockey boys and their codes; it all seemed rather archaic to me. I'd never been interested in hockey players, mostly because they got mad I could outshoot them. Sorry, my dudes! When you grew up with a Stanley Cup winner for a father, not playing hockey wasn't an option.

"Noah won't mind me staying at your place?"

"No, because he already moved in with his girl."

"He moved in with Dinah already?"

He nodded. "A bit soon, eh?"

We shared a concerned look.

Tristan's roommate Noah had been in love with their next-door neighbor for a while. She broke his heart when she broke up with him a couple of months ago. They seemed better now, but I was protective of Noah. He was like a second brother to me, and I didn't want to see him hurt again. Noah was way too nice, and I was afraid people took advantage of his kindness.

"Wait, so you don't have an open room I could use?"

Tristan abruptly cut the engine and got out of the car.

I followed him towards the elevator. "Well?"

"I have a new roommate," he said. His grim expression told me I wouldn't like whatever bomb he was about to drop on me.

"Tristan, who moved into Noah's room?" I asked.

"Benny."

"Benny?"

"Yes, Benny."

"Like...Michael Bennett?" I asked and prayed to the hockey gods he meant literally anyone else.

Please tell me he had another friend who went by the

name Benny. Please, anyone else but the six-foot-four left-winger who took one look at me and asked me if my tits were fake. There was no way in hell I was living with Benny while I searched for a place. Even if he was nice to look at with his impeccably groomed beard that looked amazing against his brown skin.

Please hockey gods, be on my side this time!

"Do you know another Benny?" Tristan asked and gave me the signature Desjardins grin.

"Oh, you have got to be fucking kidding me!"

My twin laughed the whole elevator ride up to his floor. I didn't understand why he thought this was so goddamn funny. This was my worst nightmare.

CHAPTER TWO

BENNY

Noah screwed the last leg of the bed together, and we hefted my memory foam mattress on top of the frame. Thank the hockey gods most of my teammates were like me — over six feet tall and strong. I could have put this together myself, but Noah was good with his hands and too nice to say no when you asked him for help.

Noah wiped his hands on his jeans. "That should do it, eh?"

I nodded and wiped the sweat off my forehead. Moving freaking sucked. "Thanks. I would have asked T for help, but he ran out of here in a huff a few minutes ago."

At twenty-five, I shouldn't have been happy about having a roommate. But when my long-term girlfriend and I broke up, I needed a place to stay, and TJ had come in clutch. His old roommate, Noah, had moved in with his girlfriend, so TJ offered me his vacant room. After our season ended without a playoff run a couple of weeks ago, I hightailed it back to Boston to visit my abuelos, but I came back today to move my stuff in. Mostly because my ex wanted me to get my stuff out of her house.

"Um..." Noah trailed off.

I raised an eyebrow at the pained look on his face. He rubbed the back of his neck. I spent a lot of time with the guy; I knew that was one of his nervous ticks. You don't spend a lot of time on someone's wing without learning a lot about them.

"What's up?" I asked.

"You don't know?" he asked and cringed.

"Know what?"

Noah didn't have time to explain what I didn't know because I heard the front door of the condo open and TJ's hyena laughter. Then I heard a familiar feminine voice with him, and I froze.

No. For the love of God, no.

I glared at Noah. "What is *she* doing here?"

Noah cringed. "I thought T told you since he texted me to come over here to distract you."

"That's why you came over to see if I needed help?" I asked.

I thought Noah was just being nice. The dude was a legit Canadian stereotype; I never thought he had an ulterior motive.

He ran a pale hand through his newly grown-out beard.

"Noah," I growled.

"Rox is moving here."

I felt all the blood rush to my head. I hoped he meant Philly and not here as in this condo.

Here's the thing. I never planned on having a feud with Roxanne Desjardins. When I first met her, my brain shut off at the sight of the curvy, statuesque woman. Instead of saying, "Hello," like a normal person, I blurted out, "Are those things real?" while staring at her tits.

I malfunctioned when I saw a beautiful woman, and she was one of the hottest women I had ever seen. Too bad she hated my guts.

Let's just say the animosity between us wasn't exactly one-sided anymore. It didn't stop my wandering eyes from liking what they saw, though. She made my blood boil in more than one way. Dealing with Roxanne was normally only a yearly occurrence since she lived in Canada, but if she was moving to Philly, that spelled trouble.

"Be nice, and don't stare at her chest so much," Noah said.

I opened my mouth to protest, but he sent me a piercing glare. Okay, he definitely had me there. A couple months ago, when Noah and his girl were broken up, Rox came to town to check up on Noah. He may have called me out about staring at Rox too much.

I couldn't help it, though. She might get under my skin, but she was all long legs and curves a big guy like me wanted to get his hands on. It was too bad she wanted to murder me in my sleep. She was probably a hellcat in the sack. Not that I would ever find out.

"Be nice," he said again and walked out into the living room.

I usually was nice, but she was the one who always started it, and once it started, it seemed like neither of us backed down from a fight.

With a sigh, I followed him into the other room. Noah sat on the couch next to Rox while TJ sat in the armchair. I slid into the armchair on the other side of the room and tried to avoid eye contact.

I peered over at TJ with a raised eyebrow. "What's up?" I asked.

TJ looked at me and then at his twin as if to warn us to play nice. "Roxie got a job in Philly, and she needs a place to stay for a while."

Oh no. This was what I was afraid of. There was no way we could cohabitate. We would kill each other.

Rox had her arms crossed over her chest and a scowl on her face. She looked thrilled to learn that we would be roommates for the foreseeable future. What a shocker. Not like I particularly wanted to live with someone who hated me with the passion of a thousand fiery suns.

I studied her for a second and noticed her bleach blonde hair was now as black as midnight. It didn't come to her waist anymore either, but it still looked like hair you wanted to sink your hands into. Paired with her Snow White complexion and her signature dark lipstick, the change looked great on her.

Too good.

Goddamnit, why does she have to be so hot?

My eyes tracked down her body, and I held in the groan at how sexy her long legs looked in that tight pencil skirt. At six-foot-four, tall girls did it for me. The Desjardins twins clocked in at five-foot-eleven. On T, it made him short for a hockey player, but on Rox, it made her look like a sexy Amazon.

"My eyes are up here," she snapped.

I scowled and crossed my arms over my chest. I opened my mouth to retort, but Noah sent me a frosty glare, so I swallowed it instead.

TJ kicked her foot. "Be nice."

"What the fuck for?" she asked.

I scrubbed a hand across my bearded jaw and tried to be civil. "So, where did you get a job?" I asked.

She arched a perfectly sculpted eyebrow at me. "Why do you care?"

I sighed, and Noah gave me a concerned look. Noah was too nice, so he didn't handle confrontation like this well. I wished I could be like him. I wished I could let things roll off my back, but I was a hothead.

"Sorry for making conversation!" I snapped back.

We glared at each other from across the room.

TJ pointed at us. "Can you two stop being children and be civil?"

Rox shook her head. At least she wasn't glaring at me anymore. "You know what? I'm exhausted from the drive this morning. I'm gonna head back to my hotel and take a nap."

TJ sighed. "Okay. Let me drive you."

She glared at him. "I'm perfectly capable of finding my way back there on my own, thank you very much."

"Roxie."

"Tristan."

The twins exchanged a long look, and I swear they were communicating telepathically. Finally, she huffed out a groan and nodded.

"Hey, you're gonna come over later, right?" Noah asked her.

Rox furrowed her brow. "For what?"

"Dinah and I are having a housewarming party."

Rox smiled and nodded. "Yeah, bud, I'll come over."

"Dinah will want to see you," Noah said with a smile. The dude was all smiles now that he and his lady had smoothed out their issues.

"I want to see her too. That lady gets me."

I snorted at that. Noah's girl could be blunt, so it made sense that the two women got along. Rox fixed me with another glare before storming out of the condo. TJ gave me a glare that mirrored his sister's before he followed behind her.

I sighed when they left, but Noah started laughing.

"What's so funny?" I asked.

"Benny, be honest."

"About what?"

He narrowed his blue eyes at me. "Dude! You two kinda get off on it, eh?"

I glared at him. "What are you talking about?"

"Fighting! Sometimes I feel like I'm watching some fucked up mating ritual."

"We don't get off on it," I lied.

Okay, he had a point because she looked hot when she was all flustered. I didn't do it on purpose, though. Not all the time.

Noah squinted at me for a moment. "You two should do us all a favor and finally bang it out."

"What?"

He did not just suggest that.

"You heard me."

"Dude, no."

He stroked his beard in thought. "Admit it. You've been circling each other for years."

"We hate each other. We circle each other looking to fight about nothing," I grumbled.

Like what were we just fighting about? Nothing! I asked her where she got a job, and she snapped at me. I was actually trying to be nice for once.

He squinted at me suspiciously. "You realize you blatantly check her out, right?"

I gritted my teeth but didn't deny it. I totally did that, and she caught me doing it. Again.

If she was any other woman, I would have put the moves on her. If she didn't constantly pick arguments with me, it might have been a different situation. Not gonna lie, I've had my fantasies about getting her underneath me. Or on top of me. But they were just fantasies for when I was bored and horny.

Note to self: never look at a beautiful woman and blurt out the first thing your sex-deprived, horny brain was thinking. I'd learned that lesson the hard way.

CHAPTER THREE

ROXANNE

I wasn't in the mood for a party, especially if I had to be up early tomorrow for my first day at my new job. But it seemed like it was important to Noah for me to come over, so I sucked it up and drove back to Old City after taking a nap in my hotel.

I hoped the hockey gods were on my side this time and Benny kept his distance. I was already reconsidering sleeping in Tristan's room while he was in Russia. Maybe Dinah and Noah would take pity on me and let me crash on their couch? A girl could dream.

"Hey, you came!" Dinah greeted me when she opened the door.

She handed me a beer, which I graciously took, and I bent down to hug her. "Congrats on the book!"

"Thanks! Oh, you should meet my friend Fi. Do you like young adult sci-fi?" she asked.

"Sometimes."

"She's Riley's wife."

I almost spit out my beer, and she laughed at my expression. "Aaron Riley?"

Riley was hot if you were into beefy blonde alpha males, which I wasn't, but I could appreciate a pretty face. I thought he was a guy who only hit it and quit it, though. He had hit on me a couple of times before I told him I was taken. We became friends when he figured out I could drink him under the table. I guess that meant he respected me. Men.

Her smile crinkled around her emerald eyes. "I know, right? You'll have to let Fi tell you."

That must be an interesting story. Aaron Riley with a wife. Wow. He was one of the last guys on the team I expected that from.

"TJ said you're moving here," Dinah said.

"I got offered a job with the Bulldogs on the spot."

"Oh, cool! Doing what?"

"Sales. Same thing I was doing with the OHL. It surprised me when they offered it to me so quickly."

Dinah looked thoughtful for a second. "Wait, do you have to wait around for a work visa?"

I shook my head. "Nope! Tristan and I were born in New York, so we have dual citizenship."

"Oh, I didn't know that."

I shrugged. "After Dad retired, we moved back to Canada. I think Tristan kinda forgot."

"That sounds like T."

I smirked at her and took another sip of my beer.

She pointed at my black hair. "Are you okay? With everything?"

I pursed my lips in thought.

When Lisa cheated on me, the first person I called was Tristan. The second call had been to Dinah, but only at her insistence. We weren't that close, but close enough that I knew I could unload on her. She was a good listener.

I shook my head and took a huge gulp of my beer. "Not really."

She had a sad look on her face. "I sorta get what you're going through. It was hard to let go of Jason, and Noah..."

"Is too nice?" I offered.

"Yeah. I'm not sure I deserve a second chance with him. I really messed up."

"You crushed his heart into a thousand pieces!"

She sighed. "I was scared."

I understood what she meant, but I still worried about Noah and whether she would break his heart again.

"You and Noah are good now, right?" I asked.

She nodded with a big smile. "Yeah! He made me promise that the next time I get scared, I talk to him like a grown-up. He's too good to me."

"Who knew Noah would be the adult in the relationship?"

She made a face at me, and I nudged her with my shoulder, so she knew I was just joking.

Noah was an anomaly for a hockey player. Most were complete douchebags, but not Noah. He was the epitome of niceness. If I had been interested in any of my brother's teammates, it would have been Noah Kennedy. Too bad he was like a brother to me.

"So wait...where are you staying?" she asked.

I groaned. "Next door until I can find a place."

Dinah's eyes widened. "Really? With Benny?"

I gritted my teeth. "Unfortunately."

"Okay, why do you hate him?"

"He asked if my tits were fake!"

"He apologized!"

"He's so annoying. He thinks he's God's gift to women. Why does he have to be so hot?"

Dinah bit her lip and tried not to laugh. "So you hate him because... you think he's hot?"

"Shut up!"

She laughed that throaty laugh of hers, but then someone tapped her on the shoulder and distracted her. I wandered off into the dining room. I finished my beer and then switched to water while I gazed out at the city skyline.

Moving to a new city with zero plans was impulsive. What did it say about me that I was moving to a different country? If my brother didn't live here, I might have reconsidered. But working for an NHL team was a step-up for my career. I would have been a fool not to take the job.

I felt a presence sidle up beside me. It didn't surprise me when I flicked my eyes to the side and saw Benny standing next to me. *Oh, here we go.* I didn't feel like fighting with him right then.

My eyes tracked over him. He was wearing a red flannel button-down shirt that clung tight against his broad chest. He had rolled his sleeves up to his elbows, showing off his toned brown forearms.

Oh my God, those forearms! Why did this infuriating man have to be so hot?

"Can I help you?" I asked, with a hint of venom in my voice.

He held his hands up in surrender. "Just saying hi."

"Mmmhmm."

"Can I ask you something?"

"No," I growled.

I looked down at the floor and tried not to stare at his forearms or at how nice his beard looked. I loved a nicely groomed beard on a man; it was a huge turn-on. Benny's beard looked so good against his dark complexion. I would have appreciated his hotness more if he wasn't such a jerk face to me.

I was having a hard time focusing on getting him to leave me alone when he crossed his forearms over his broad chest. "Rox?"

I glared. "What the fuck do you want?"

"Tell the truth. Why do you really hate me?" he asked.

"Because you're an asshole."

He smirked and stepped closer to me, caging me in against the wall. He leaned down and bent his lips to my ear. "Then why are you looking at me like you want to ride my dick?"

A shiver ran down my spine at his breath purring in my ear. Then my brain processed what he had said.

Wait...what the fuck?

I pushed against his chest. "That's why! You're such a dick!"

He smirked at me, and his brown eyes walked down my body. "Come on, Rox. Tell the truth. You love how I get you all riled up. You know you want to—"

I cut him off by throwing my cup of water right in his face and storming off.

I'd admit it was an immature thing to do, but it was my knee-jerk reaction. Sometimes I was a volatile asshole, and he seemed to bring it out in me. Tristan being the person who shoots the puck first and hopes it goes into the net? Yeah, I was exactly the same way. It was great on the ice deking past a defenseman, but not so much in real life when your emotions got the better of you.

As I headed for the door, I heard my brother calling me. He grabbed my wrist to keep me from leaving. "Roxie, what did he say to you?"

"He said I looked like I wanted to ride his dick!" I seethed.

Tristan tried not to laugh, but he couldn't help himself. "I'm sorry. I made him do shots. He's pretty drunk."

"That's not an excuse!"

Tristan sighed and pulled something out of his wallet. "Here." He pressed the object into my palm, and I realized it was a key. "I fly out early tomorrow, so you'll need a key."

I shoved it back at him. "I'm going to get a hotel until I find a place. Or maybe Dinah and Noah will take pity on me and let me stay on their couch."

"You can't do that. Just play nice with Benny, okay? For my sake?"

"You're not gonna persuade me to stay tonight?"

He shook his head but pressed the key back into my hand. "Nah, you're in a shitty mood."

"Bye, hoe!"

"Bye, slut!"

I left in a huff and made the trek back to the parking garage. When I got behind the wheel of my car, I realized Benny was right. I *had* been looking at him like he was a snack I wanted to eat up.

It wasn't lost on me that the man was ridiculously attractive. If I was being perfectly honest with myself, sometimes I wasn't sure if I wanted to punch him in the dick or put it in my mouth. Maybe a little of both sometimes. I may have thought Lisa was my endgame, but it didn't make me any less bisexual. I still recognized a hot guy when I saw one.

One thing was for certain: I needed to get laid. Before I did something even more reckless than moving to a different country. Like hate banging my nemesis.

CHAPTER FOUR

BENNY

My head felt like someone had been bashing it with Thor's Hammer. That's how I always felt after I drank with TJ. I ran a hand down my face and scratched my beard. Memories of my behavior last night came flooding back to me in a rush.

Rox was right to hate my guts.

I couldn't believe the shit I said to her last night. I never would have said that if I was sober, but my drunk, horny brain took over. When I saw her from across the room, all I thought about was how to get her beneath me and moaning my name.

What is wrong with me?

I blamed TJ for forcing me to do shots with him last night, even though I should know my limits. If Rox didn't hate me already, she definitely did now, and I didn't blame her.

I picked up my phone when it beeped with a text notification.

TJ: *You're a dick, but seriously please don't kill each other while I'm in Russia. Be the big man and apologize.*

I put my phone down and dropped my head back against the wall. TJ was right; I owed her an apology. I had been a massive jerk last night, and she hadn't deserved that. I knew I should be the bigger person and apologize, and I knew I should do it in person.

Hungover and feeling like hot death, I hopped in the shower. After, I crawled back into my bed and wanted to hide for the rest of the day. I didn't handle hangovers well. During hockey season, I limited my drinking because I was very careful about what I put into my body. I took my nutrition and my career seriously. Despite my size, I should have been able to handle my liquor, but not as much as my teammate TJ.

My phone beeped with another notification, and I saw a text pop up from my ex.

STEPHANIE: *Come get the rest of your shit.*

I rolled out of bed with a groan and went into the kitchen to make coffee and toast. I needed coffee before I did anything else and food to soak up all the alcohol in my system. I'd probably need to rope one of my teammates into helping me get the rest of my things, too. Riley still owed me a favor, so I'd call him later.

I had just set my plate and coffee mug down at the island when there was a knock on the door. I walked over and opened the door and wasn't surprised in the least to find Noah behind it.

Good. Now I was roping him into helping me today.

"You're a dick," he said and walked inside.

I groaned and sat back down at the kitchen island. I took a bite out of my toast and sipped on my coffee. I wasn't even sure I could keep this plain toast down. I never learned my lesson about drinking with TJ. I didn't think that dude had ever been hungover in his life. Not sure what it was with the Desjardins' genes, but the twins could drink an entire hockey team under the table.

Noah sat next to me and stared at me without saying a word. He was one of the younger guys on the team, and I saw his immaturity shine through when he and Dinah were going through their rough patch. However, he was always the guy to tell you when you messed up and to help you fix it. He was one of the good ones.

"I don't know what came over me," I admitted.

Noah smirked at me. "I can't believe you said that to her."

I didn't need to ask who told him. Noah and TJ were tight, and before Rox stormed out, I saw her talking to her brother. I didn't blame her for hating me even more after last night. I acted like the dickhead she thought I was.

"You got it bad," Noah said with a lopsided grin.

I grunted in response.

"You should apologize."

"I want to do it in person."

His eyebrows shot up in surprise.

I glared at him. "Don't look at me like that."

He held up his hands in surrender. "What are you up to today? You want to get some training in?"

"Actually, I need your help."

"What's going on?" he asked.

I laughed. "Why are you so nice?"

"Maybe you could learn from me."

I ignored that, even though he was probably right. Noah was a saint. A lot of the guys gave him shit for being a 'stereotypical Canadian,' but I think that was just his personality.

"I still have stuff at Stephanie's, and she wants me to get it today. We better do it now while she's at work. Can you lend a hand?"

"Of course!"

I finished up my breakfast and listened to Noah tell me about Dinah's three older brothers grilling him last night. Dinah's brothers were super protective of her, but she didn't let them get away with it. I was glad Dinah and Noah had figured things out because I had never seen my linemate look happier.

I hated to admit it, but I was jealous of what they had. I'd been happy with Stephanie, but she wanted more. A lot of women said they didn't want marriage and kids, but in my experience, that was a lie. When Stephanie asked if I ever thought marriage was in our future, I couldn't lie to her. I didn't want to get married or have kids.

Noah followed me to Stephanie's place, and we spent a couple of hours packing up my stuff into our respective vehicles. I owed Noah one. I then left my key on Stephanie's kitchen counter with a note that read 'sorry' in my sloppy handwriting. I wished things had gone differently, but there wasn't any room for compromise when you wanted different things.

I spent the rest of the day unpacking my stuff in my new condo, even though I was half wondering if I should get in my SUV and drive up to Boston until training camp.

Eventually, I called my sister because I needed her advice.

"What's this? A call from my baby brother?" Liliana teased when she answered the phone.

"Hi, dweeb," I said.

"Hey dickhead," she joked back.

I groaned. "I really am."

"What do you mean?"

She laughed for a long time after I explained everything that had happened.

"That was bad, right?" I asked her.

She laughed her ass off some more. "I can't believe you asked her that! And told me!"

My sister and I were pretty close, so me telling her this wasn't that weird. I was the first person she came out to. It hadn't gone well with our parents; they disowned her, and Liliana went to live with our grandparents while she finished high school. I had wanted to go live with them, too, to escape the insufferable fights my parents had day in and day out, but Dad wouldn't allow it. I'd have more sympathy for my mom if she didn't look my sister in the eye and tell her she wasn't welcome in their home. Since leaving for Colorado after I got drafted, the only home I went back to was my grandparents.

"Why did you ask her that?"

"I don't know," I sighed. "I was very drunk."

"Michael!" my sister scolded. "Tell the truth!"

"Did you use your 'mom' voice on me?"

"Yes! Tell the truth."

"I don't know." I paced around my room in annoyance. "She annoys me. She's still mad about what I said the first time we met."

"You asked if her tits were fake; I don't blame her."

"That was three years ago! And I didn't mean to say it out loud!"

Liliana laughed. "Oh, brother, you have it bad."

"I do not!"

"You don't? You basically asked if she wanted to fuck you. Please, explain to me how you don't?"

I spluttered before blurting, "I wanted to know why she

hated me so much. The other part was because I drank too much tequila with her brother."

"She hates your guts because you ask her rude questions!"

My sister wasn't wrong. I knew I messed up, and I'd own up to it. I was trying to be nice to Rox last night, but when she glared at me, my lizard brain chanted, *Say something really rude to her to piss her off. She's hot when she's mad*. No other woman ever made me react that way, so out of character. I didn't know what it was about Rox.

"Why did you ask that?" my sister asked again.

I sighed. "Because she's hot when she's mad. And maybe it's fun to poke the bear."

"Jesus. Look, you need to apologize. You should make her dinner."

I didn't think I heard her right.

"What?"

"She started a new job today, right? She's probably super stressed from trying to learn everything at once. Make dinner when she gets home tonight and apologize. Try to bridge the gap so you can leave the past in the past."

"TJ said she's going through a hard time, and Noah told me her long-time girlfriend cheated on her."

Liliana swore on the other line. "You remember when Kelly cheated on you?"

Kelly had been my high school girlfriend who stayed in Boston when I got drafted by Colorado. It hadn't lasted long. I came home to surprise her in her dorm room, and she wasn't alone. My chest ached thinking about it.

"It really hurt. I was miserable for months."

"Exactly. She's probably really hurting. Maybe her lashing out isn't about you right now. Try to be nice to her—and stop saying rude things!"

My sister always had the best advice. "Thanks, Lil."

"Mmmhmm. Hey, make her your pozole."

I stroked my beard. It wasn't a bad idea. Making pozole was kind of my specialty.

Growing up, my grandmother made me and my sister learn how to cook authentic Mexican food in her kitchen. She wanted us to keep in touch with our mother's roots and remember where we came from. I loved that as a kid, especially on those days when my parents' fights got to be too much, and we retreated to our grandparents' home for comfort. I was a pretty good cook thanks to my grandmother, and I inherited her love of cooking for others. My sister teased me and said making food for others was my love language, whatever the fuck that meant.

"It's not a bad idea."

"See, I'm always right. Make her dinner and then you two can finally get married and have cute babies."

"Liliana!" I scolded.

"What?"

My family didn't get that I didn't want the whole marriage and kids thing. I loved my nephews, but I never wanted kids myself. My family had a hard time understanding that.

"You know how I feel about that. Besides, making her pozole doesn't mean any of that will happen."

She laughed. "I don't know about that one, buddy."

"Ugh, why did I call you? Wicked annoying!"

"Calm down. The Masshole is coming out."

"Bite me!"

"Admit that you want to have giant, hockey-playing babies with Roxanne Desjardins."

"I don't!" I huffed.

"Whatever you say!" she teased. "I gotta go; I have a client coming in."

"Give my love to Nina and the kids."

I hung up with my sister and started drafting up my grocery list for dinner. I'd hit up the local Mexican-owned grocer, so I could get the best ingredients to make my pozole as authentic as possible. Maybe if I fed Rox, she wouldn't be as angry with me. A guy could dream.

CHAPTER FIVE

ROXANNE

I checked my lipstick in the mirror of my car for the fiftieth time and smoothed an invisible wrinkle from my skirt. To say I was nervous for my first day was an understatement. I had been a sales associate with the Niagara Tigers in the OHL for the past couple of years, so this sales manager position with the Bulldogs was a promotion. I would also be in charge of a team of people for the first time in my career. Naturally, I was terrified.

What if they figured out this was a mistake?

I wanted to call Tristan so he could talk me down like he always did, but I wasn't sure if he had landed in Russia yet. Or if he had, what time it was there. I was excited to move to the same city as my other half, but now I felt abandoned with him on the other side of the world.

With a sigh, I got out of my car and headed into the office. I could do this. I was starting over here. I was starting a new life and leaving all that heartbreak back in St.

Catharines. Philly would become my new home. Eventually.

I greeted Cindy, the office manager, at the front desk, and she walked me to Quinn's office. She gave me a reassuring smile and walked off as Quinn looked up from her desk at my approach. "Oh, you're early," she said.

I gave her a sheepish look. "Sorry. I didn't know how long it would take me to get here."

"Rather early than late," she said with a smile. "Come on, let me show you your office, and we'll get you all set up."

"Office?" I asked while I followed her down the hallway.

"Oh yeah, I forgot to tell you. Since you're a manager, you get your own office."

I expected to sit in another cubicle, but it was a pleasant change of pace that I had an office. Even though anxiety was crawling up inside me that the Bulldogs would realize they made a mistake hiring me. What if I was bad at being a manager?

Quinn showed me my office and took me around to meet all my coworkers. I tried to remember their names, but it would take me some time. She left to run to a meeting, and I spent the rest of the morning filling out paperwork down at HR and double-checking that IT had loaded all my systems properly. I was glad the IT guys seemed to know what they were doing. With the Tigers, I had to figure everything out myself. It was a nice change.

Around lunchtime, Quinn popped back into my office. "Hey, since it's your first day, I was wondering if you wanted to grab lunch together?" she asked.

"Oh, yeah, definitely!"

"I'll drive."

I laughed when we ended up at Eileen's Tavern. It was

the local hockey bar in South Philly I had been to a couple of times when I visited Tristan. When Noah and Dinah broke up, that's where I found a very heartbroken Noah. I was glad they had worked things out; I liked them together. Even if their height and personality differences were comical.

"Oh, have you been here before?" Quinn asked with a smirk.

"Yeah! This is where the boys always end up after games."

"True. The owners are both ex-Bulldogs. I guess we like to keep the Bulldogs family together. You're good with it?"

I nodded. "Definitely. I love pub food."

"Same, girl!"

I had a feeling Quinn and I would get along great, and the anxiety that had been bubbling up inside me evaporated. We ordered and talked about the upcoming season while we waited for our food. When our food arrived, we both dug in for a bit until Quinn turned the conversation back to work.

"I have to admit, I felt bad when I asked you to start right away, but I needed the position filled."

I waved her away with my hand, dismissing her apology. "It's fine. I'm staying with my brother until I find a place of my own."

"But he's in Russia for Worlds, right?"

I nodded.

"So why Philly?" she asked.

I shrugged while I swallowed my food. "I needed to get out of my hometown. I've been going through a bad breakup, so I figured it didn't hurt to apply. I never expected you to hire me on the spot."

"I've been having a hard time getting suitable applicants. I offered it to Maxine twice, but she didn't want it."

I wracked my brain for the names of all the people I met today. Maxine was the petite blonde sales associate. She said she started as an intern in college and had been there since. I wondered why she didn't want it; it would have meant more money, and it would have looked great on her resume.

"Why didn't she want it?" I asked.

Quinn shrugged. "Not sure. It would have been great for her. Honestly? I know she loves working for the team, but I don't think she particularly likes the job itself."

I made a mental note to remember that. I didn't want someone on my team who hated their job. I wanted my employees to like what they did. I wanted the team to be successful. If Maxine enjoyed working for the team, maybe we could find her something more suitable.

We spent the rest of lunch talking about sales strategy for the upcoming season. Since the Bulldogs failed to make the playoffs again this year, it would be a tough selling season. But Philadelphia was a hockey town, so Quinn wasn't concerned; there were always diehard fans in this city. It reminded me of the market in Toronto. The Wolves might have sucked forever, but tickets to see the team were always in high demand and expensive.

My anxiety about the job was dissipating. Maybe I made the right choice when I took this job on a whim. Now I just had to find a place to live. I had no interest in sharing a condo with my sworn enemy. The sooner I found a place, the better.

❄

I keyed into my brother's condo and was hit by the smells of spices and a good home-cooked meal. I spied Benny in the open-concept kitchen, hunched over the countertop and garnishing two bowls of some sort of stew that smelled way too good to be poisoned.

"Um, hi?" I asked, confused by what he was doing.

"Hey! I made dinner. I hope you like authentic Mexican," he said.

He looked back at me with a grin, and I noticed for the first time that he had a beautiful smile.

"I do," I said as I toed off my high-heels and walked into the kitchen.

The words coming from my lips felt foreign to me. Without venom and spite, I didn't know how to talk to him.

He smirked. "I was hoping you would say that."

I caught myself staring when his biceps flexed in his too-tight black t-shirt. It fit across his broad chest in all the right places. I spied a colorful tattoo peeking out beneath his shirtsleeve. I wondered what he would look like without that shirt.

Get it together, Roxanne! This is Benny! He might be hot, but he's 100% an asshole.

I took a bowl from him and set myself up on the barstool in front of the kitchen island. I hesitated to bring a spoon to my lips. It smelled amazing, but I was also suspicious. After how rude he was to me last night, I had my hackles raised, ready for another fight.

"It's not poison," he said as he took the seat beside me.

I put the spoon in my mouth and took my first bite. A wonderful combination of pork and spices filled my mouth. Wow, Benny could cook. I thought all hockey players were as useless in the kitchen as my brother.

"This is amazing...but why did you make me dinner?" I asked.

"It was my sister's suggestion. I wanted to apologize for last night. I was an asshole, and I'm sorry."

I stared at him, wide-eyed. "Holy shit, hell has frozen over."

He glared at me. But instead of poking the bear, I shoved more food into my face. I told Tristan I would try to be civil, but it would be a challenge. After dinner, I would start researching where to move so I could get out of here as soon as possible.

I had to admit it was nice to come home to a meal I didn't have to prepare. Not that I was going to get used to it. It was nice sitting here with him and not trying to tear his eyeballs out, though.

Huh. Maybe *I* had always been the jerk all these years.

No, I knew I had been. Tristan always roasted me for being such an asshole.

I cleared our plates and started loading up the dishes after we finished dinner. Benny stood up and stalked over to me. "Stop! Let me clean up."

"No! You cooked, and it was totally unnecessary."

Why was he arguing with me about who did the damn dishes? He made dinner, so it was only fair I did the clean-up.

He stared daggers at me and took a step closer to me. I backed up against the kitchen countertop.

"I was trying to be nice. But no, can't do that, not for Roxanne Desjardins," he fumed.

"You don't have to be nice to me," I growled back. "Let me clean up since you did all the cooking. Seriously, why are you arguing with me about this?"

"Fine!" he spat through gritted teeth.

He was a little too close to me now. If he stepped one-foot closer, we would be chest-to-chest. He had an intense look on his face; he was mad as hell, and I hated to admit it, but he looked so hot.

Okay, *maybe* I pushed his buttons on purpose.

"Benny, why are we fighting about who does the dishes?" I asked.

"Because you're the most frustrating woman I've ever met," he whispered, but his hands gripped the counter behind me, boxing me in between his thick biceps.

I watched the cords of his muscles flex at the motion, and I couldn't look away. I wasn't a tiny woman, I was curvy and tall, but Benny was a big, burly guy. Now that I thought about it, I was pretty sure he was the biggest guy on the team. Being caged in-between the countertop and his gigantic frame made me feel small, and that wasn't something I felt often.

"I'm tired of this, Roxanne. I'm tired of all the fighting and hating each other. I don't want to hate you."

"Then don't be such a dick!"

His dark eyes flashed in anger, and his fingers gripped the countertop tighter. His hard chest pressed closer, and my traitorous nipples pebbled underneath my bra. God, I hoped he didn't notice that. Even if I didn't exactly like him, I couldn't help but admit he was attractive.

My breath hitched in my throat as I looked up into his annoyingly pretty face. His eyes were like melted pools of chocolate as they bored into me like he was seeing into my soul. I wrenched my head back to keep myself from getting lost in them.

"Why do you have to always pick fights with me? I don't set out to be a jerk to you, you know," he snapped.

"Then fuck off! We hate each other. We don't have to

eat dinner together and hang out while I'm living here. I'll be out of your hair as soon as I can."

"Why do you think *I* hate you? *You* hate me!"

"What? Of course, you hate me. You're such an asshole every time I see you. If you didn't hate me, you wouldn't say the things you say to me. Fighting is what—"

I couldn't finish my last thought because he grabbed my face and kissed me.

Wait, what?

My brain must have been on autopilot because without thinking, I relaxed into the kiss and threaded my hands through his dark, silky hair. It was soft and lush and with enough length for me to grip while I bit his lip and kissed him back.

The kiss was angry, like instead of getting into a screaming match, we used our lips to boss each other around. I didn't hate the feeling of his mouth on mine or his facial hair rubbing up against my face as we deepened the kiss. His tongue slid across my bottom lip, and I opened to him without hesitation. I gripped his hair hard between my fingers, and we fought for dominance. We were still fighting, but this time with our tongues in each other's mouths instead of snarky comebacks or screams of frustration.

I whimpered when he lifted me like I weighed nothing onto the countertop. His big hands gripped my thighs as he parted them, and he stepped in between them so he could bridge the gap between our bodies. His mouth was a hot trail of kisses until he reached my neck. I clutched at his shirt and tried not to whimper again as he kissed and sucked on that spot on my neck that always got me going.

Holy hockey gods, this insufferable man was good at kissing. He was probably good at fucking too, and I suddenly had a craving to get underneath him.

He abruptly pulled away from me. We panted and searched for air. I glared because I was still mad, but now I was mad because he broke that amazingly passionate kiss. I didn't want him to stop kissing me; I wanted my hands in his hair and his on my thighs while he kissed me into submission.

I needed *more*.

"Well, if I'd known that was how to shut you up, I would have done it years ago," he said with a grin.

Then he promptly walked away into his room and slammed the door. I sat on the kitchen counter, staring at the closed door to his bedroom, absolutely dumbfounded.

Did that actually just happen?

I touched my swollen lips and fanned myself. Who kissed someone like that and then walked away like it was nothing? Was it bad it pissed me off he hadn't kissed me all over? Or thrown me over his shoulder and taken me with him behind his bedroom door?

Yes. It was very bad.

Damn, I needed to get laid.

CHAPTER SIX

BENNY

I couldn't believe I did that and then walked away like a Grade-A douche. Time after time, I proved to her I was exactly who she thought I was. Why couldn't I stop being such a jerkoff? I didn't even know why we were arguing over who did the dishes, but she got under my skin about it. Just like she always did. I was honestly surprised she hadn't pushed me away and punched me in the face after I ambushed her with that kiss.

Fuck, that kiss was *so* good.

I sat on my bed and smoothed down my hair. It had gotten messed up from Rox gripping on it. I had to admit; I didn't mind the pain at all. It kinda made my dick hard, which was a problem. I stripped out of my clothes and went into my bathroom, hoping a cold shower would calm me down.

The shower didn't help.

I was so hard it was painful. My brain kept playing back the sound of Rox's moans when I peppered her neck with kisses. I wanted to memorize the feel of her lips on mine and my hands on her curvy body. I placed a hand on the tile wall as I pumped my dick while replaying the memory of kissing her until I spurted my release down the drain. Not gonna lie, that kiss would play on repeat in my spank bank for the foreseeable future.

After I showered, I lay in my bed staring at the ceiling, wondering how I'd survive tomorrow. Surely Roxanne Desjardins would murder me in my sleep. I didn't regret kissing her, though. Not one bit. I had wanted to do it for years. Every time we got into our spats, in the back of my mind, I thought, 'What if I kissed her right now? That would shut her up.' I was right, but now I kinda feared for my life. Rox wasn't a woman to be trifled with. She might cut me with a skate blade in the morning.

I didn't have time to think about smoothing things over with Rox because I saw my sister-in-law Nina's name come across my phone. Nina rarely called me, so I knew something important had come up. My heart raced as I immediately thought something was wrong with my grandparents, or my sister, or the twins.

"What's wrong?" I asked.

"I'm sorry. I should have waited until the morning. Lil's fine. It's Abuelo."

I jumped out of bed and frantically started packing stuff into a duffle bag. Abuelo had a bad heart. He was getting older, and it killed me that he was all the way in Boston while I was in Philly. Lately, I'd been debating if I should ask for a trade.

"I'm on my way," I said.

"He's fine. His blood pressure was a little high. They're keeping him overnight. I didn't want to call you, but Liliana insisted."

"I'm still coming," I argued.

"Don't! Lil just wanted to let you know what was going on."

"Nina, he's my grandfather; I want to be there."

I hated feeling like I wasn't taking care of my family when I made a silly amount of money playing a game. Liliana and I had argued about it a lot. When I got traded to Philly, I seriously considered asking my agent when I could ask for another trade. Liliana didn't want me to jeopardize my career that way. Abuelo had given me shit for it, too, because he said he wanted me to 'live my life' and that I already did enough for the family.

"I was just letting you know. We're not asking you to drive up here tonight."

"But I'm gonna."

"You're just like your sister. Stubborn as an ox, I swear."

"I'll probably get in late tonight."

"You don't have to come."

"But I want to. It's probably best if I get out of Philly for a while anyway."

She laughed. "Was dinner that bad? What did you do to piss her off now?"

I groaned. I didn't need to ask her how she knew; my sister and her wife told each other everything. "I kissed her."

"That's it? What's wrong with that?"

I cringed. "And then walked away and said something like 'if I knew that's how to shut you up, I would have done that years ago.' I think she might stab me tomorrow."

The line was silent for a moment, and then she burst out laughing. "Liliana wasn't wrong. You have zero game with this woman."

"I don't know why I act like that around her. She frustrates me."

"Yeah, sexually. You probably need to bang it out."

I sighed. "Not you, too."

"I love you, but I've heard you talk more about this woman in the past three years than any of your girlfriends. The entire family has a pool on when you'll finally get together."

I banged my head against my pillow. "You do not."

She laughed. "We do! Because we all know you're gonna marry that woman and have the most ridiculously cute babies."

I groaned. My sister and her wife were sometimes worse than my grandparents about nagging me about when I would settle down. Liliana even took me to task for not considering marrying Stephanie.

Growing up and watching my parents have the worst marriage ever definitely had something to do with my opinion on the institution. My grandparents and my sister might have been shining examples of great marriages, but it wasn't something I ever wanted. But in my family, continuing the line was always important to us, especially to my grandparents. I loved my nephews, and I loved that my sister and her wife had the family they wanted, but having kids wasn't something I wanted for myself.

"Nina, you know how I feel about that," I said.

"But she's wicked hot, and you'd have such beautiful hockey-playing babies," she argued.

"Not if she's gonna murder me in my sleep."

She laughed. "So you're saying you could change your mind."

"NINA!"

"So I'll see you later?" she asked.

"There isn't seriously a family pool, right?"

Her laughter was all the answer I needed.

"I hate all of you."

"You love us!"

I hung up on her and gathered my things. I was leaving tonight, and I didn't care if I got to the house really late. I wasn't about to deal with whatever Rox had in store for me. I couldn't believe I'd kissed her.

The worst part? I still couldn't stop remembering the sound of her moans.

❄

"There he is!" my grandmother said when I came down the stairs the next afternoon. I hadn't intended on sleeping in so late, but I got to my grandparents' house late last night.

"Morning, Abuela," I said to her and hunched down to hug the petite older woman. "How's Abuelo?"

She waved a hand at me. "He's fine; they already brought him back. He's in the den. You didn't need to come."

She poured me a cup of coffee, and I thanked her silently. I grabbed a yogurt and a spoon and took a seat at the table. I knew my grandmother would try to make me a big breakfast if I didn't do that, but I needed to stick to my nutrition plan, especially during the off-season.

"I wanted to. I feel like I don't do enough for the family."

She gestured around the room. "Mijo, you paid off our mortgage, you gave your cousin Sal that loan for his bar, and you paid off your sister's student loans. You do enough. We know you care."

"But I'm not here," I argued and shoved a spoonful of yogurt into my mouth.

"We're proud of your accomplishments. You don't have to be in Boston for us to know that you're here for us, okay?"

"But what if I—"

She put her hands on her hips. "Don't you dare ask for a trade, you hear me?"

I sighed and sipped on my coffee. "Okay, okay."

It didn't mean I wasn't still thinking about it.

"Good. Now tell me about the woman."

"Abuela," I groaned.

She shrugged. "What? Your sister told me you made her your pozole. You only cook my recipes when you're trying to impress a woman."

"No, I don't," I grumbled, but when I thought about it, my grandmother was right. The first thing I did when Stephanie and I got serious was make her one of my grandmother's recipes.

"Did she like it?"

"Yes," I muttered.

"This is the woman you have issues with, right?"

I snorted. "We hate each other."

My grandmother frowned. "I don't think it's that."

"Nina told me about the pool."

Abuela smiled at me. "We only want you to be happy. Maybe this is a woman you could settle down with, no?"

"Nope. She hates me. Besides, you know how I feel about marriage."

She waved her hand to dismiss me.

I drained my coffee cup and put it in the dishwasher along with my dirty spoon. I chucked the empty yogurt into the bin. My grandmother peered over at me, and I knew she wanted to press me more. I was pretty sure I would hear it again when my sister and her wife got home from work, too.

I loved my family, I really did, but they could be all up in my business about my love life sometimes.

"I'm gonna go see what Abuelo's up to," I said and escaped into the den to find my grandfather.

He was sitting in his chair with the sports news on like nothing was wrong with him. The old man was probably gonna outlive me.

"How ya doing?" I asked as I took a seat next to him on the couch.

He shrugged and waved me off with his hand. "Oh, who me? Ah, you didn't have to drive up to see me."

"I was worried," I said in a voice that was smaller than I intended.

"Ah, you shouldn't be worrying about a big, strong ox like me," he said with a chuckle and pounded his fist on his chest.

I smiled at him. "Well, I was due for another visit anyway."

"You were just here."

"I wanted to see you."

He squinted at me suspiciously. "Your sister told me you're having lady troubles."

I was going to kill Liliana. "Uh, yeah. She wanted to settle down, but that's not my thing."

He waved a hand at me. "Ah, not that one—the other one. The one you always fight with."

Okay, maybe I have ranted to my family about how Rox annoys me so much. And maybe Abuelo had gotten a wicked smile on his face every time I talked about her, but I always deflected. The first time I mentioned that my teammate's sister hated my guts, the old man swatted me upside the head and demanded to know what I had done. No way I would tell my grandfather I asked a woman if her tits were fake.

I ran a hand down my beard in frustration.

"Liliana said she's living with you," Abuelo said.

I groaned inwardly. Of course, my sister said something to our grandparents.

"She got a job in Philly, so she's staying with us while her brother's overseas."

"Hmm."

"What does 'hmm' mean?"

He had an amused look on his face, and then he tipped back his head and laughed. "I've watched you rant about this woman for years. If you can't figure it out, I don't know what to tell you."

"What do you mean?"

He laughed again. "Why do you let her get under your skin?"

I picked at my nail. "Because she's the most insufferable and annoying woman I have ever met. She makes me so mad."

He raised an eyebrow. "Just mad?"

"Yes," I lied through my teeth.

She also made me seriously horny, but I wouldn't tell him that.

"Okay, you keep telling yourself that, but I think we both know you enjoy fighting with this woman, or you wouldn't bring her up all the time."

"That's not true."

He pointed a finger at my chest. "What are you doing here? You didn't need to come all the way to see me. I'm fine. You should go back home."

"Why?"

He gave me an annoyed look. "To make amends with

that woman! Sweep her off her feet and finally admit you've been circling each other for years."

"Abuelo..." I sighed.

I didn't understand why he was pushing this subject. Rox and I would never see eye-to-eye. We just had to learn to live with each other until she found her own place. I hoped I didn't make her hate me more by kissing her last night, even though I really wanted to do it again. Maybe I should stick around here until training camp. It probably would have been better for both of us.

"Promise me something, mijo?" Abuelo asked.

"Yeah?"

"Don't ask for a trade because you're worried about me."

"Abuelo—"

He cut me off with a glare. "Don't do that. You do so much for us already. I want you to be happy and to live your life."

"I could be happy back home."

"You like your life in Philly?" he asked.

"Well, yeah, but—"

"Then there's no reason for you to upend your career. Especially if a pretty lady's living with you now."

I narrowed my eyes. "How do you know she's pretty?"

He smiled at me. "Your sister showed me her picture."

"Abuelo, it's never gonna be like that between us. We don't get along."

"You need someone to challenge you. From what you've told me over the years, I don't think she hates you either. I think you're both pretending."

"No, we're not," I argued.

He raised an eyebrow at me. "Go back home, woo your lady, and don't even think about dropping your entire life for me. We know you feel guilty not being here, but you do enough already."

"I want you to be proud of me. I want to be a good man, like you, not like my asshole dad."

He made a face at the mention of my father. "I wish your mother would divorce him."

"She made her choice when she kicked Liliana out," I argued.

He nodded in agreement. "You're not like him; you're a good man. You bought this house, paid off Liliana's loans, gave Sal money for his bar, and you have a college fund for the twins."

I did all that stuff because that's what you did for your family. Abuelo had instilled that in me growing up. My sister and her wife weren't happy with me when I told them I wanted to start the college fund. They both prided themselves on being independent women who could provide for their children, but college was expensive, and I made a lot of money playing hockey.

"I'm proud of you, Michael. More than you could ever know. But you don't need to sacrifice your happiness because you think I need you right here. Don't ask for a trade, okay?"

I hung my head but nodded.

The old man was stubborn, but I loved him. I couldn't make that promise; my family was too important to me. I was still going to ask my agent if a trade with Boston was a possibility. Even if my grandparents didn't like it.

"And besides, maybe you could finally settle down and give us more grandkids."

"Abuelo!"

CHAPTER SEVEN

ROXANNE

I wasn't sure how to deal with Benny kissing me last night. Did we pretend it never happened? Should we have a conversation about it? After he left me horny and unsatisfied on the kitchen counter, I took a shower, hoping to forget. I wasn't that surprised when I got out and discovered he had disappeared.

He wasn't home when I left for work this morning, either, so I pushed all my thoughts about our kiss to the back of my mind and focused on my work.

I was knee-deep in spreadsheets and having what I called 'sad desk salad' when Quinn knocked on my open office door.

"Hey. Oh no, are you having sad desk salad lunch?" she asked with a smile.

I laughed. "Girl, you know it."

"Oh, honey! Please don't be like me; you gotta get out at lunch. Yesterday was the first time I've left for lunch in months."

"I'm trying to get up to speed on everything."

She sat down across from my desk. "The group of us usually do happy hour after work on Thursdays. Would you like to join tonight?"

"Sure!" I responded a little too quickly. "I'm new to the city, and I haven't made many connections yet."

She gave me a funny look.

"The players don't count; they're my brother's friends. I'm friendly with a few of the WAGs, but it's different when you're just a sibling."

Quinn laughed. "You really picked up your whole life for this job, huh?"

I shrugged. "New me, new city, new hair."

"New hair?"

I pulled out my phone and went to my Instagram page, then scrolled down a bit to find the last photo I had posted when I was still sporting my long bleach blonde hair. I showed it to her.

Her mouth formed a little 'O.' "You look better with darker hair."

I took my phone back and held up my hands in frustration. "I wished someone had told me that sooner. I've had blonde hair since I was thirteen. The black is a little darker than my natural color, but it's growing on me."

"It makes you look more like TJ."

I made a face at that.

We talked about strategy until she had to run to another meeting. I was glad for the distraction, but then I hunkered down and got back to work. She came round much later to grab me to go out with everyone.

In my last job, I worked with all men, and none of them seemed to want to include me. More and more, I felt like taking this job was the right decision for me. Not only was the pay better, but I liked my new boss. I definitely wanted to make sure I got to know my coworkers.

A couple of hours later, we were at Eileen's, laughing over a couple of beers. The other girls in the office were nice, even if they kept on making fun of me for saying 'eh' too much.

"I don't say it that much!" I argued and downed the last of my lager.

Quinn laughed hard with her hand over her face. "Girl, you do!"

"I'm not as bad as Noah Kennedy," I muttered.

Kat laughed. "He does say it a lot. I thought it was a Canadian thing."

"Noah's such a stereotype," I said and rolled my eyes. Like truly, thanks Noah for making these Americans think we were all so sugary sweet nice! But that was just Noah's way. He was too pure for this world sometimes.

"Yeah, but he's one of the good ones," Maxine argued.

I pointed at her. "You're not wrong."

"It was so sweet last season when he came to me to get tickets for his girlfriend," Maxine said with a dopey smile on her face.

"He adores her," I said with a shake of my head.

Kat nodded. "Dotes on her! Seamus told me how down he was when they broke up."

I forgot Kat was the rookie goaltender, Seamus Metz's, mother. I didn't talk to Metzy all that much. Goalies were the weirdest guy on the team, and Metzy was intense. Kat was the GM's assistant, but Quinn said that basically meant she ran the place.

"How long have you worked for the organization?" I asked Kat.

"Since my twenties when I was an intern. I love it," she answered.

"Oh, me too," Maxine cut in.

Kat and Quinn scoffed at her.

"You don't count; you're still a baby," Quinn complained.

It was nice to feel like I belonged, and I was glad we could all chirp each other. I had already transitioned to my glass of water when the server came over and slid another Yuengling in front of me. Yay for two-dollar Yuengling during Happy Hour, but I didn't order another beer.

I furrowed my brow at her. "Um, I didn't order that."

She pointed a thumb behind her at someone at the bar. "That guy over there wanted to buy it for you. He's cute," she said with a wink before walking away.

"Uhh..."

Quinn nudged me. "You should go talk to him."

I put a hand on my face in embarrassment. "I haven't gone out with a guy in a long time."

Maxine nudged me. "Go for it, girl!"

I leaned across the table and saw a dark-skinned man with a shaved head and a beard raise a glass at me over at the bar. Huh, he was kind of cute.

"Oh!" Maxine cheered. "That's Keith Collins."

I gave her a confused look.

"Beat writer for the Bulldogs at the newspaper," she explained.

"Ohh..."

Quinn practically pushed me out of the booth.

I grabbed my drink and strolled over to him. He was cuter up close, and he had a bright smile. What the hell? Maybe I should get back on the horse and try dating again. I was so sexually frustrated that I had been ready to screw

Benny last night. If nothing else, that had to be a sign it was time to put myself out there again.

I stuck out a hand to the stranger. "Roxanne."

"Keith," he greeted and shook my hand.

I slid onto the stool next to him and sipped the lager. "I've heard. Thanks for the drink."

"Didn't peg you for a Lager girl, but I'm impressed."

I wrinkled my nose. "Wine's gross."

He laughed. "So, Roxanne, what do you do for a living?"

"Sales," I stated flatly but didn't ask a question in return.

"You kind of look familiar to me."

I looked down at the maple leaf tattoo on my wrist. "Oh, yeah. You probably pester my brother for a lot of interviews."

He cocked his head quizzically. "I'm sorry?"

I sighed. "I'm TJ Desjardins' sister."

His eyes lit up in recognition. "Ah, that's what it is. You look a lot alike."

"We're twins," I explained.

"I know this is forward, but can I take you to dinner?"

It must have been the second beer because I found myself saying yes, and I exchanged numbers with him. When I walked back to the table where my coworkers sat, they all had big smiles on their faces.

"Well?" Quinn asked with a sparkle in her eyes.

"He's taking me to dinner," I said and shrugged like it wasn't a big deal, even though it was an extremely big deal.

"Damn, girl. How long have you been in this city? Two days and you already have a date?" Maxine asked.

I shrugged, but inside, I felt like spiders were crawling

around inside my skin. I hadn't been on a date in a long time, and I wasn't sure how I felt about it.

❄

I didn't know what to wear on my date. Quinn and I were friendly, but I didn't think it was appropriate to ask my boss for advice on what to wear on a first date. Dinah and Noah had gone up to Winnipeg to visit his parents, so I couldn't ask her. I ended up video chatting with Natalie instead.

"Hey!" she cheered when she answered the call.

"I need your fashion guidance," I said.

She raised an eyebrow. "Do you have a date already? OMG! Is it with Benny?"

I scowled. I would never tell anyone I had kissed Benny; I would take that to my grave. It didn't matter how good his lips felt on mine or how much I loved the pressure of his hands clutching onto my hips.

...and now I was thinking about those hands doing other things to me. Some very X-rated things. I needed to get laid.

"Fuck no! Just some guy I met while I was grabbing drinks with my coworkers the other night."

Her question about Benny reminded me he hadn't been home for a couple of days. When he disappeared after our kiss, I assumed it was because he feared my reaction. I didn't blame him; I could be a petulant asshole, and I had expressed my undying hatred of him for several years. I hadn't thought much about his disappearance until I was on the phone with my brother last night, and he mentioned Benny went to visit his family in Boston.

"Oh! You haven't gone out with a guy since university!" She narrowed her eyes. "Why do I feel like you're withholding something?"

"I'm not!"

She glared. "Rox."

I sighed. "He's the beat reporter for the Bulldogs."

She pursed her lips, and I waited for the screen to catch up because it lagged again. It went back into focus, and she glared at me. "That's not it."

"Okay, fine. I kissed someone."

"Ooh...who?"

"It's not important. Help me with what to wear for this date."

Her mouth hung open. "You kissed Benny, didn't you?"

I stared at my computer screen.

"Oh, my God! Finally!"

"Shush. Focus, Nat! It was an accident, and it's never happening again."

"Oh, I'm sorry, did you trip and break your fall on his lips? Oooh, is he a good kisser?"

I gave her the finger. "Enough about him. Help me out. I don't know how to dress for a date with a man anymore."

She laughed. "Look hot and show off your big boobs."

I glared. "Help me!"

"Show me some outfits, and I'll see if I can help."

I pulled out a red wrap dress with white flowers that showed some cleavage and a simple black A-line dress and held them up to her.

"The black one, right?" I asked.

She put a finger on her chin. "Hmm. What else you got?"

I rolled my eyes at her, and I heard her tiny giggle from the speakers of my computer.

I opened up my suitcase and pulled out a floral print maxi dress. "What about this?"

She cocked her head to the side, debating the choices.

"The red one," a deep voice said from behind me, and I nearly jumped. Benny was standing in the hallway. He had a bag over his shoulder and was wearing his signature leather jacket. He had a guilty look on his face when he saw my reaction, and he ran a hand through his hair nervously. "You look good in red."

Before I could utter a reply, he went into his room and shut the door.

"Oh my God, girl. I can see the sexual tension through the screen," Natalie quipped.

I hushed her and shut the door to Tristan's room. "Hard pass."

Natalie smiled. "Put the dress on, and let's see if he's right. Plus, if you already kissed him, it seems like you didn't take a pass."

I grumbled.

She arched an eyebrow. "Was it more than a kiss? Tell me what happened!"

I balled my hands into fists. "Nothing. We got into an argument and kissed. He stopped it before it could go further, and I haven't seen him in a couple of days."

She waved a hand in front of her face, fanning herself. "Oh, my God. You need to cancel your date and climb that mountain of a man instead."

"HARD. PASS!"

She giggled, and I felt my face getting hot just thinking about it. "The lady doth protest too much."

I glared back at her.

I slid into the dress and tied it around myself. Shit, my tits were out. No wonder Benny picked this dress.

"Shit, you look HOOOOOT. You should wear red lipstick, not the usual plum you wear. And what shoes are you gonna wear?"

I held up the black wedge heels I was planning to wear, and she nodded her head in agreement. "Thanks, Nat. I don't have a lot of friends here yet, and you know—"

"Your ex is a dick," she interjected. "Just so you know, Lisa told everyone you cheated on her. I'm glad you got out of here; it's a sign that Philly's the place for you."

I sighed heavily. I didn't think Nat was that close with me, but her saying that made me feel emotional.

"Oh, sweetie, don't cry."

"I'm sorry! I swear Tristan's so dead inside because I absorbed all the feelings in the womb."

She cackled at that. "You might be right. Although..." She trailed off and had a guilty look on her face.

"It's in the past," I said.

Nat was rather cruel to Tristan in high school, but she had been going through some shit back then. It took a while for me to forgive her for how she hurt him, but eventually, I did. I think he did too, but she was probably why he was such a commitment-phobe.

"You look happy, though, so go enjoy your date. Get some!"

"I'm trying to."

She rolled her eyes. "Love you, sweetie. Text me if you go home with this guy, okay?"

I nodded. "Yes, Mom."

We ended the call so I could finish getting ready. I did my make-up and hair and put on a black blazer over the dress because it was only May and still a little chilly outside. Benny was in the living room watching the playoffs. When I called out goodbye, he didn't respond. I was pretty sure he hadn't even seen me leave.

Okay, we were going to ignore what happened last

week. That was fine with me. I'd rather pretend he didn't exist instead of fighting all the time.

I told Keith I would meet him at the restaurant because I didn't like getting into cars with strange men. I had even insisted we have dinner at Eileen's since it was one of the few places in the city I knew. I felt safe there, especially since the owners were ex-hockey players. Hal, one of the owners, was old friends with my dad, and he already told me the other night that he'd look out for me. I didn't tell him I wasn't on speaking terms with my dad, but I didn't think that mattered. It made me feel safe at his bar.

I was a little paranoid because Natalie made me promise to text her my date's address if I went home with him. I didn't think I was gonna go home with him, but I was keeping the option open. Since that kiss with Benny, I found myself sexually frustrated. Like killing my vibrator daily type of sexually frustrated.

Keith was seated at a booth when I got to the bar. I slid into the seat across from him and gave him a smile. It puzzled me when I noticed there was a bottle of wine on the table and no menus.

Who ordered wine at a sports bar? And didn't I tell him I didn't like wine?

As soon as he opened his mouth, I realized it had been a mistake to even shave my legs tonight.

CHAPTER EIGHT

BENNY

I hadn't planned on coming back to Philly until training camp. The further I stayed away from Rox, the better. However, my family was nosy busybodies who kept razzing me about her. I loved my family, but they had boundary issues.

I wasn't sure what my play was with Rox, but I knew I should apologize. When I walked into the condo and saw her getting ready for a date, I swallowed that apology. Maybe it was best to pretend it never happened. I didn't even say goodbye when she left wearing the red dress I recommended. Red really was her color. That dress was bad news for me—that was the one she had been wearing when we first met, and it looked amazing on her.

I sighed and pulled up Riley's contact on my phone. Riley was one of our top defensemen on the team and my best friend. I shot off a quick text to him.

ME: *Just got back in town. You want to grab a drink?*
RILEY: *Yes! Fi shoved me out the door.*

ME: *Why?*

RILEY: *Too distracting when she has to write.*

I laughed at that.

Riley was the last person I'd thought would settle down. When I met Fi, it explained a lot about him. Like why he never got serious with anyone and why he hooked up a lot. They seemed pretty happy together now that they'd figured everything out.

A part of me, deep down, wanted that. Maybe not the marriage part, but finding a person to spend my life with. It was hard to find a partner who didn't want marriage, kids, and the white picket fence, though. Especially when you were a monogamous guy.

I took a quick shower and met Riley for drinks at Eileen's. The team hung there since it was a hockey bar. Riley wanted to sit at the bar and watch the playoffs because, of course, he did. Dude was a stats fiend.

"How's the family?" he asked.

I shrugged. "Okay, I guess. You ever thought about asking for a trade to Minnesota?"

He narrowed his eyes at me. "Nah, but it's on my list if they ask me if I have any place I want to go. What's up, man? I thought you liked it here."

"I do. But I feel guilty being so far away from my family."

I took a swig of my beer and glanced up at the game on the TV above the bar. I winced when I saw the replay of a blatant headshot that didn't get called. "That looked rough."

I didn't pay attention to his next sentence because my phone vibrated in my pocket and distracted me. I saw a text message notification pop up from an unknown number.

UNKNOWN: *Can you be my emergency call?*

I furrowed my brow in confusion at the message. Riley

gave me a questioning look, but I ignored it when I saw a second text come through.

UNKNOWN: *Tristan gave me your number for emergencies. It's Roxanne.*

Riley nudged me. "What's up?"

I stared down at my phone as the dots moved across the screen, showing her typing.

"It's Rox. What's an 'emergency call'?" I asked him.

He laughed. "It means she's on a shitty date and needs rescuing."

Another few text messages popped up on my phone.

ROX: *Please send help! This date is awful.*

ROX: *He ordered for me! I hate wine!*

I furrowed my brow as I reread what she sent.

ME: *Wait, you went on a date with a guy?*

ROX: *Yes! Still bisexual, you dick!*

ROX: *HELP ME, ASSHOLE! You're the only one I knew who was around.*

ME: *Hmm... I think I will just let you suffer instead. I mean, if I'm your last resort.*

ROX: *You're such a fucking dick.*

ME: *Where are you?*

ROX: *Eileen's Tavern.*

I chuckled and glanced across the restaurant, then saw her sitting in a booth on the other side of the bar. Riley turned around and waved when Rox noticed us. Her date turned around, too. Keith Collins from the paper. Why would Rox go out with someone from the media?

"Okay, what's a good emergency to get her out of this date?" I asked Riley.

He raised both eyebrows and ran his hand down his clean-shaven jaw. "You forgot your key?"

I stroked my beard. "Hmm...that might work."

"She seems pissed; you should take her home," Riley suggested. There was a grin on his face like he knew something I didn't. He stood up and fist-bumped me, and seconds later, he was out the door.

I downed the rest of my beer and threw some dollars on the bar for a tip. I took a deep breath and strode over to Rox and Keith. Keith's eyes lit up with recognition, but Rox had her signature scowl plastered across her face. I wasn't sure if it was for me or him this time.

"Oh, hey Keith," I greeted pleasantly. "Listen, I'm sorry to cut your date short, but I locked myself out, and Roxie here is the only person in the country with another key."

She glared at me at the use of the nickname she only let her brother use. "Honestly, Benny!" she exclaimed in exasperation, but her eyes told me 'thank you.' She looked at Keith with a grief-stricken expression. "I'm sorry."

She dug around in her purse and threw down some money. Keith seemed to balk at that and tried to give her the money back, but she waved it away. "No, no, take it. I'll see you around."

She hopped down from the booth, and we walked together toward the exit while I called a car. She ground her teeth and looked pissed beyond belief. Was it bad that I was turned on by the look on her face? Very much, yes. Did I care? That was a big nope.

"He knew I hated wine," she said, spitting venom. "When he asked me out, I told him I didn't like wine because he said he didn't peg me for a beer drinker."

"He's an ass," I agreed.

She balled her hands into fists while we stood together on the street, waiting for the car. She ran her hands down her face in obvious agony, but my eyes focused on cataloging how sexy she looked. That dress hugged her ample breasts in all the right places and accented her deliciously curvy body. My mouth watered at the sight of her, all soft and feminine, and holy fuck Roxanne Desjardins made me hard again.

She rubbed her hands over her arms, and without thinking about it, I had to be a smart-ass. "I thought you Canadians didn't mind the cold?"

She glared at me. "You think you're a real funny guy, eh?"

I smirked but shrugged out of my leather jacket and put it around her shoulders. I felt her freeze as my hands lingered on her shoulders. "Here," I breathed a low whisper into her ear.

If this was any other woman, I would have made a move and placed a gentle kiss on her neck. But this was Rox—a move like that might get me murdered.

"I don't need your jacket!" she snapped.

I held up my hands but didn't remove my jacket from her shoulders. She was ready to pounce again, but then the car arrived, so we got inside and had a very tense ride back to the condo. She shoved the jacket into my face when she got out of the car. I let her storm off and leisurely made my way back up to the condo. I didn't think she was mad at me but about the whole situation. When I keyed into the condo, she was pouring two shots of vodka at the kitchen island.

"Come on, take this shot with me," she said. She gave me a pleading look I couldn't say no to. Her bright red lips were all pouty, and I felt my dick twitch behind my zipper.

I threw my jacket on the back of the armchair and toed off my shoes. When she bent over to grab her shot glass, I saw the cherry blossom tattoo on her right shoulder blade and a new tattoo of a white flower on her left shoulder blade. I wanted to trace the lines of her tattoos with my tongue and kiss them slowly until she begged me to fuck her. I shouldn't have been having thoughts like that about her, though. I was already skating on thin ice here.

I was cautious when I walked over and took the shot glass out of her hand. We clinked glasses, and I winced as the alcohol burned my throat.

"You want to talk about it?" I asked carefully.

She groaned. "First, I hate when they order dinner for me. Second, he spent the whole date goading me for information on Tristan. He *knew* who I was when he bought me that drink. What a fucking fuckety fuck!" I tried not to laugh at her cursing, but she noticed and slapped my shoulder. "Don't laugh about it!"

"I'm sorry. I'm not laughing at you, just your colorful language."

She ran a hand down her throat, and my gaze dropped to her ample cleavage. God, this woman was a goddess. Was it wrong of me to fantasize about running my hands and my mouth all over her curvy body?

I realized I was staring when she placed her hands on her hips and glared up at me.

"We gonna talk about that kiss? What kind of person kisses a girl like that and then fucks off for a couple of days?" she seethed.

I exhaled. "I was trying to not get murdered. Sorry!"

She growled and muttered another insult that I couldn't hear.

"Not that it's any of your business, but I went to see my family," I tried to explain.

She sighed and gave me an apologetic smile. "I'm sorry. I'm making this about me."

My eyebrow shot up in surprise. "Holy shit. Mark this

day. Roxanne Desjardins has apologized to me, Michael Bennett, for snapping at me for no reason!"

She gave me the finger. "Shut up! I'm just..." She trailed off and didn't look me in the eye as she searched for the right word. "Frustrated."

"Frustrated how?"

She gave me a pained look. "Horny."

"Oh."

"Anyway, why did you kiss me that night? You hate me!"

I placed my hands against the kitchen island behind her, boxing her in and staring down at her. "We need to talk about you thinking I hate you."

"You do!" she snarled.

I gritted my teeth. This woman and her constant need to argue was grating on my last nerve. As much as she infuriated me, I'd never said that I hated her. Sure she got under my skin, and she was combative as hell, but hate was a strong word. The same couldn't be said for her, though; I thought she lived to hate me.

"I don't hate you. You make me so goddamn frustrated, you infuriating woman."

"*I'm* infuriating? Are you for real?"

"You want to know why I kissed you?" I growled at her.

"Yes! I wouldn't have asked if I didn't want to know. I swear, you're the most insufferable man I've ever met!"

I leaned into her, closing her in against me so she couldn't escape. She looked up at me with wild eyes that looked equal parts pissed off and horny. That was sure interesting to my lizard brain right about now.

"I kissed you that night because you were annoying me, and it shut you up."

"Yeah? Is that what you want, to shut me up again?"

"Is that the only way to get you to stop yelling at me? Do I need to shove my tongue or my dick in your mouth?"

"You don't have the balls."

"Fucking watch me," I growled.

She cocked a dark eyebrow at me as if daring me. "Watch you do what?"

I grabbed her face in my hands and slanted my mouth against hers. She growled into the kiss, biting my bottom lip so she could get the upper hand. Rox was a hellcat, but I didn't know I would enjoy angry-kissing her this much.

I let her take the lead, her tongue in my mouth and her hands gripping my hair. I snaked my hands down her luscious curves and gripped her hips. She moaned when I lifted her up onto the island and spread her thick thighs open. Instantly, she wrapped her long legs around my waist, and I gripped her thighs tighter as we deepened the kiss.

She angrily pulled at my hair while our tongues battled for dominance. I wondered if this was what sex would be like for us. Instead of screaming at each other, would we fight with our bodies instead? Would we wrestle for who got the upper hand? I really wanted this stubborn, angry woman underneath me right now. Or on top of me.

She yanked my head toward her neck, and I took her lead by pressing hot, angry kisses along her neck until I was sucking on the soft flesh below her ear.

"Oh, fuck..." She moaned and unclenched my hair from around her fingers.

Her hands slid down my back, and she pulled me flush against her. My dick was a hard spike, begging to be inside her warm center. She had to feel it against the thin material of her dress.

The sound of her moans brought me back to earth. I realized I was kissing Rox, and if I didn't pull away right now, she was going to straight murder me when she came to her senses.

I pulled away suddenly. I could smell her arousal, but if I didn't stop now, we would do something I knew we would both regret. Well, I wouldn't regret it, but she would.

"Rox," I panted.

Hazel eyes flashed open in anger. "What the fuck!"

"I'm sorry. We shouldn't—"

"Kiss me again," she demanded as she gripped my t-shirt. Her eyes were ablaze with fury and desire. In my wildest dreams, I never thought she would look at me that way.

"I...what?"

She sighed, grabbed my shirt in both hands, and pulled me back to her lips. My hands went into her hair while I angled her head to kiss her better. I couldn't help it.

But I pulled back slowly. "Roxanne."

Her eyes snapped open again. They were a storm of desire in greens and browns. "Stop thinking so hard."

"We should stop."

She rolled her eyes at me. "Haven't you ever hate-fucked anyone? You said you're tired of fighting all the time, right? So why don't you try to fuck it out of me? Come on, big guy. Punish me for being so mean to you for all those years."

I raised a dark eyebrow and kissed her neck again. I nipped at her earlobe and whispered in her ear, "Is that what you want? You want to be punished, you bad girl?"

She grabbed my face in her hands and kissed me again in response. That was all I needed to know. Oh, if hate-sex was what she wanted, I would give it to her good. She'd be screaming my name tonight—and for once, not out of anger.

CHAPTER NINE

ROXANNE

I sighed into his mouth and loved the way he aggressively pulled me towards him, gripping my hair in between his fingers. I wound my hands around the back of his neck and sunk my fingernails into his skin. His cock pressed into my thigh, and let's just say, Benny being the biggest guy on the team wasn't just about his muscles.

Maybe we should have done this sooner. I wanted him so badly. I was finally going to admit it — maybe I didn't hate him. I just hated the way he made me jump out of my skin when he looked at me. Michael Bennett was too pretty of a man to be interested in someone like me, and maybe my hatred for him was a wall I put up to protect myself. Guys like him didn't go for the curvy girl.

His lips traveled down my neck to that spot below my ear again. I couldn't control the moan that sprung from my lips when he nipped and sucked at the sensitive spot. I moaned again when I felt his hand snake up to cup one of my breasts.

"Your tits are so nice," he breathed into my ear.

"Oh, yeah? And real, eh?" I teased.

"Yeah..." He panted into my ear and continued to fondle me. "They fit so nicely in my hands. Like they were made for me."

I bit back a moan at that. He had huge hands, and I wanted them all over me tonight. I wanted to have rough, hot, angry sex with this man. I squeezed my legs around his back and threaded my hands through his hair. He lifted me off the island and carried me into his bedroom, never once breaking the kiss. I was impressed; the big guy had skills. He kicked the door shut and pressed me up against it.

Oh my God, was he going to fuck me up against the wall?

"Rox..." He moaned into my neck, and I wrenched his head back up to my lips.

"Shush. Less talky, more get inside me," I growled before I bit his bottom lip.

He yanked his head away and went back to kissing my neck. I was practically humping him to feel the friction of his cock against my needy pussy.

"I want to be inside you so bad," he panted into the hollow of my throat. "Are we really doing this?"

"What part of shut up and fuck me do you not understand?" I asked with a hiss.

He didn't respond to that, but he ground his hips into me, and I moaned at the feel of him, hard and aroused. I wanted his cock inside me right now. He pulled at the tie on my dress while I pulled his t-shirt over his head. He had an impressive body, but running my hands over the hard lines of his chest and his defined abs was a completely different story. My fingers grazed across the colorful skull tattoo on his upper arm. I wanted to ask him about the meaning of his tattoo, but I was too horned up for real questions.

He pulled back and dropped my legs to the floor, but he held my hand so he could spin me out of the dress and drop it to the floor. He traced the white trillium flower tattoo on my left shoulder blade.

"This is new," he said, and I nearly died when he pressed a soft kiss to my skin. Before I could process it, he spun me back around so I could face him. His eyes were ablaze with lust, and he drank me in hungrily, looking at the strapless red push-up bra and matching panties.

"You're so sexy," he growled and unclasped my bra with one hand in an impressive move.

My hand went to his jeans, but he slapped it away and pushed me against the wall again. He pinned both of my hands above my head with one hand while his other slowly slid my underwear off.

"So sexy," he whispered, more to himself than to me.

I wrinkled my nose at that. "You don't have to flatter me. I know you've been with women who are way hotter and thinner than me."

I wasn't ashamed of being a curvy woman, I knew I was a big girl, and I was fine with that, but guys with six-pack abs and biceps like that weren't interested in women who looked like me. Hockey players went for the supermodel-looking woman, and we weren't talking about the Ashley Graham type.

Fire flashed in his eyes, and he pulled me flush against his naked chest. He grabbed my hand and put it on his cock through his jeans. "You feel that?" he gritted out.

"Uh-huh."

"If I didn't think you were sexy as fuck, I wouldn't be so

hard right now it hurts. So when I say you're sexy, shut the fuck up and take the compliment."

He kissed me hard. Our tongues tangled until I pulled back to bite his bottom lip. My hand gripped the back of his neck angrily. "Don't tell me what to do."

He smiled and bent down to nip at my neck playfully. He kissed up to my ear until his breath was on the shell of it. "Get on the bed, Roxanne."

"Or what?" I asked with a raised eyebrow.

His hand bit into my ass in a playful slap. "You infuriating woman. You're going to get it good."

"Yeah?"

"You gonna listen now? Or do I need to spank that cute ass of yours? Huh, bad girl?"

I let a whimper out, and he smirked because he knew I was into the domineering thing he was pulling right now. The idea of him bending me over his knee and spanking me? I was into it. Why was I into that? I yelped as he picked me up again and threw me onto his bed. I sat up and watched as he took his jeans and boxers off.

Benny crawled into bed with me and kissed me roughly. I gave in to the feeling of letting him take control. His hand pinched my nipple while the other slow-crawled down between my thighs. I sighed in satisfaction as he pumped two thick fingers inside me. I moaned when he kissed down my chest and swirled his tongue across one of my nipples. He sucked on it in time with his pumping fingers, and I arched into his hand.

He lifted his head up from my chest. "Are you gonna come for me?"

"Uh-huh."

"You want my cock inside you, baby?" he asked while he slammed a third finger inside me.

I made a sour face at that term.

"What's wrong? Am I hurting you?"

"Don't call me baby," I said. I put a hand on his arm. "But thanks for checking in."

He nuzzled my chest again, and his beard felt rough across my skin. "I want to make sure you feel good. If you don't feel good, you tell me, okay? I don't want to hurt you."

Oh my God! This man could be aggressive and alpha-male in one breath, but in the next, he was making sure this was good for me too. Who was this guy? Was this the same guy I had been fighting with for years?

He searched my eyes in concern.

I nodded. "I don't like being called 'baby.' We're pounding one out; I'm not your baby."

"You sure you want to do this?" he asked, and I whined when his fingers stopped pumping inside me.

I shamelessly rocked myself against his fingers, getting myself off without his help. "You have your fingers inside me, and you were just sucking on my tits, but you still need to ask?"

"I want to be sure. We can stop anytime."

That was actually sweet, and it surprised me. I totally thought he was just another cocky jock who took what he wanted. Maybe I didn't know Michael Bennett at all. Maybe I was the asshole, not him.

Fuck. I *was* the asshole. I always was.

I nodded. "I'm good. I want this." I lifted a hand to his jaw and kissed him slowly. "Do you have protection?"

"Of course. Rox, I would never do that to you."

I was still rocking against his hand, and I felt him chuckle into my neck. His fingers returned to pumping in and out.

"Mmm, please don't stop," I begged.

"Come for me," he ordered while he kissed my neck. His fingers glided in and out as I arched my hips off the bed and pressed myself into his hand. His thick fingers sliding inside me felt so good. I didn't want to admit it, but he was good with his hands. Too good.

I moaned when he curled those fingers up and found my g-spot.

"Oh, God," I moaned as I came all over his fingers.

He pulled his fingers out of me and looked at me deeply while he licked my juices clean off of them. His dark eyes bored into me as he did it. It was the hottest thing I had ever seen. Not that I would ever admit that to him.

He reached into the bedside table drawer and pulled out a condom. I watched him slide it down his length, and then he pulled out a bottle of lube and spread the liquid down onto his cock. Watching his hand pump down his hard length was an erotic sight. He reached down and spread the excess lube along my slit. I didn't know a lot of men who used lube during sex, but I appreciated the gesture.

He flipped me over onto my stomach so I was on all fours. I panted at the sudden motion in surprise. He pushed my hair off my back and pressed small kisses on my tattoos. His other hand reached down to caress me again.

I gasped while his finger rubbed a small circle on my clit. That was definitely helping me relax. "Good?" he asked.

"That helps...and the lube. Thanks for using it."

He kissed the side of my neck and whispered in my ear, "I might be about to pound into you so hard you can't walk tomorrow, but I want you to enjoy it." The hand not rubbing my clit gave me a small slap on the ass.

That should have pissed me off, but it didn't. I liked him being aggressive with me in bed.

He positioned himself behind me and inched inside me slowly while rubbing my clit to relax my body. I moaned when he had fully seated himself inside me. I hadn't had sex with a man in a long time, but Benny's dick felt so good.

His hand trailed down my back in a gentle caress, but I didn't want gentle tonight. Especially not with him.

"You okay?" he asked. He removed his hand from my clit and gripped both hips tightly while he bucked slowly behind me.

He was being sweet. Why was he being so sweet to me?

"Stop being nice to me," I growled.

I felt the vibration of his laughter down my back, but then he listened and quickened his pace. I gripped the sheets in my hands when he finally slammed hard into me. Then he did it again and again as if all the frustration we had built up over the years was coming out in how hard he moved inside me. I loved it. I moaned in response and was even more turned on when he slapped my ass again and his thrusts got harder, wilder even. I wanted him rough; I wanted him to make it hurt.

I groaned when he halted.

"Why did you stop?" I asked and pressed my ass back against him.

"I want this to last. I want to remember how good it felt being inside you."

"Fuck me hard," I demanded.

"Not yet, bad girl."

"Ugh, I hate you so much."

"Quit lying."

"I'm not lying! You're the worst!"

His hand bit into my ass again, and he nipped at my

neck. "And yet, you begged me to punish you with my dick. I want to enjoy this..." He paused and slid in and out slowly, torturing me instead of crashing into me like I wanted him to. "I want to enjoy watching my dick sliding in and out of your pretty pussy."

I moaned at his words and gripped the sheets in front of me. "Your dick feels so good...but I need more."

He didn't quicken his pace. Instead, he continued to slowly stroke me from behind, almost like he was torturing me.

Oh my God! He was doing it on purpose.

"Benny, please," I begged. "Stop tormenting me. I need you to fuck me like a wild animal. Like you can't control yourself."

He rolled his hips and quickened his pace again. He gripped my hair in his fist. "Then you better come all over my cock. Right now, bad girl," he growled.

Fuuuckk.

I liked when he called me a bad girl. I shouldn't have liked that shit, but I *was* a bad girl. I was an asshole, and I liked that he was punishing me for all my misdeeds by pressing his dick deep inside me.

I moaned when he let go of my hair, reached a hand between us, and gently caressed my swollen clit. He rubbed small, torturous circles around it while pounding inside of me hard and fast. That sent me over the edge, and I cried out loudly as my orgasm crested. While I was coming down, he drove into me uncontrollably until he was growling out his release.

He pulled out and went to get rid of the condom in his trash can while I collapsed onto his bed in a heap of sexual satisfaction. I didn't care that I'd just slept with Benny or what it meant for our weird feud. Nothing else mattered after how he made me feel tonight.

I wasn't sure if he liked to cuddle after sex or if he wanted me to leave. Either was fine with me. I felt the bed sink underneath me, and I got up to clean myself up in his en suite bathroom. When I looked in the mirror, I saw my make-up was a wreck. I washed it off with some of Benny's face wash and patted my face dry with a clean washcloth.

I wasn't sure what to do then. Did he want me to come back to bed? Or should I go to sleep in my brother's room? He was in his bed with his eyes closed when I came out of the bathroom, so I started putting my undergarments back on and scooped up my dress.

"Hey," he called out groggily.

"Go back to sleep."

He sat up. "I'm not asleep."

He was only wearing his boxers now, and looking at his incredibly fit body, I wondered if I could go for round two. I was grateful he had fingered me with three fingers to get me ready for him and used a lot of lube. Men never knew that they needed to use lube! I didn't think it completely helped, though. Benny was bigger than average, and I would be sore tomorrow. So worth it though, because much as I hated to admit it, sex with Benny was amazing. Even if he had tortured me a bit. I kinda liked that too.

He scratched his beard nervously. "That was okay, right?"

"The sex?" I asked with a furrowed brow. "Or that we did that?"

"Both. Do you still hate me?"

I smiled at him. "Right now, my pussy loves you, but ask me again the next time you piss me off."

"Definitely not trying to piss you off. I'm glad I got to know for sure."

"What?"

"That your tits aren't fake. They're quite nice and big."

I didn't mind what he did to me tonight. His soft touches and kisses were like he was expelling all my anger, and it had been exactly what I needed.

"Ass!" I yelled, but I smiled at him, so he knew it was okay.

"You were okay with me being aggressive like that?" he asked.

"Uh-huh."

"Really?"

"Well, I told you to hate fuck me."

He beckoned me with a finger. "C'mere."

"What?" I asked. I dropped my dress on the floor and walked over to the bed.

"Stay?"

"What? I'm gonna go to sleep in the next room."

He reached a hand out, brought my wrist up to his lips, and gently kissed my maple leaf tattoo. It was a sweet gesture, and I didn't know what to make of it, but I liked it. "Please. I like to cuddle after sex," he explained. "I'm sorry if you're sore. I didn't mean to hurt you."

That's not what I had been expecting to hear. "I know you didn't, but I asked for you to be rough. I wanted you to punish me."

His lips quirked up into a smirk that I shouldn't have thought was cute. "Yeah, you did, you bad girl."

I rolled my eyes at him, but I slipped into the bed and was the big spoon. Or tried to be. I was tall, but he was a giant of a man. I ran my hand over his dark hair, and he sighed at my touch. I didn't think a man had ever asked me to cuddle with him after sex. I was usually the needy one who wanted to be held after sex and made to feel like I was loved. Lisa used to get right up and into the shower after sex. She made me feel like I was too clingy when I wanted to lie in bed with her arms around me.

"Do you think we just had pent-up sexual tension?" I asked.

He shifted his position, so he was on his back, and my arm was across his toned abs. "All signs point to yes."

"Don't be an ass."

He shrugged. "I don't know. Why?"

"Do you think we can stop hating each other? Can we be friends?"

He had a quizzical look on his face, but he nodded. "I'm tired of fighting with you. If I had to fuck your brains out and make you come multiple times to stop, I can live with that."

I punched him in the shoulder. "Nope, you're still a jerk. You only made me come twice."

He smirked at me. "Not true. You came when you watched me lick your cum off my fingers. Don't even lie, I saw the look in your eyes. You know it turned you on."

I glared. He was right, but I'd hoped he hadn't noticed. I hit him again. "Again, you're still an asshole."

He grinned again, and it pained me to admit he looked so cute. He turned onto his side, and I pulled him closer to my chest and wrapped my arm around his flat stomach. I stroked his hair until I heard his breathing slow. I had every intention of sleeping next door, but I drifted to sleep holding my arch-nemesis.

CHAPTER TEN

BENNY

"Stop breathing down my neck!" a sharp voice snarled and startled me awake.

"What?" I groaned, still half asleep.

I leaned into the soft body beside me, tightening my arm around her waist as I nuzzled into her soft hair. She'd kill me for that, but I pretended I was asleep and enjoyed holding her in my arms.

I was still in disbelief that I'd spent the night with Rox in my bed, but my dick sure wasn't. I could blame it on morning wood, but having this sexy goddess-like woman in my bed got my blood pumping.

"Benny."

"Hmm?"

"Will you get that thing away from me?"

"Why, you don't want a repeat?" I whispered into her ear.

She growled and elbowed me in the ribs. "Dick!"

I chuckled into her neck.

"Dude, get off!"

I rolled onto my back, sat up in bed, and rubbed the sleep from my eyes. I didn't regret the night spent with her, but I wondered if, in the morning light, she regretted what we had done. I never wanted a woman to wake up the next morning and regret sleeping with me. It was why consent and checking in with whoever I was intimate with was important to me.

She ran a hand down her face and laid on her back. "Sorry. I'm not a pleasant person without my coffee."

"Holy shit, we should check outside," I joked.

"Why?" she asked.

"To see if the apocalypse has started."

She punched me in the shoulder and glared up at me.

"Are you okay?" I asked.

She furrowed her brow. "Yes?"

"I mean, are you sore?"

She laughed and brought her forefinger and thumb together. "A little, but I'm okay. It's sweet of you to check."

I stretched and pulled my phone out to check the time. I had three missed calls and a bunch of text messages from her brother. My heart beat loudly in my head at the reminder that I had slept with my teammate's sister. TJ was one of those guys who believed in 'the code.' He couldn't find out Rox and I had succumbed to our desires.

I scrolled through the text messages.

TJ: *Do you know where my sister is?*

TJ: *My ex Natalie is friends with her and is worried she hasn't heard from her. Apparently, she had a date tonight?*

TJ: *Now I'm getting worried.*

"Shit."

"What's wrong?" Rox asked while she sat up in the bed.

"You need to call your friend Natalie."

"Shit!" she exclaimed and ran into the other room.

Not gonna lie, I watched her ass as she left. I couldn't help myself with her. I shook the dirty thoughts from my horny brain and texted her brother back.

ME: *Sorry, I was asleep. She's fine.*

I put my phone down and walked into the kitchen. Rox was leaning against the island with her phone to her ear. It wouldn't have given me pause had she bothered to put clothes on. My mind was still trying to wrap around the fact that I had been inside her last night, and now she was standing in my kitchen in her underwear. If I wasn't already sporting morning wood, that image would have gotten me hard in an instant.

I turned around to make coffee but mostly just to distract myself.

"I'm fine!" she insisted into her phone. "The date was a bust."

She paused, and I couldn't hear the person on the other line, but I could tell they sounded annoyed. "You said you wanted to know if I went home with him, and I didn't. Ugh, girl, bye!"

I handed her a mug of coffee. "Everything okay?" I asked.

She nodded. "Sorry you had to get involved in that. My friend Natalie wanted me to text her if I went home with that douche and his address."

"That's actually smart."

"Yeah, she's all about staying sexy and not getting murdered. I guess she wanted to know that I got home safe regardless, which wasn't what she said yesterday. I left my phone out here last night, so she panicked."

I sipped on my coffee. "It's good you have a friend who wants to make sure you're okay."

She nodded. "Yeah, I think she might be my only friend back home."

I reached out a hand and touched her arm; it surprised me when she didn't try to bite it off. Maybe something had shifted between us now that we had worked out our tension in the bedroom. I hadn't lied to her the first time we kissed; I was tired of fighting with her. We didn't have to be best friends, but it would be nice if we could be civil with each other.

"You want to talk about it?" I asked.

She looked so broken, and that didn't track with the stone-cold woman I'd known for the past few years. Maybe I had misjudged her; maybe I was the jerk she always claimed I was.

She looked contemplative for a second. "She cheated on me."

"Rox, I'm so sorry."

"And since it was her apartment, she kicked me out. I stayed with Nat for a while, but I wore out my welcome. I overheard her husband ask when I would leave one morning, so I had to find somewhere else soon anyway. I was couch surfing a lot before I moved here."

"You couldn't have gone to your parents?"

"No!" she snapped. That was the type of reaction I was used to whenever we interacted, but it made little sense to me.

I held up my hands in surrender. "Sorry I asked."

She sighed and ran a hand through her hair, pulling it up into a bun on top of her head. "Sorry. We're estranged. I don't like to talk about it. I forgot you don't know."

"What happened?" I asked.

"My mom's biphobic."

I furrowed my brow. Bisexuality wasn't something I

truly understood, but that also might be because Rox was the only bisexual person I knew.

"What's that mean?"

She sighed. "I'm attracted to more than one gender, right?"

"Okay..."

"My mom thinks that doesn't exist. When I came out, she said I needed to choose if I was gay or straight. She thought me coming out as bi was a warm-up."

"Why would she think that?"

She sighed. "Sometimes people think, 'oh, she's just doing it for the attention' or 'she's too afraid to say she's a lesbian.' But that's not it! I'm fucking bisexual! The gender of my current partner doesn't define my sexuality."

"I'm sorry."

She shrugged but had a sad look on her face. "Sometimes I feel like I'm not accepted in the gay community either; there's a lot of biphobia among queers, too. My mom and I have never seen eye-to-eye, but I thought she loved me unconditionally, so it really stung."

"What about your dad?"

"He just sat there. They both have reached out a couple times since, but I have nothing to say to them. They made it clear they don't support me."

She looked ready to cry, and that made me angry for her. I couldn't say I understood what she went through, but it reminded me a lot about what my parents put my sister through.

I put my coffee down on the island. "C'mere."

"What?"

I pulled her towards me and rested her head against my chest. She leaned into my embrace while I stroked her hair. "You don't owe them anything."

My heart twisted when I felt tears sliding down my chest. Seeing Rox be so vulnerable in front of me told me last night had changed everything between us. Even if we both tried to deny it.

She pulled away after a few seconds and wiped her eyes. "Sorry. You know I'm the emotional twin, right?"

"Is that why TJ's such a robot?"

We both laughed at that.

"I'm sorry, I know you didn't ask for the crying lady in your kitchen this morning."

"Hey, I don't talk to my parents either."

She gave me a look of surprise. "You don't?"

"They're super religious, and when my sister came out, they kicked her out. She went to live with our grandparents, but once I got drafted and shipped off to my first team, I never looked back. I might not get how you feel, but my sister sure does."

"I didn't know your sister was gay."

I nodded. "Oh, yeah. She's got the wife and kids and everything. I love Nina. Abuela introduced them."

She smiled up at me and wiped the rest of her tears away. "I think I like your grandmother."

"She's awesome, but..."

When I looked away, she reached a hand up and guided my face back to her. Her soft touch against my beard was a pleasant sensation. "Hey, what is it?" she asked, and she sounded sincere.

"I hate being so far away from my family. My grandparents are getting older, and I feel bad Liliana and Nina are the ones bearing the burden. I'm considering whether I should ask for a trade to Boston."

"Oh. You really want to play for Boston?"

I shrugged. "They're my home team. Don't get me

wrong, I love playing for the Bulldogs, but I feel so guilty being away from my family."

"Have you talked to your family about this?"

I gritted my teeth. "They don't want me to ask for a trade. They think I already do too much for the family, but I feel like it's not enough. My grandfather said he wants me to be happy, and that doesn't mean I have to be in Boston."

She went to say something, but then her phone beeped. "Shit, I gotta get going."

I furrowed my brow. "Got big plans?"

"I'm gonna look at apartments today. Hey, do you know the best way to get to UPenn? The first one I'm looking at is near there. Should I take SEPTA, or should I drive?"

"I'm coming with you," I said sternly.

She balked and shook her head. "No!"

"You don't know the city, and these landlords could take advantage of you because of your Canadian accent."

"I don't have an accent!" she protested.

I stared her down.

She growled. "Fine, but I'm getting a shower, you dick."

She stormed off to TJ's room to use the shower, and I started making breakfast because I wasn't dealing with a hangry Rox. Just when I thought we'd come to an understanding, I pissed her off again.

I was plating some eggs and toast when I heard her heels click-clack against the hardwood floor. She looked all professional in a black pencil skirt and a smart white blouse. I scratched my beard and decided I should shave it. It got too hot during the summer, and Philly humidity was the worst. Plus, the clean-shaven look might help with appearances.

Why did I care about that? I wasn't looking at apartments; she was.

"Oh, you didn't have to do that," she said. She took the plate I offered and sat down to eat. I shoveled food into my face and then went to go shower myself.

She was doing the dishes when I got out of the shower.

She glanced at me and then did a double-take. "You shaved."

I rubbed my hand over my jaw. "Yeah, it gets too hot in the summer."

She squinted at me.

"What?" I asked. I didn't like the look she gave me. Did she like the beard?

"Hmm."

"What does 'hmm' mean?"

She shrugged. "You looked better with the beard."

"Yeah?"

"Yeah, hides all the ugly," she said, but she smiled, so I knew she was teasing me.

I rubbed my face. Huh. I didn't know that she had a thing for beards.

"Benny?"

"Hmm?"

"About last night..."

I smirked. "You want a repeat?"

She glared at me. "Why do I even try? You aren't coming with me today, you ass."

"Relax, feisty. What's on your mind?"

She dried her hands on the hand towel and bit her lip. "Can we keep that to ourselves?"

Oh, that was the problem. I guessed she realized that explaining it to any of our friends could get awkward. If word got to Noah, I was sure he would tell TJ I banged his sister. He would break the bro-code if he didn't. If last night was a one-time thing, it was better to not tell a soul.

It made me feel like a dick because I wasn't ashamed of what we did. I didn't do one-night stands, so this was unfamiliar territory for me. I didn't want to hide that I slept with her, but I understood why we needed to keep it a secret. It was just sex; it wasn't like Rox and I were dating.

"It's none of their business," I said.

"My brother doesn't have to know. I know he believes so strongly in 'the code,' but that's a load of bullshit."

I pointed at her. "Agreed."

"Really?"

"Yeah. What a load of misogynistic BS! What, I can't date your sister because we're teammates? Pretty sure women have their own brains."

"I've really misjudged you all these years."

"To be fair, I might have goaded you into arguments over the years."

She put her hands on her hips, which just made me notice her tits more. I snapped my eyes back up to her face, but by the scowl across it, she caught me staring.

Again.

"My eyes are up here! And what does that mean? Why would you do that?"

"Rox, don't be dense. You know why."

"Why?"

I walked towards the front door and grabbed the keys to my SUV. AKA far enough away from her that she couldn't hit me for what I was about to say next.

I gave her my cockiest grin, the kind I gave a woman before I was about to go down on them like it was my last meal. "Because I think you're hot when you're mad."

I heard her shrieking, but I was already out the door.

CHAPTER ELEVEN

ROXANNE

In hindsight, I was glad Benny came with me to look at apartments. Mostly because the landlord, who sounded very sweet on the phone, stared at my tits the whole time he showed us the apartment.

Benny looked around the apartment with a grimace and his lips in a tight line. When the listing said, 'Near UPenn campus,' that hadn't been entirely truthful. The landlord didn't like that I brought a man with me. I didn't protest when Benny slipped his hand into mine. Or when he squeezed my hand and called me 'baby' in front of the guy, even though I hated being called that.

The next apartment was a studio in a house across the street from UPenn's main campus. Despite the small size, I didn't mind the apartment, but I was concerned with how hot it would get inside during the summer. It already felt like it was a thousand degrees inside, and it wasn't quite summer yet. It was also next to a frat house, which I didn't love.

The landlady was a nice old lady who asked us how long we had been married.

"Oh no," I corrected her. "We're just—"

"Friends," Benny answered for me.

She eyed him and then turned to me. "Oh, good idea to bring someone with you, dear. You never know with some people."

Benny gave me a triumphant look, and I glared back at him. "When is it available?" I asked.

"July."

That was too far away for my liking. I needed to find something sooner unless I was okay with crashing on the couch when Tristan returned from Russia at the end of the month.

I frowned. "I'll have to think about it. I'm looking for something sooner."

She nodded. "I understand. I'll call you if I have anything sooner."

We left the attic apartment and moved on to the next place, but it ended up being worse than the first. It was an absolute dump. I wondered if it was a better idea to move out to the suburbs. Or would that be worse because of the Philly work tax? I had no idea.

"Well, that was a bust," I said when we left the last apartment. I climbed into the passenger seat of Benny's SUV in defeat.

It surprised me he didn't have something flashier, like my brother's Maserati. Perhaps I'd misjudged him. I hadn't been the nicest person to him over the years. Okay, I had been a colossal bitch, but not fighting with him today had been nice. Having a genuine conversation with him without wanting to throw something at him felt surprisingly natural. Maybe he did fuck the hate out of me last night.

"You'll find a place. Are you glad I came with you?" he asked with a grin.

I glared at him.

He looked so weird without his signature beard. Benny was a beautiful man, but I liked beards, and the clean-shaven look on him looked wrong. On the flip side, I was glad to see him clean-shaven because I was less tempted to jump his bones again. Not gonna lie, it had been nice waking up this morning to someone holding me. Sometimes it was nice to feel loved, even if that's not what it had been.

He put the SUV into drive and started the drive back to the condo. "Are you glad I came with you, though?" he asked again, with that cocky grin across his face.

"No," I lied.

The grin got bigger. "Liar."

"Fine," I huffed. "Thank you for coming with me and...I'm sorry I'm always such a bitch to you."

He put a hand on my thigh and squeezed it gently. My breath hitched in my throat at his hand on me again. "It's okay, Rox. Like I said, you're hot when you're mad."

I gaped at him and then slammed my mouth shut. I didn't believe him when he said that. I thought that was just his horny brain. Guys who looked like him didn't chase after the curvy girl.

Benny went to the gym with Riley when we got back to Old City. I was grateful for the quiet when he was gone. I needed to search for some new apartments, but the challenge was finding something in a decent area within my budget. I could have used Dinah's knowledge of South Philly right about then, but she and Noah were still in Canada, visiting Noah's parents. She was a phone call away, but I didn't want to bother her.

I scrolled through my phone and landed on Riley's

wife's number. Dinah had given me Fi's number when they left town, in case I needed anything. I hadn't even had the chance to meet Fi at the housewarming party since I threw a drink in Benny's face and stormed off. I cringed at the memory. That was such a typical asshole Roxanne Desjardins move.

I tapped my fingernails against the counter in thought and hit dial on my phone. I pressed the phone to my ear and waited for her to pick up. "Hi, Fi. We haven't met, but Dinah gave me your number."

"Um...hi?" the voice on the other line responded.

I cringed at the fact that I didn't even introduce myself. "Sorry, it's Roxanne Desjardins. You got a minute?"

She laughed on the other line. "Oh, I didn't know who the hell this was. Sure, what's up?"

"How well do you know Philly?"

"Not as well as D. She's a native."

"Shit. I thought you were a Philly girl."

"Nope, Minnesota born and raised. Riley and I grew up together."

Huh. I didn't know that. Dinah gave me no clue about how and when Riley got married. His marriage seemed sudden, but it made sense if they were childhood friends. I think I read a few romance books like that.

"Well, I won't keep you then."

She laughed. "Girl, what's up?"

I sighed. "Oh, I'm still looking for an apartment. Checked out some places in West Philly today that were a bust."

"Why were you looking there?"

"Because I don't know where to look."

"I used to live in Fishtown. That's kind of the hipster area, according to Riley. You know what?"

"What?"

"Let me call you back. I'm gonna call my old landlady and see if she has anything available. She loved me. Give me a bit."

"No rush. I appreciate it."

I hung up with her and paced around the condo in frustration. And not just about my current living situation. No, my brain had used the apartment hunting to distract itself from the fact that I slept with Benny.

I was glad he went to train with Riley because I couldn't stop thinking about last night. He knew how to kiss, and I wanted him to kiss me again. How could I be so horny when he practically fucked me into submission last night? I kept reminding myself that it was a one-time thing to get it out of my system, but my libido had other ideas.

I took a cold shower to calm myself down. Benny and I had agreed we wouldn't talk about it with anyone, but I felt like I needed to talk to get it off my chest. I itched to call Nat back and tell her what happened, but I was afraid she would tell Tristan. Not that they were on speaking terms, or so I thought, but I couldn't afford my brother finding out I slept with one of his teammates. My brother took that code business way too seriously.

I didn't have time to completely process how I felt because I saw Fi's name come across my phone screen.

"Hey."

"What are you doing right now?" she asked.

"Brushing out my hair," I answered honestly.

"Want to meet me in Fishtown to look at a one-bedroom?"

"Fi, you're a lifesaver."

She laughed. "Okay, meet me in like a half-hour."

AGAINST THE BOARDS

❄

"Hey!" Fi called out to me from the entrance of the apartment building.

I had spied her bright red hair and tall, slender figure the moment I stepped out of my car and onto the sidewalk. I only knew what she looked like because I creeped on Riley's social media until I found a photo from their wedding. He didn't post a lot. I had to admit, his wife was a smoke show. If they weren't married, I might have asked her out.

When I approached her, she gave me a hug, which I thought was kinda weird since this was the first time we were meeting.

"Oh...was that weird since we just met?" she asked.

I laughed and held up a forefinger and thumb together. "A little."

She shrugged and flipped her long hair over her shoulder. "Come on, let's go inside. Mrs. Lee is waiting for us. You toured some apartments in West Philly?"

I followed her inside and down the hallway of the first floor. "Yeah. Benny insisted he go with me. I'm glad he did because some of the landlords were creeps."

She raised a red eyebrow. "I thought you didn't get along."

From the look on her face, I could tell either Dinah or Riley had given her the rundown on Benny and me 'not getting along.'

"Yeah, we had a lot of misunderstandings."

"You know, Rox, I don't know your history with Benny, but he's a good guy. You should give him a chance," she said.

"We're trying to be civil since we have to live with each other."

She raised an eyebrow at me again but didn't press me.

Was it all over my face that I slept with him? Could she tell that being civil meant me begging him to fuck me hard? I didn't know Fi, but I knew Dinah was observant because she was a writer. I wondered if it was the same for Fi.

She stopped at a door to our left and knocked on it. An older Asian woman answered, and her eyes lit up when she saw Fi. The landlady hugged Fi and asked her how she was doing. Fi smiled at her and asked how her grandkids were and then gestured to me.

"Mrs. Lee, this is my friend Roxanne. She needs an apartment. You said you had an opening?"

The older woman nodded and shut the door behind her. We followed her up two flights of steps, and she showed us into the apartment. It was a one-bedroom but was kinda small. I was okay with that since I didn't have a lot of things. It had old hardwood flooring, which I liked because it was easier to clean. There wasn't a dishwasher, but it had laundry on-site in the basement.

"What do you think?" Fi asked.

I nodded. "I think this could work for me. I live alone, so the size wouldn't be an issue. When could I move in?"

"Beginning of June," Mrs. Lee said.

That was only a couple weeks away, so it was doable. It was nice, but I wasn't sure if I should hold out for a better place.

"I need to think about it. Can you give me a day to decide?"

Mrs. Lee nodded and smiled at Fi. "Call me in a couple of days and let me know what you think. But I'm not gonna hold the place for you."

I nodded and thanked her. I wanted to sleep on it first before I decided.

I thanked Fi for helping me out and hugged her goodbye. She was a friendly person, and I was glad she didn't push the conversation about Benny. Honestly, I hoped she forgot about it. I drove back to the condo in Old City and tried to weigh my options.

Benny wasn't back when I returned, and I was grateful for more time alone to think. It appeared the hockey gods wouldn't let me have any peace today, though, because my phone buzzed with multiple missed text messages.

I groaned when I saw they were all from Lisa.

LISA: *Baby, I miss you. Please come home.*

I rubbed my temples, collapsing on my brother's bed. I didn't have the patience for Lisa and her mind games today. She missed me? She missed me so much, she brought another woman into our bed and then let me be homeless. And she knew I hated being called 'baby.'

I stabbed out an angry response.

ME: *Find someone else to warm your bed. You didn't have a problem doing that last time.*

LISA: *Baby, please.*

ME: *No. I moved to the States. We're done.*

I dropped my phone onto the bed. I didn't need this; I was done with her, and I wasn't looking back. I had upended my life and moved to a different country because she broke my heart into a thousand pieces. Philly and this job were my clean break. I wouldn't get back together with someone who cheated on me and then acted like it was my fault. Like I wasn't enough for her.

I tossed down my phone when I heard the front door open and saw Benny walk in, fresh from a post-workout shower. He smiled at me as he shed his leather jacket. I loved his smile.

"Hey, did you eat?" he called out to me.

I sighed and walked out into the kitchen. He started

pulling out pans and was flipping through a cookbook on the counter.

I leaned against the island and watched him. "You don't have to make dinner again. I'll probably eat a salad."

"I don't mind. I love cooking for other people."

I bit my lip and nodded. "Okay."

He turned to me and raised an eyebrow. "What's up?"

I shook my head. "Nothing."

"Rox, are you okay?"

I plastered on a fake smile. "Fine. Do you want help?"

"Nope. You sit your fine ass down and let me cook."

I crossed my arms over my chest and glared at him. "You can't say that stuff about me."

He started getting ingredients out of the fridge and chopping vegetables on the cutting board. He glanced back and made an obvious look at my ass. "Why not? You've got a nice ass."

"Benny! I thought we talked about this. I don't want people to know we slept together. You know what would happen if my brother found out. You can't say that sort of shit in front of anyone else."

He held up his hands in surrender and then opened the fridge and handed me a beer. "Here, drink this and go watch the hockey game while I make us dinner, okay?"

I yanked it out of his hand and stomped over to the couch. I flipped on the Boston-Toronto game, but I was only half paying attention. Truthfully, I wasn't mad at Benny. Lisa irritated me, and I took it out on him. He didn't deserve that, but I held my tongue and sipped on my beer. I was being a bitch to him for no reason, but in typical asshole Roxanne Desjardins fashion, I wouldn't apologize.

CHAPTER TWELVE

BENNY

After an early morning workout session with Riley, I was beat, and it wasn't even ten a.m. yet. I knew something was up when I walked through the door and saw Rox pacing in TJ's bedroom. She had her phone pressed up against her ear, and she looked pissed off. She should have been at work already, so something was seriously wrong.

She had been off last night when I got back from training with Riley. I didn't think things would have completely changed, but she snapped at me when I joked about her fine ass. I got why it annoyed her, and I had to admit she had a point. I couldn't say stuff like that when we wanted to keep the fact that we'd slept together a secret.

She had gone quiet for the rest of the night while we ate dinner in front of the TV and watched the hockey game. I never thought Rox was a quiet woman, so it had unnerved me, but I didn't want to press her in case she snapped at me again. When she went to bed after the game, she looked kind of sad, and I didn't like that, but I didn't know what to do about it, so I left her alone.

I dropped my gym bag on the floor and peered into the hallway. I tried not to eavesdrop, but she was yelling into the phone.

"Because you cheated on me! I'm not taking you back," she yelled into the phone. "Fine, I'll come get all of it today." She groaned in frustration and threw her phone down on the bed. That's when she looked up and saw me staring at her from the hallway. "What?" she asked, her eyes flashing in anger.

I held up my hands. "I didn't say anything."

She put a hand over her face. "Shit. I'm sorry."

I crossed the threshold into the room. "What's going on? Shouldn't you be at work?"

"My ex is demanding I get the rest of my stuff. I'm going to have to take a personal day so I can drive up there," she said and looked down at the floor.

I lifted her chin up so she looked into my eyes. Her eyes were shiny, and though she was putting on a brave face, my heart wrenched in my chest when a tear slid down her cheek.

"Aw, Rox, I'm so sorry," I told her as I wiped the tear away with my thumb.

She wrenched her head away from my grasp. "I don't want your pity!"

"Rox, it's okay to be upset."

"It's none of your business."

I clenched my jaw and tried to weigh my words carefully. I didn't want to piss her off right now, even though I knew she wasn't actually angry at me.

She sighed and wrung her hands in front of her. "Shit, I'm sorry. I'm not mad at you; I'm just taking my anger out on you."

I raised an eyebrow. "Wow, an apology from Roxanne Desjardins!"

She glared. "Oh, fuck off, Benny."

"Sorry. I'm being a dick. What are you gonna do? Drive the seven hours there and back tonight just to pick up some stuff you need?"

She shook her head. "I'm gonna have to take tomorrow off, too. I'll probably stay the night."

"You can't wait until the weekend?"

She shook her head. "You don't know my ex. I think she'll throw all my shit out if I don't show up today."

"Okay," I said firmly and went into my room.

I grabbed my passport from my bedside table and a backpack from my closet. I shoved a change of clothes in the backpack before swinging it over my shoulder. I paused for a second and opened the drawer of my bedside table again. I stared down at a pack of condoms and a bottle of lube. Then I shoved them in the bag, too, just in case. I didn't think we would sleep together again, but I liked to be prepared for anything. A man could dream.

I walked out of my room and found her pacing in the kitchen. She looked frustrated, but I couldn't help noticing how good she looked in a low-cut Bulldogs t-shirt and how her jeans hugged her sweet ass. My gaze lingered on her cleavage for a little too long, and when I shifted my eyes upward, she met me with a familiar scowl.

Would I ever learn?

"Can I help you?" she asked and crossed her arms over her chest.

"Nope! I'm gonna help you. My SUV has more room than your little Civic. Are you ready?"

"What?"

"Will you let me help you? Christ, you're so difficult."

"It doesn't involve you. I'm fine," she argued.

I wanted to scream at her. She was so damn stubborn. A Desjardins family trait, I was sure of it.

"Rox, will you let me help you?" I asked, trying not to straight-up growl at her. The caveman inside of me wanted to pick her up, swing her over my shoulder, and drive her to Canada.

She marched over to me with an angry scowl on her face. "Why do you care?"

I looked down at her and gulped as I got a direct look down her shirt. Why was she wearing a sexy lace bra? This woman was killing me.

She pushed me away before I could say anything. "Stop looking at my tits!"

"I'm tall. What do you want from me? They're in my line of sight!" I growled.

Her hands balled into fists. She looked so hot when she was all riled up. My lizard brain was chanting, "kiss her, kiss her, kiss her." I wanted to, but that was wildly inappropriate right now.

I growled to myself in frustration. "Rox, I held you while you cried after you told me she cheated on you. Let me help you today."

She was quiet for a moment.

"Okay," she muttered meekly.

"Okay?"

She nodded firmly. "Let's go."

I grabbed my keys from the bowl at the front door while she darted back into TJ's room. She came out with her briefcase and a backpack and followed me out the door. She had her phone pressed to her ear.

"No, I'm okay..." She said into the phone and paused

while the person on the other line said something I couldn't hear. "Thanks for being so supportive, Quinn... No, I have someone going with me... Okay. I have my computer, so I'll try to catch up on stuff later."

She hung up as she climbed into the passenger seat of my SUV. "Sorry," she said.

I waved my hand at her as if to dismiss her. "It's fine. You got an address for me?"

She nodded and plugged her phone into my infotainment center. The GPS map popped up on the screen. Six hours and thirty-four minutes. That was a long drive just for her to tear open this old wound. This would be rough.

In a bold move that would probably get my hand cut off, I grabbed her hand in mine once I hopped onto the turnpike. "Hey, it's going to be okay. I promise."

She yanked her hand away and nodded while looking out the window with her chin in her hand. She looked so sad, and I hated that. This was going to be a long drive.

An hour went by before she finally said anything. "I'm sorry for being such a bitch."

"You're not being a bitch."

She laughed. "No, I am. I own that shit, but I'm angry right now, and I shouldn't have taken it out on you. It's not your fault my ex sucks. I'm sorry."

"I'm sorry about what you're going through. Break-ups suck. Trust me, I know," I said. She was hurting, and no matter how much we fought and bickered, it broke my heart to see her so downcast. "You were together a long time, right?"

"Three years. We were best friends before that, though, so it really hurt."

"Do you still love her?"

She sighed.

"You don't have to answer that."

"It's okay. I don't think so. I haven't been in Philly long, but I was broken before I came here. She broke me. She's trying to get me to come back to her, and I'm half wondering if this is a ploy, so I don't know what we're gonna walk into today. But I'm ready to move on."

"Maybe this will give you closure."

She sighed again and looked out the window. "I hope you're right."

I was glad at least I could get her to stop looking so sad. Honestly, I preferred her scowls and glares over that disheartened look.

"I'm sorry," she said after a few moments of silence.

"I don't mind driving."

"No, I snapped at you for no reason yesterday. She started pestering me last night. I was in a bad mood, and I took it out on you."

I reached out a hand and squeezed her thigh. "Rox, it's okay. You had a point."

"I did?"

"I can't make comments like that in front of my teammates if it's supposed to be a secret."

She nodded. "Right. Yeah."

"I don't regret what we did. We both had a good time, and it's nobody's business."

"I appreciate your discretion. I had a good time too."

"I'm kind of mad that everyone was right."

"What do you mean?" she asked as she fiddled with her phone and changed the music to some indie rock band I'd never heard of.

"Noah and my sister-in-law both said we needed to bang it out."

She tipped back her head and laughed. I pulled my hand away from her thigh and focused on the road.

"Noah Kennedy said that?" she asked.

"Yup."

"We talking about the same guy?"

"Dude, you all think he's like the nicest guy you know, but he has a dirty side."

"I think that's Dinah's influence."

"Christ, I don't want to know about that."

"You know she's the one in charge in that relationship."

"I don't want to know that!"

"She likes to be on top," she teased.

"I don't want to know that about my teammates!"

"Too late."

I shook my head and drove while she laughed to herself. I didn't want to admit it, but she was probably right. Dinah was a cute little thing, but she also was pretty blunt, and Noah was a lovesick puppy around her. I didn't want to know about their sex life, though. I already knew enough about Riley and Fi's sex life from when I lived with them before our season ended. I would rather be blissfully ignorant.

CHAPTER THIRTEEN

ROXANNE

I felt bad Benny had dropped everything to drive to Canada with me. I attempted to get some work done via phone, but as soon as we hit upstate New York, the signal dropped off. I had been pretty quiet since we crossed the border, but that was partly because I was tired of fighting with Benny. I was a bitch earlier when he was trying to be nice to me.

"I'm sorry if I ruined your plans tonight," I said.

"No plans! I was gonna get a drink with Fi and Riley. They wanted you to come too, but they understood when I told them what was going on."

I winced. "Shit, I'm sorry. You didn't have to come with me."

He shook his head. "It's fine. I'm sure they're fucking each other's brains out, anyway."

I nearly choked at that.

He turned to me with a smirk on his face when we hit a

red light. "Did I tell you I lived with them for a little before moving in with your brother?"

"Nope."

He hit the gas when the light turned and made a right turn onto Lisa's street. It was still early afternoon, so I was hoping she wasn't home yet. Maybe her new girlfriend or whatever would let us in. Fat chance of that since she demanded I come get my stuff today. I had a feeling she and the woman she cheated with weren't together anymore anyway. When I found them together, the other woman didn't know Lisa had a girlfriend or that we lived together. She felt bad, but I was too angry to consider that Lisa had done both of us wrong.

"Yeah..." Benny trailed off. "They aren't subtle or know how to be quiet."

"Oh my God!"

"That's why I went to Boston as soon as our season was over."

I laughed too hard at that. My phone buzzed in my pocket and distracted me from saying anything else.

LISA: *Are you coming?*
ME: *We're almost here.*
LISA: *We?*

I looked up from my phone and eyed Benny's profile. How pissed would she be if she found out I was dating him? So pissed. Especially since she insinuated I enjoyed fighting with the man whenever I complained about him. I didn't want her back; I wanted to move on. The fact I had hopped into bed with him already meant I was ready to move on. Not with him but with someone else down the line.

Benny parked in one of the visitor spots at Lisa's apartment complex and turned off the engine. He caught me looking at him. "What's wrong?" he asked.

"Um...so how do you feel about being my fake boyfriend?" I asked.

He laughed. "What?"

"Pretend to be my boyfriend in front of my ex-girlfriend, please?" I begged.

He shook his head with a laugh but then nodded. I grinned and squeezed his bicep in thanks. I went back to my phone to respond to Lisa.

ME: *My new boyfriend. Are you home? We're here to pick up my stuff.*

LISA: *Yeah.*

Oh, one-word answer. Yeah, she was pissed. I complained about Benny anytime my brother was in town or I went to visit him, so Lisa knew I couldn't stand him. I wondered how she would react to him being my boyfriend. I hated to admit this because I had loved Lisa, but sometimes she could be biphobic. She never liked that I liked men. Not everyone who was bi was attracted to men, but I was.

Benny came up behind me when I got out of his SUV and gently guided me towards the entrance of the apartment building. My heart jumped into my throat at his touch, and I had to remind myself to breathe. I hit the buzzer for Lisa's apartment and opened the door when she let us in. Benny followed me to the elevator, and once inside, I hit the button for Lisa's floor.

"How much stuff do you have?" he asked, cutting through the tension.

I shrugged. "Not a lot. My books and hockey stuff."

"Hockey stuff?" he asked. His brow furrowed in confusion, and he looked at me curiously.

"Like my old trophies and jerseys. Oh, and my skates. I

guess that's why I wanted to come get my stuff. I want my hockey stuff back."

He gave me an appraising look. "Wait, you played?"

"Pretty much my whole life. After university, there isn't a good option for women. There's the NWHL...wait, sorry, they just rebranded themselves as the Premier Hockey Federation; I keep forgetting to call them the PHF. But they're still growing; it's not as viable as a career like the NHL. Most of the women who play in the league also work full-time jobs."

I didn't want to talk about how my hockey career ended. I wanted to get my skates back, but that didn't mean I wanted to get back on the ice.

"I didn't know," he said, and he gave me an impressed look. "What position?"

I grinned. "Left-wing."

He grinned back. "Maybe that's why we never got along."

"We're too similar!"

He laughed with me. "I want to see you on the ice."

I shook my head. "I haven't put on skates in three years."

"Really? But Rox…"

I squeezed my eyes shut and held up a hand to cut him off. I didn't want to talk about this. It was bad enough Tristan kept trying to get me back on the ice. I loved playing hockey with every fiber of my being. Not playing the sport I loved, not being on the ice, felt like there was a hole where my heart should have been. That accident my last year at university and the concussion that followed fucked me up, though. I couldn't think about getting back on the ice without thinking about that night.

"Benny, I love hockey, and I miss it, but that part of my life's over. It's okay."

He seemed bothered by that, but he didn't push it. Instead, he changed the subject. "Are you gonna be okay with this today?"

I couldn't answer him because the elevator dinged, and we were on Lisa's floor. I went to her door and knocked on it with Benny close on my heels. I couldn't believe he was doing this for me. We fought and argued, but after the night we spent together, it felt like we finally understood each other. He still frustrated me, though. Stubborn man. After three years of fighting, one good fuck and a few favors didn't mean he was automatically going to become my best friend.

Lisa opened the door in a huff. Her blonde hair was up in a messy bun, and she had dark circles under her eyes. She didn't look good, but I didn't care. She looked past me at the man behind me, who stood with his arm around my waist. His fingers dug into my hipbone, almost possessively.

Where did that come from? And why do I like it?

"Hi," I said to her. "I'm here for my shit."

She crossed her arms and eyed Benny up and down. "Really, Rox? Michael Bennett? You hate him."

I opened my mouth, but Benny's thumb stroking across my hip made my breath catch in my throat. "She just thought she did. There's a fine line between hate and love," he said, and he bent to kiss my temple. I wanted to slap his hand away, but I had asked him to do this. I could be mad at him later. I schooled my face so she couldn't tell I was annoyed with my 'boyfriend.'

She opened the door and gestured to the boxes sitting on the floor in the living room. I walked over to them and knelt beside them. She had done a good job of getting my stuff together, but some of my books were missing.

"You got everything, baby?" Benny asked, and he tried to suppress a grin.

I wanted to glare and give him the finger, but I knew he was calling me that because of Lisa and because I hated it. Dick. I shook my head and walked into the office. I peered at the bookshelf and felt Lisa walk in behind me.

"Some of these are mine," I snapped at her.

"Really, Roxanne? You're dating that guy?" she asked, apparently not caring about the book issue.

"Yup. He's a good guy. Hot too."

She groaned. "What are you straight now?"

I gritted my teeth. "You're worse than my parents. Dating a man doesn't take away my bisexuality. Ugh, you never understood me. I'm soooo glad you cheated on me and this ended."

While Benny packed up the full boxes and took them out to his SUV, I collected my remaining books and put them in the empty boxes. I walked back into the bedroom and opened the closet. I had packed most of my clothes when she kicked me out, but I had a few things shoved back into the closet I wanted to take with me.

Lisa came into the bedroom while I started throwing hockey jerseys and work dresses on the bed to sort through.

"Please, Rox," she begged. "Let's get back together."

I shook my head. I folded up the clothes and took them into the living room. I threw them in the boxes as Benny walked back into the apartment. He eyed Lisa with a glare but then looked at me carefully. "What else do you need help with?" he asked.

"I think this might be it," I admitted. I chewed my lip. "I don't have a lot of stuff."

"What about your jewelry?" Lisa asked.

I glared at her. "I don't want anything you gave me. We're done, Lisa."

"Please, Rox, I'm sorry."

Benny grabbed the last box. "You ready, baby?" he asked me, ignoring my crying ex-girlfriend.

I gave him a fake smile. He would pay for that later. "Yeah, babe."

"Please, Rox, I'm so sorry. I want you back," Lisa pleaded.

I sighed. "Lisa, you cheated on me. I'll never go back to someone who did that to me. I moved on, and so should you."

"So you're never gonna come back home?"

"Philly's my home now," I told her.

That wasn't a lie. Even though I was still living at my brother's condo, Philly felt more like home to me in the last couple of weeks than when I had lived here.

Benny gave me a questioning look, but I shooed him away, and he went back down to the car. Lisa was still crying, and maybe it was cold of me, but I didn't care.

I went to the jewelry box in the bedroom and pulled out a few pieces like the bi pride necklace Tristan gave me when I graduated from U of T and statement pieces I bought myself. Anything she gave me, I left for her.

I felt her eyes boring into my back while I dug around in the jewelry box. I didn't understand why she wanted to get back together all of a sudden. She was the one who cheated on me and then kicked me out. She left me when she knew I couldn't go home to my parents and my brother lived in a different country. That wasn't something you did to someone you loved. Her texting me out of the blue last night that she missed me and then demanding I get my stuff didn't make any sense. Nor did the waterworks she had going on. If she wanted me so badly, she wouldn't have cheated on me in the first place.

I turned back around and saw her face stained with tears. I took a deep breath and tried to ignore her obvious play at my emotions.

"Lisa, why do you want me back?"

"Because I miss you," she cried.

I raised an eyebrow. "Do you? Or do you just miss having someone to warm your bed? It doesn't matter if it's me or some other woman?"

She stared at me for a second, and then her eyes narrowed to angry slits. "Fuck you, Roxanne."

"You cheated on me. You did this. Goodbye, Lisa. Have a nice life."

"Are you really dating Benny?" she asked incredulously.

"He's not who I thought he was," I admitted. That was true.

"You hate him."

I smirked. "Yeah, well, he's fantastic in bed. Goodbye, Lisa."

I walked out of the apartment for the last time, and I felt relieved. Like someone had lifted a tremendous weight from my shoulders. I didn't think Lisa wanted me back; she just didn't like to be alone. I had been heartbroken when she cheated on me but getting the rest of my stuff today felt like closing a door, like I could finally move on. I didn't want to move back to St. Catharines; I was going to make Philly my home. I was on to a new chapter in my life.

I walked outside and found Benny leaning up against his SUV.

I glared at him. "Really, dude? You had to call me baby?"

I marched over to him and punched him in the arm.

He rubbed his arm. "Ow! Damn, you hit like a man."

"No shit. Who do you think taught me how to punch? My dad's Alain Desjardins."

He grinned. "Okay, I guess I deserved that. You okay?"

I nodded. "I feel...closure?"

"That's good. You weren't lying when you said you didn't have a lot of stuff; that didn't take very long. We should have flown instead of driving."

I shrugged. I hadn't thought of that when we left this morning. I hadn't been in the right frame of mind when Lisa demanded I get everything today. I was angry and hurt and wanted to be done with her. I should have known it was a ploy to get me back. If I had been thinking straight, I might have called in another favor from Nat instead of roping Benny into driving up with me today.

"It's fine. We should probably find a hotel," I said.

"I took care of it."

I glared at him. "What?"

He grimaced. "But don't get mad at me."

"Why?"

He sighed and ran a hand through his hair. "They were full up. There's only one bed."

CHAPTER FOURTEEN

BENNY

I prepared myself for the worst. It didn't surprise me when she glared and screeched, "What?"

"I'm sorry. Maybe I can find something else?"

She sighed and ran her hand through her hair in frustration. "It's fine. We've slept in the same bed together before. We can handle it for one night."

We let her sentence hang in the air. We both had to be thinking about our night together. It was getting harder for me to not stare at her lips and wonder why our mouths weren't fused together. Or why I wasn't inside her again.

I was such a horny bastard when I was around her.

"Okay. How about we get settled into the hotel?" I offered, trying to ease the tension.

She rubbed her hands down her arms because it was a little cold outside. I wanted to wrap my leather jacket around her, but I wasn't trying to get my hand cut off.

She nodded. "Please. I need to get some work done. I also need to call this landlady back."

"You found a place?"

She nodded. "Yeah, Fi helped me out, and I think I'm gonna take it."

"That's great!"

"It's high time I got out of your hair."

I didn't want her out of my hair; I wanted her all up in my hair.

"Where?" I asked.

"Fishtown."

I nodded. Fishtown was kinda the hipster side of town, but I remembered moving Fi out of her old apartment, and it was in a decent area.

I gestured with a thumb to my SUV. "Come on, let's get going."

She was quiet on the ride to the hotel, but she was probably exhausted. We should have flown up instead of driving several hours to spend barely an hour getting her things from her ex. I didn't think about suggesting it this morning because I didn't know how much stuff she had to bring back. It wasn't much, a handful of boxes and no furniture.

When we got to her ex's apartment, it was apparent the whole thing was a ploy to get Rox back, especially when Rox asked me to pretend to be her boyfriend. I had heard her ex accuse her of being straight while I was loading up the boxes, and that pissed me off. I never said I understood the spectrum of sexuality, but her ex seemed like a jerk. I didn't like how she hurt Rox and then tried to reel her back. I hadn't minded pretending to be her boyfriend if only to help her get the closure she needed.

We checked into the hotel, and she protested when I handed over my credit card. I shushed her while the concierge looked between us with a smile. When we got into the room, Rox set herself up on the bed with her computer while I dropped my backpack on the floor.

"Are you sure you're okay with this?" I asked. "I can sleep on the floor."

Luckily, I booked a room with a king-sized bed, and it looked big enough for us to sleep comfortably on it. My feet might dangle off the end, but I was used to that with my height.

"I think the bed's big enough for the two of us. It'll be fine," she said and started typing on her computer.

"I'm sorry. I booked it without looking at the description."

She shrugged. "It's fine. It's just one night."

"Right."

I took my shoes off and sunk into the bed next to her. She leaned against the headboard with her computer on her lap, and her long legs stretched out in front of her. I leaned onto my side towards her and reached a hand out to lie against her thigh.

"Are you sure you're okay?" I asked.

She nodded, but I noticed she didn't swat my hand away. Interesting...

"I'm good. Sorry, I have to catch up on some work emails and call that landlady. Maybe we could get dinner in an hour?" she asked.

I nodded and eyed the book she had lying on the bed in between us. I removed my hand from her thigh and picked it up. On the cover, there was a half-naked guy flexing his muscles, and he had a pair of hockey skates around his neck.

What? Who does that?

I didn't realize she read books like this. I saw Fi read a lot of romance books when I lived with her and Riley, but I didn't realize there were ones about hockey. Or ones about hockey and hate banging your enemy according to the description on the back. That sounded eerily familiar.

"Oh my God!" she squealed when she saw what I was doing. "Give me that!"

I held it out of her reach. "Nuh-uh. What are you reading?"

She grimaced. "It's a romance book. Stop making fun of me."

"Not making fun. It's about hockey?"

Her cheeks tinted pink, and it looked so cute. "Yes," she gritted out in embarrassment. "Sports romances are a big sub-genre of the romance genre. They're my favorite."

I laid on my back and flipped to the first page to read. "Why do you like them so much?"

She shrugged as she tapped away on her keyboard. "I like sports. I played hockey, I like hockey, so I enjoy reading any sort of book that has to do with it. Fi leant me that one."

I raised an eyebrow. "Really? I think she's working on a romance novel."

"Wait, really? I need to read that!"

I held a finger up to my lips. "Baby, shush, I'm reading."

That got me another glare and the middle finger, which made me laugh. I didn't know why I insisted on making her angry all the time. Probably because it made her chest heave, and her eyes got all dark and sexy. I was in over my head with this woman. Sleeping with her didn't get it out of my system. Not by a long shot. Sleeping with her made me desperate to pin her underneath me again, but I knew that wasn't an option.

I stopped bothering her while she worked, and I read. I had to admit the hockey stuff was pretty accurate, so that was cool. I didn't even mind the kissing stuff in it, especially when it got very detailed. Holy fuck, people wrote this stuff? I felt my dick thicken against my thigh and my palms sweat. How did words in a frigging book get my motor going like this?

I jolted when Rox leaned over and placed a hand on my thigh. My dick was rock hard, and her grip was edging a little too close for comfort. "Benny," she said into my ear.

"Uh...yeah?" I asked and shifted so she wasn't touching me.

She smirked. "I asked if you wanted to get dinner."

I closed the book, not caring if I lost my place, and laid it down on the bedside table. I swung around to the other side of the bed and shifted myself in my pants so she couldn't see I had a boner. From a freaking book!

"Um, yeah, that's good. Did you get your work done?" I asked.

She packed her computer away and walked over to the mirror to reapply her dark lipstick. "Not really, but it's okay. Quinn was good with it."

I walked across the room to stand behind her. Watching her rub her lips with her make-up didn't help my downstairs situation. Now I was thinking about her lipstick smearing across my dick as she went down on me. I needed to stop thinking about her this way.

I ruffled my hair and tried to fix it from its messy bedhead state. I combed my hair with my fingers and fixed it naturally. I rubbed a hand across my jaw. My stubble was coming in all scratchy now that I was trying to grow my beard back out.

"You ready?" I asked.

She nodded, and we walked out the door together. We ended up sitting at the bar, so we had a prime view of the DC Senators and Carolina Thrashers series. We ordered lagers and food in what I felt was an uncomfortable silence.

"Senators are gonna take it, eh?" she offered as her eyes darted around the screen, chasing the players on the ice.

I peered up to watch what she was watching. She groaned at a hit right in the numbers that didn't get called. I shook my head. "That's bullshit; that guy left his feet!" I exclaimed.

"What do you know?" the guy next to me heckled me. He slurred his words, clearly a little drunk. I clenched my hand around my beer glass tightly and was surprised by the warm sensation of Rox's hand on my wrist. "Don't," she mouthed.

I shook my head. "If anyone did that to one of my guys, I would drop the gloves so fast."

She laughed. "You don't fight that much."

I cocked an eyebrow at her. "You keeping tabs on me, Desjardins?"

Her dark-colored lips curled up into a grin. "It's kind of my job now. Gotta figure out how to sell those tickets. But seriously, you still fight even with everything we know about concussions?"

I gulped down more of my beer and mulled over her question.

Concussions and CTE were still a tremendous problem in the league. I luckily never had a concussion, but it was a fair question. When I thought about what I loved about the game, fighting wasn't my main thought. I got where she was coming from, but she was wrong. Most concussions were because of the speed and nature of the game.

"I get what you're saying, but fighting only causes a small percentage of concussions. It's the speed and hits that cause more damage."

"Okay, fair, but the fighting stuff still worries me."

"Aw, don't worry about me, Roxie."

That got me her signature glare, but then she got serious for a second. "I worry about Tristan. He fights too much."

Ah, that made sense. It wasn't a secret that the Desjardins Twins were codependent, but with TJ away in Russia, I hadn't seen much of that yet.

The conversation ended because our food arrived. I tried to be healthier with the grilled chicken salad while Rox went for the burger. I had to focus on drinking my beer while she moaned in pleasure as she ate. My dick lifted up in interest at the sound of that coming out of her mouth. The man downstairs definitely remembered her moaning like that and was interested in hearing it again.

"Oh my God, I was so hungry." She groaned and finished her beer. The bartender filled her up again.

I eyed her while she closed her eyes and ate her food. She was getting greasy juices all down her chin, and it was enough to distract me. I thrust a pile of napkins at her. "Here."

Her eyes snapped open, and she gave me a sheepish look as she carefully wiped her mouth so she didn't smear her lipstick. I dug into my salad and tried not to look at her.

"Thanks," she muttered, but her eyes were on the screen watching the game.

A smile curled around my lips. "You miss it."

She nodded. "Yeah..."

"You know, you can still play if you love the game. What's so bad about playing in a beer league?" I asked.

She took a sip of her beer. "I don't know. I think...I'm scared."

"Of what?"

She wouldn't look at me. "I didn't play for most of my last year at university."

"Oh?"

She downed more of her beer at an alarming pace.

I put a hand on her shoulder. "Hey, you don't have to tell me."

She shook her head. "I took a nasty hit earlier in the season and got a severe concussion. I finished out that year, but I've barely been on the ice since."

"Shit, Rox, I'm sorry."

Her worrying about concussions and CTE made sense now. She was scared about that happening again or to someone she cared about, and I didn't blame her.

I put an arm around her shoulder in comfort and was surprised when she didn't yank it off. We finished our meal in silence, but I was glad I was slowly unraveling the mystery that was Roxanne Desjardins.

CHAPTER FIFTEEN

ROXANNE

I didn't know why I told Benny about my concussion fears. There was something about him calmly asking me that made me reveal that secret. He was right, though; I missed being on the ice. I missed the skshh-skshh-skshh sound of my blades biting into the ice and the thwack of my stick against the puck. I had lived and breathed this sport for years, but like most women hockey players, it ended with my collegiate career. He was right. I could join a league for fun if I missed the game, but I wasn't sure I wanted to do that.

I was mulling it over in silence and on my third beer when the guy next to me tapped me on the shoulder. He was a bearded, middle-aged guy with greying hair old enough to be my father. Gross.

"Can I buy you a drink?" he asked.

I held up my current bottle. "I'm good." I turned back to Benny to ask him about the call on the ice I had missed, but the guy grabbed my arm. "Hey!" I yelled in protest.

"Come on, just looking for a little conversation," the guy said with a slur. He was way drunker than Benny, who narrowed his eyes and clenched his hand around his nearly empty beer.

"I'm not interested," I said to him. "Thanks, but no thanks."

"And people say chubby girls are easy," he spat.

In a flash, Benny had risen to his full height and stood over the guy. "What the fuck did you say to her?" he asked through gritted teeth.

"Benny!" I yelled.

The guy sneered at me. "Bitch knows what I said. Fat girls are supposed to appreciate men interested in them."

Benny stood over the guy. "Apologize to the lady, right now."

"Benny! Stop!" I shrieked at him.

"Fuck you, man," the guy scoffed.

I grabbed Benny's arm and dug my fingernails into his skin. "Benny, calm down."

He looked down at my hand on his arm, and his eyes softened as he met mine. He had been nursing his beer all night, so I didn't think he was drunk, but I didn't want him to cause a scene. He couldn't be getting into bar brawls and jeopardizing his career because some asshole called me fat. I pulled him back toward his seat next to me.

I mouthed sorry to the bartender. "Can we get the check?" I asked her.

She nodded, printed out the receipt, and handed it to me. Benny yanked it out of my hands. "Give me that!" he snapped. He handed her his card, despite my protests.

The drunk guy moved on, but Benny looked pissed, and I was fuming at him for his outburst. We needed to get out of there before someone recognized him, and we caused a bigger scene. What that guy said was rude, but it wasn't the first time a drunk asshole called me that.

Benny signed the check and threw down a hefty tip. "Come on, let's get out of here."

When he took my hand in his, I didn't protest, although I might have squeezed his hand a little too tight. Like I was trying to break his hand for trying to be the tough guy who defended my honor. I waited until the elevator doors slid closed before I fixed him with a glare and wrenched my hand out of his.

"Dude, what the fuck?" I asked with a sneer.

He looked confused. "What? That guy was being a dick!"

"I'm aware, but you don't need to do that whole alpha-male thing and defend me. It's not like I haven't heard that shit before."

His nostrils flared. "What?"

"Men have called me fat before because I've rejected them. You can't afford to be getting into a brawl. Think of your career."

He growled in frustration. "I hate that people say that shit to you."

"Why does it matter to you?"

The elevators dinged on our floor, and I stomped down the hall with him hot on my heels. I didn't care what people thought of me, and he didn't need to defend me. I didn't ask him to come with me, and I didn't need him getting into a fight in the off-season.

Benny had it harder as a player of color. Despite what the NHL said about hockey being for everyone, they scrutinized him for his actions on and off the ice way more than his white teammates. It wasn't fair, but I didn't want to fuck up his career because he was trying to defend me.

I stomped into the room, but before I could go to bed angry, he spun me around and grabbed my shoulders. "Why are you mad at *me*?"

I pushed at his chest. "Because I don't need you to defend me. I don't give a fuck what people think about me."

"I do," he admitted in a small voice.

"Why?" I asked.

His eyes trailed down my body, and he hooked two fingers through my belt loops. "Because your curves are sexy, and it pisses me off when people don't see you the way I see you."

I pulled back. "Benny, you're drunk."

"I'm not. I had two beers." He wound his hand through my hair, and I couldn't help the way my breath hitched as he touched me.

"You're such a frustrating man," I growled out, but I wasn't pulling away this time. I *wanted* him to touch me...but the other part of me wanted to punch him.

My feelings about this man were a constant contradiction. I was supposed to hate him, but I didn't hate the way his hands felt on me. And I didn't hate the night we had spent together.

He gripped my hair tightly, and I felt a slight tug of pain on my scalp, but I was kind of into it. "And you're such a frustrating woman. You make my brain stop working," he hissed.

I glared at him, but I didn't pull away from his grip. I snaked my arms around his neck and dug my fingernails into his skin. "You can't go all caveman when some drunk guy is rude to me. I can take care of myself."

"Rox, stop arguing with me!"

"Why are you so anno—"

He cut off the rest of my retort by crushing his lips up

against mine in an angry kiss. I relaxed into the kiss and opened to him when his tongue caressed the seam of my lips. I moaned at his tongue tangling with mine again. His grip loosened on my hair, and his hands trailed down my back. He lifted me up into his arms, and I wrapped my legs around his waist and clung onto his shoulders.

His hands went to my ass to hold me up, and he squeezed while he trailed kisses down my jaw. His lips were like fire across my skin, and if his arms weren't holding me up, I might have melted into a puddle on the floor. I tipped my head back in pleasure when that hot trail of kisses led to the soft skin below my ear.

"Put me down. I'm too heavy for you," I complained.

He nipped at my neck. "Shut up. You know how much I lift, right?"

"No..." I moaned while he licked and sucked at my flesh on that spot that got me going.

"More than you weigh, so shut up and let me."

"Mmm," I moaned and angled my head to give him more access to my neck.

"Is that the only way to get you to stop arguing? Huh, bad girl? Kiss you senseless?" he whispered into my ear.

His voice rumbled in a combination of frustration and desire, matching the heat building up inside my body. This man frustrated me to no end, but he was also my weakness. I wanted him to touch every part of me until I was begging him to stop. I knew I shouldn't want that with him again—he was supposed to be my mortal enemy forever—but I didn't think about my grudge against him when he held me in his arms and kissed me.

"Uh-huh," I mumbled.

Suddenly the world spun, and I was on my back as he settled me on the bed. I looked into the dark eyes of the giant kneeling in-between my legs. He hovered over me, and his hands gently caressed my face. He was a man of contradiction. Gravely voice and brutish aggression, but his caresses were feather-light and gentle. When he stopped kissing me, I remembered why I was so mad at him.

"Are you gonna be a good girl now and stop arguing with me?" he asked.

I glared up at him. "Fuck no! I'm still pissed at you for trying to start a fight."

"I was trying to protect you."

"I don't need your protection. Who says I need you to protect me from drunk assholes?"

"I love your curves," he whispered. His hand slid down from my chest to my torso; his fingers hooked onto the belt loops of my jeans.

I ground my teeth at him, even though the other part of me didn't want him to stop touching me. "You didn't have to do that!"

"You don't deserve for people to treat you that way."

I glared at him. "Don't you think I already know that?"

"That's what I like about you."

"What?" I screeched.

I thought we were still fighting. Why was he talking about liking me?

"You don't give a single fuck what anyone thinks about you. You're feisty and confident. It's so sexy."

I gripped his shirt in my hands and pulled him back down to my level roughly. "Get back down here and kiss me like you mean it."

He obliged, but like the tease he was, he only kissed me for a split second. "I'm gonna show you how much I mean it. Show you what you deserve."

I arched an unimpressed eyebrow at him. "Oh yeah? What do I deserve?"

"To be worshipped like the goddess you are." He kissed my neck and nipped at my earlobe. His breath was hot in my ear. "I'm going to shed you of all these clothes and worship every inch of your body until you beg me to stop. Until I've drained you of every last drop of pleasure."

"Fuck…"

"And then I'm gonna keep going."

"Then what are you waiting for? Do it!" I growled. I needed him inside me. I needed him to make me feel like I was loved.

"Patience, bad girl," he cooed. "I want to savor you."

He gave me a cocky smirk when all I could do in response was whimper at how painfully horny I was.

CHAPTER SIXTEEN

BENNY

She looked up at me with eyes full of desire. Her dark hair fanned out against the pillow, and in that moment, she looked like an angel. I loved that with every moment of me being aggressive; she gave it right back. When I heard that guy call her fat, I nearly blew a gasket. I liked her soft, feminine body, from her full breasts to her round hips and everything in-between. I loved it all, and I wanted to show her that.

She grabbed the collar of my shirt and pulled me back down to her lips. "C'mere, you," she growled.

I cupped her face and kissed her. She nipped at my bottom lip, and I opened to her, letting her tongue slide into my mouth and giving her the control she desperately wanted. I straddled her hips, locking her legs underneath my bigger body, and pushed her t-shirt up to reveal her smooth white skin.

I pulled back to look at her.

"What?" she asked, almost annoyed that I had stopped.

"You sure you want to do this?" I asked.

She bit her lip. "I do, but you seem drunker than me. Are you sure?"

"I'm not drunk, just a little tipsy."

"Yeah, but for a big guy, you're surprisingly a lightweight. I don't want to take advantage of you," she admitted.

I laughed. "Yeah, I never hear the end of it from the boys. I just have a low alcohol tolerance."

She smirked. "I don't have that problem."

"Enough about that. Let's get you out of those clothes." I helped her sit up, and I pulled her shirt over her head. I ran my hands across her lacy bra. "Rox, you're so sexy."

She frowned. "You're just saying that to get into my pants."

I kissed her neck and nipped at her earlobe. "When will you get it through your thick skull that you're sexy to me? You're confident, sassy, and a real ball-buster. You intimidate me and make me say all the wrong things. It's why you hate me."

She pushed me off her. "What do you mean?"

I laid back on the bed next to her with a groan. "I don't know how to control my filter when I'm around you. So I say rude things that make you hate me."

She leaned over and swung her legs over both of my hips, straddling me and holding me down with her hands pressed hard against my chest. I slid my hands up her jean-clad thighs.

"I don't think I hate you anymore. At least not as much."

Then she started laughing.

"What?" I asked.

"Oh my God, I knew this would happen as soon as you told me there was only one bed."

I frowned up at her. "You know I didn't do this on purpose, right? I had no intention of getting tangled up in bed again."

She ran her hands up and down my chest. "Oh, are you saying you don't want to fuck me?" She pressed my wrists above my head, locking our hands together, trying to prevent me from flipping her over onto her back. It was cute that she thought she could restrain me.

"Oh, no. I'm gonna fuck you real good tonight," I promised. "I want to worship your body."

She smirked down at me. "Good, because 'there's only one bed' is like one of the biggest romance tropes! There's only one bed, so now we have to fuck. It's the rules."

I smiled up at her. "Yeah? I like those rules."

"You really think I'm hot?"

"Shut up—you know you're sexy. Now get these jeans off and get on your back."

I used my legs to flip her over. Our hands were locked together, but I had the upper hand. She bit her lip seductively at me, so I knew she liked that power move.

I removed our interlocked hands and brought her tattooed wrist up to my lips to kiss it. I dropped her hand and fumbled with the button of her jeans. She arched her hips up to help me pull her jeans down her legs, and I tossed them to the floor. I shed my clothes and tossed them to the other side of the room without a care.

I ran my hand down her chest and noticed her bra had an open clasp. *Oh hell yes.* I flicked the clasp open with one hand and revealed those perfect round globes. It was like she was offering a sexy gift for me to lick and suck as much as I wanted. She shimmied underneath me, and I helped her remove the offensive article.

She pulled me back down to her lips aggressively, and

we melted into another passionate kiss. She moaned into my mouth. I trailed my kisses down her jaw, traveling towards her chest. I swirled my tongue over a nipple, smiling into her skin when the bud sharpened to a point on my tongue. I switched to the other one, sucking long and hard until her back arched and she writhed in pleasure.

"Benny..." she moaned.

I placed tiny kisses that made her laugh along her ribs until I reached the waistband of her black lace panties. I stripped them off and spread her legs to make room for my body. I kissed her inner thigh, teasing her by not going to the place I knew she wanted me to go.

"Tell me where you want me to kiss you next," I demanded into her skin.

"You know," she snapped at me.

"You want me to kiss you here, angel?" I asked and placed a soft kiss on her swollen clit while I parted her with my thumb.

"Benny, please!" she begged.

"Please, what?" I asked. I ever so lightly flicked my tongue over the sweet bud.

"Get down there and lick me," she said and shoved my head down where she wanted me.

My laugh rumbled into her pussy, and she squeezed her legs around my head in response. Most women moaned and said thank you when I went down on them, but not Roxanne Desjardins. I loved how feisty she was in bed.

I licked at her clit and slid a finger inside her entrance. I continued to lick and suck at her while she writhed in pleasure until I pumped a second finger inside. I curled my fingers up and hit her sensitive spot. Her breath hitched under my ministrations, and I took my time pleasing her until I felt her shake with a thunderous orgasm. She shuttered and moaned, and I licked across her sensitive clit while she came down from it. And then I did it again, tasting her and moaning into her until she was whimpering and begging for my dick.

"I thought you were a guy who didn't do that," she said and pulled me back up to her. She kissed me, not caring that I still tasted of her.

I pinned her arms above her head. "I love eating pussy. Did you love coming on my tongue?"

She laughed at me. "Uh-huh. But now I want your cock in my mouth."

I grinned at her. "Holy fuck, really?"

She nodded vigorously but then frowned. "I haven't done that in a long time."

I nosed across her skin and laughed into her neck. "It's okay. You don't have to."

"But I want to," she whined. "I'm just bad at it."

"Rox," I growled. "The fact you want to do it at all does it for me."

"I don't want it to be bad," she admitted with a small frown.

I cupped her face and kissed her tenderly. When I pulled away, I rubbed my thumb across her plump bottom lip. "Nothing you do could ever be bad."

"You don't know that," she argued.

I didn't argue with her. Instead, I moved to my back and fisted my cock in my hand. "You want this?" I asked her.

She nodded and licked her lips.

I stroked myself and watched her with hungry eyes. "You want to put it in your mouth?"

She nodded again. "I do."

I crooked a finger at her. "Then get over here and suck my cock."

She kissed her way down my body until she was kneeling in-between my legs and nuzzling my rock-hard dick with her face. I held in a breath of anticipation. She looked up at me seductively and flicked her tongue across the head, never once dropping her eyes from mine. One of her hands held the base while she took me in her mouth.

"Oh, fuck." I gathered her hair up in my hands to keep it out of her face, but mostly so I could watch my dick sliding in and out of her sweet mouth.

"Mmmhmm," she moaned with her mouth full of my cock.

She was such a liar; she wasn't bad at sucking dick at all.

I had to focus on trying to not finish while she took me deeper and sucked on me hard. She teased me, pulling me in and then pulling back so she could lick me from root to tip, then she sucked on me again.

"Rox..." I moaned while I gripped her hair tighter.

She must have sensed I was close because she suddenly released me with a wet pop.

"When was the last time you did that?" I asked.

Her on her knees with her lipstick-smeared mouth near my cock was a sight I never wanted to forget. I wanted to burn the image into my retinas, memorize it and never forget this night. It would be the star image for my spank bank, that was for sure.

"Not since university," she admitted and wiped her eyes. "Shit, that made my eyes water."

"Damn girl, I'm sorry."

"You don't think I'm bad at it?"

"Fuck no! You were moaning while sucking my dick; that was hot."

"But I can't even deep throat."

"Rox, I don't care. Your lips wrapped around my cock felt amazing."

She smiled up at me and returned to her spot beside me on the bed.

I got out of bed and went to grab a condom from my wallet. I slid it on my cock and found the lube in my bag. I squeezed a liberal amount out and worked it down my length, then wiped my hand off with a tissue and climbed back onto the bed.

I traced my hands down her face, across the planes of her body, until I gripped her hips in my hands. Her body was luscious and curvy, and yet she felt so small beneath my muscular bulk. I cradled her in my arms, afraid I would break her, while I kneed her legs open and slid home.

"Fuck, you feel so good," I groaned.

"We should have done this sooner," she admitted while she wrapped her legs around me.

I didn't disagree with her. I pumped into her slowly until we found the pace together, me driving into her hard while she bucked her hips up and met me pound-for-pound. Her fingernails dug into my back as we rocked and writhed together.

"You're so beautiful," I whispered across her skin while I kissed her neck.

She wrenched my head back by my hair, forcing me to look into her passion-filled eyes. "Don't say that. Don't tell me things you think I need to hear."

I adjusted my position and pressed my hand against where we were joined. "I thought we went over this. I'm not lying," I seethed through gritted teeth and rubbed tiny circles on her clit in time with my thrusts.

"I'm not what men like you want."

"Yes, you are. Stop overthinking this, and let me give you this pleasure. Let me worship your sexy body."

"Benny, I'm not—"

I cut her off with a kiss while I pumped into her and gave her feather-light touches on her clit. "You're such a frustrating woman. I love your body, and I want to please you. Give in."

"No," she growled.

"Give in," I demanded.

She ground her teeth. So fucking combative, but I loved it.

"Please, angel? Let me get you there," I urged her while I buried myself deeper inside her hot heat. Her resolve was slipping with each thrust, and when she closed her eyes and rolled her hips lazily to meet me, I knew I had won.

"Oh my God. Please..." she moaned.

"Please what, angel?"

"Please unravel me."

"Let go. I've got you," I urged her. I removed my hand from our connection so I could cradle her in my arms and look her in the eyes while I took her over the cliffs of pleasure.

"Please," she cried out.

"Come for me, angel. I've got you."

Our bodies slapped together, and she lifted her hips up to meet my thrusts. I was unraveling the sexy woman who used to want to murder me but who relinquished her control to me. It was a sexy thing when a strong-willed, opinionated woman like Roxanne gave up control to let me have the reins.

"Fuuuckk," she moaned while she shuddered beneath me. Her legs slipped back down to the bed, and she pressed her hands into my chest.

"What the—" I started, and then somehow I wasn't inside her anymore and was on my back, looking up at the woman hovering over me.

She pressed her hands flat onto my chest. "I want to be in charge," she snarled at me while she slid down onto my cock in one swift motion.

"Hey!" I growled back. My hands bit into her ass while she rode me, and from her gasp, I knew she liked it. I grinned wickedly at her. "I should spank that ass of yours for being such a bad girl."

She ground herself on top of me and gave me a cheeky grin. "I want to break you like you just broke me. I want to watch you come undone beneath me until you're moaning my name," she growled.

"Roxanne, please, take what you want. I'm yours," I moaned beneath her.

She leaned down to kiss me, and I sneakily slid my finger to her clit. She might have thought she was in charge, but I knew how to have her falling apart in my hands. I circled the tiny bud with my finger until she cried out in release, riding me hard and digging her fingernails into my chest. I loved watching her let go like this, trusting me with this intimate part of herself. Watching her tip back her head in passion while she came on top of me was a beautiful sight.

"That's it, angel. Ride my dick like the bad girl you are," I said and dug my hands into her hips.

"I am a bad girl," she agreed.

I slapped her ass. "So fucking bad."

She ground on top of me. "Come for me, Benny. Please?"

She didn't have to ask me twice; I held her hips down

onto me and thrusted up inside her uncontrollably until I was coming in long, hot spurts.

We were both panting and glistening with sweat. She reached down to push a sweaty chunk of my hair out of my face. Then she did something that surprised me; she cupped my face and gingerly pressed her lips to mine. It was a sweet gesture, but the kiss was over before I could process it, and then she hopped off of me.

I got rid of the condom while she was in the bathroom, but when she came back, she laid down on the bed beside me, still naked and beautiful. Like a fucking angel. She shifted onto her side so her arm was around my waist, and she stroked my hair with her other hand. I smiled that she remembered how much I liked to be held after sex.

"Are we gonna talk about you calling me angel?" she asked.

I closed my eyes. *Shit*. I had called her that. "You said you don't like being called baby. Is it okay if I call you angel?"

"Why did you call me that?" she asked.

"Because you looked like an angel laid out on the bed for me."

"You're not gonna ask if I fell from heaven?"

I laughed and turned in her arms. "No, because we both know you crawled up from hell to annoy me."

"Ass!" she screeched and pinched my side.

I pinned her arms above her head and straddled her, my cock thickening in interest again already. This feisty woman made me so hard. "Admit it, Rox. You love bickering with me."

She gave a sheepish look and nodded. "Fine, you're right, I kinda do. You're hot when you're all riled up."

I let go of her wrists and rested my head against her

naked chest. She wrapped her arms around me and kissed the top of my head. Her fingers stroked my hair lovingly, and I sighed at the sensation. This woman was frustrating but also sweet in these quiet moments.

"Full disclosure?" I asked and looked up into her eyes. I continued when she nodded. "I may have picked fights with you on purpose over the years because you're also hot when you get all flustered."

Hazel eyes flashed in anger. "Dick!"

"Admit it—you love our fights. You look forward to them."

"No..." She trailed off, but she wasn't fooling me. "Shut up."

I cuddled down into her soft curves and hugged her waist tightly. "Nope."

"You really like to cuddle, eh?" she asked.

"I love cuddling, but my ex called me a 'soft boy' because of it. What the fuck does that even mean?"

She laughed. "Oh, that just means you're sensitive and in touch with your feelings. Getting to know you lately, I don't think she was wrong. Although, I think you're more of an Alphamallow."

I frowned. "A what?"

She bopped my nose. "You're all growly and aggressive in the bedroom, but really you're a teddy bear. It's sweet how you don't want to hurt me. I also like a man who's not afraid to use lube."

I ran my hand down her arm and brought her tattooed wrist up to my mouth for a kiss. "I want it to be good for you."

"I appreciate that."

"Can I ask you something?"

"What?"

I removed myself from her chest and laid back on my pillow. I turned and looked into her eyes. The swirls of browns and greens were a storm of confusion. "Can we be done fighting and hating each other?"

She shrugged. "Only if you don't go all alpha-male and try to fight every douchebag who says something mean about me. I'm still mad at you for that."

"But you don't hate me anymore?"

Her eyes twinkled, and her lips curled up into a grin. "The jury's still out."

She yelped when I grabbed her hips and swung her across my lap. I gripped her jaw between my fingers, and I pressed another passionate kiss to her lips. Her hands immediately tangled in my hair, and we fought for dominance again.

"Stop being so difficult," I growled at her.

She giggled into my ear while she sucked on my neck. "You can't tell me what to do."

I growled at her again. "Do I have to fuck it out of you?"

"What?" she asked and nipped at my earlobe.

"Your hatred for me."

"I'd like to see you try," she snarled.

"That's it, bad girl. You're gonna get it good now."

I was glad I remembered to throw extra condoms in my backpack—and the lube. Lube was great. Especially if you were planning on throwing down with a feisty woman all night long. She was going to have to beg me to quit before I was through with her.

CHAPTER SEVENTEEN

ROXANNE

Later, when I was brushing out my hair and Benny was brushing his teeth, I realized I didn't hate him anymore. Maybe it was too soon after years of animosity, but when he kissed me, I got lost in the sensation. Like I was flying or skating down the ice on the breakaway. I was in *trouble* because if I didn't hate Benny anymore, that meant I felt other things for him, and I didn't want to think about that.

I drug the brush through my damp hair and stared at my reflection in the mirror. Benny may have worshipped my body tonight and told me how much he loved it, but that didn't change the insecurities I felt. Not like it mattered since he was going to ask for a trade.

He brushed my hair over my shoulder and leaned down to kiss the nape of my neck. "Stop it," he whispered in my ear.

He wore only his towel after we had round three in the shower. I'd never had shower sex before, but he made me think wild thoughts. I was going to be sore tomorrow, but I didn't care. I never thought I was a woman who craved cock, but Benny's was amazing.

"What?" I asked.

He wrapped his arms around my waist and peppered my neck with kisses. "I can see the gears in your head turning. I know what you're thinking."

I glared at him through the mirror. "You do not."

"You think we don't fit together. You think I couldn't possibly love your body."

"No..."

He spun me around and put a finger to my lips. "Don't lie; I can see it in your face." He pressed his hips against mine, and my eyes widened at the semi-hardness I felt on my leg. "You wouldn't do *that* to me if I didn't think you were sexy."

"How? Again?"

He laughed and gestured to the towel wrapped around me. "You in nothing but a towel. Fuck, it makes me horny all over again."

"I don't believe you!"

He turned me around to face the mirror and pressed up against my back. I felt his cock poking me while he fingered the knot on my towel.

He bent his head to my ear. "So sexy. I want to bend you over the sink and watch our reflection in the mirror while I fuck you from behind."

I breathed hard and tried to look away from him. "I need to blow dry my hair."

He nuzzled my neck, and I gasped when he untied the knot and the towel dropped to the floor. "Let it air dry," he said in my ear.

"Benny..." I sighed. "You can't seriously want to go again."

He chuckled against my skin. "Oh, Rox. You don't understand; I can't get enough of you."

I looked up, watching him in the mirror as he unceremoniously dropped his towel on the floor. My eyes tracked down the hard lines of brown skin, from his six-pack abs to the delicious V above his hips before landing on his cock. Romance novels always talked about wanting to lick the hero's six-pack abs, and I never understood that until Michael Bennett was standing naked in front of me. Now I wanted to lick every part of his body. Even though we had sex three times tonight, I ached for him.

He ran his hand over my body, stopping to cup my tits, and then he continued to roam. He made a little noise of pleasure as his hands skated down my rounded stomach and inched towards my mound. Then the little tease gripped my hips in his hands instead.

"Benny..." I groaned as if I was in pain.

"Love these sexy curves," he said and tapped my ass playfully. "Stop thinking I don't want you, that I don't like what I see. That I don't like what I'm holding onto right now."

"Benny."

"Yeah?"

"Do we have any more condoms?"

He grinned at me through the mirror and gave my ass another little tap. "Don't you fucking move."

"Don't tell me what to do!" I snapped back at him.

"Do as you're told," he said and gave me another slap on my ass.

I gave him the finger, and he laughed while he walked out

to the main room. I bit my lip, watching him through the mirror when he walked back into the bathroom. He had already rolled the condom on his cock, and he gave me a cute smirk as he fisted it. He positioned himself behind me and pushed my legs apart while I leaned my arms against the sink in front of me.

He slid his hand around me, crawling down my body until his finger slid across the bud of my clit. "Look at you," he breathed.

"What about me?" I gasped as he touched me. His hand slid down past my clit to explore my depths. He pumped two thick fingers inside me, and I bucked against his hand, ready for him again.

What was wrong with me? I was never this horny before.

"So sexy. Love that you're ready for me again," he purred into my ear. He kissed my neck while his fingers worked their magic on me.

"Give it to me, big guy."

He pulled his fingers out and entered me from behind in a smooth motion. I was going to be so sore tomorrow. I'd never had sex with someone this many times in one night. I couldn't get enough of him, though. Maybe I was just trying to fuck any hostility for him out of me. When he touched me, kissed me, was inside me, all of those old feelings melted away. I unraveled myself into him, letting my guard down and giving in to the pleasure of it all. Maybe Canada put this spell on us, but I would take it.

His hands dug deep into my hips as his thrusting got faster and harder. I moaned, and we locked eyes in the mirror. We looked wild with our desire for each other. No one else had ever looked at me the way he looked at me. Like he wanted to eat me up—and I would let him.

"So fucking hot, Rox," he moaned into my neck in-between thrusts.

"What is?" I asked and gripped the sink tighter.

His motions were sending me up and up until my orgasm was about to crest. I didn't even know I could come again. I had lost count of the number of orgasms this man had given me tonight. Too much, not enough; I wanted more and more. I wanted him to take what my body could give until I was exhausted and spent.

"Taking you from behind and watching you as we fuck and fuck and fuck," he growled and punctuated each word with a hard thrust, sending my tits bouncing. He grinned as he watched through the mirror, and his grip on my hips tightened.

"So good," I moaned in agreement. I squeezed my eyes shut while the pleasure took over.

"That's it, angel."

I opened my eyes so I could watch him through the mirror behind me. His hands clenched tighter, and he thrusted hard and fast until I was about to come apart at the seams.

"Say my name," he growled.

"Benny," I moaned and leaned into the sink more.

"No. My first name, I want to hear you moan it."

I frowned. Nobody called him by his first name; sometimes, I forgot Benny was a hockey nickname.

His fingers dug into my skin. "Say it, angel."

"Michael."

"Good girl."

"I'm not a good girl!"

He slapped my ass and grinned big at me. "Damn right you're not. You're my bad girl, huh?"

I nodded while I felt that tingle up my spine as he angled his cock where I needed it.

"Come with me, Roxanne. Come all over my cock," he ordered.

"Michael," I moaned in response.

Pleasure coursed through my body, and I let it take over me. He pounded hard and needy inside me. His hands dug into my hips until his lips were on my neck, and he groaned into my ear while he came with me.

We locked eyes in the mirror again. "That was hot," he panted out and kissed my shoulder.

I laughed. "It was. Now get out because I still need to fix my hair."

He pulled out and threw away the condom, but then he came back to me and kissed my cheek. "You look beautiful."

I gave him a sour look.

"I love your come face. It's the hottest thing I've ever seen."

I shook my head at him but was grinning as I shooed him out of the bathroom. "Get out of here!"

He walked back into the main room, and I heard the TV turn on. I surveyed myself in the mirror. My hair was a bit of a wreck, so I had to brush it out again to get all the tangles out. At least he didn't pull my hair this time. It could have been worse.

I flicked on the hairdryer and ran it through my hair until it was dry enough. I then hung up our dirty towels on the hook and padded into the main room. I went to my bag, where I produced clean clothes to sleep in. It was cold in the room, and I had only brought a tank top and shorts to sleep in. I ran my hands down my arms.

Benny sat on the bed against the headboard with his long

legs stretched out in front of him. He wore a pair of black sweatpants and a Bulldogs t-shirt. I was silently thanking the hockey gods for that because if he was shirtless, oh boy, I might have made some poor decisions. We'd had sex four times tonight. How did I still want to jump his bones?

He arched a dark eyebrow at me. "You cold?" he asked.

I nodded and got into bed next to him. He hefted himself off the bed and dug around in his bag. When he returned, he handed me a Bulldogs sweatshirt. I thanked him and put it on, surprising myself by thinking that it smelled like him, and that comforted me.

Wait, what?

He climbed back into the bed, but instead of next to me, he slid in behind me and shifted my body so I was sitting in-between his legs with my back against his front. His arms came up behind me to hug me around the waist. I leaned my head back against his chest and watched the game while I settled into his arms. This was weird, but I liked that he was such a cuddly guy.

It was a little late, so the St. Louis Walleyes and the Winnipeg Whitecaps game was about to start the third period.

"Who you got?" I asked while listening to the intermission report.

"St. Louis."

I glanced up at him. "Really? Caps all the way."

He chucked, and I felt the rumble in his chest on my back. "What? Is that like Canadian law or something?"

"Yup!"

He wrapped his arms around my middle again, and I couldn't help the smile break out on my face. This gigantic man was such a cuddly teddy bear, and I didn't hate it. I leaned back into his chest, loving the feeling of his body pressed up against mine. I felt oddly safe in his arms. He was chipping away at my armor and had unraveled me completely.

"Oh, wow, you aren't glaring at me. I need to take a picture because I know that won't last," he joked.

I jabbed him in the ribs with my elbow, but I smiled when he picked up his phone and took a selfie of us. I smiled at the camera when at the last second, he kissed my temple. I angled my head up towards his face, and he ducked his head down to meet me in a kiss. I reached my hand up into his hair, and I smiled into the kiss when I heard the click of his camera again.

"Send those to me?" I asked when we parted.

He nuzzled my neck and gave me feather-light kisses. Even though his short stubble was still scratchy, I loved the feeling of it across my smooth skin. "Of course."

"Benny?"

"Hmm?"

"What's happening between us right now?"

He paused for a moment, and then he lifted my wrist to his mouth and kissed my tattoo. I swear he was obsessed with that spot, but I liked the sweet gesture. "Whatever you want."

I chewed my lip but didn't have an answer for him because I didn't know what I wanted. I liked being in his arms and him holding me close as we watched the sport we loved. He was so strong, and his enormous arms made me feel so safe that I didn't want to let go of the cocoon of his embrace. His kisses made me feel alive. They were like him, aggressive yet kind, and I didn't want them to stop.

He squeezed me around my middle and kissed my cheek. "Do you still hate me?" he whispered into my hair.

"Hmm. I don't know..." I trailed off until he tickled me, and I giggled uncontrollably.

He pushed me onto my back again and held my face in both of his hands while he hovered over me. "Say it!" he teased.

"Fine, stop!" I laughed. "I guess I don't hate you anymore."

"Damn right, you don't," he grinned, and he bent down to press another kiss to my lips.

This kiss differed from all the others. Those had been passionate, aggressive kisses between two people at odds with their feelings. I wasn't sure what was happening between us, but I melted into him every time his lips touched mine. Chills went down my spine when he touched me, and my heart was getting big foolish ideas when he brushed my hair behind my ear and looked deep into my eyes. His dark brown eyes stared back at me like he was reaching into my soul. Like he knew every fear and thought inside my head, and he wanted to kiss them all away. I wanted him to do that. I never wanted to leave the comfort of his arms...but he was asking for a trade, so I couldn't let my heart get any ideas.

"Rox, why did it take us this long?" he asked in between kisses.

I tangled my hand in his hair. "Because I'm a bitch?"

He nipped at my neck in anger. "You're not. You're stubborn, difficult even, but not that. I never thought that about you."

My heart softened at his kind words, but I wasn't sure why he never thought of me that way. I made his life difficult every time our paths crossed. I was a Grade-A bitch to him while he had been patient with me.

Something had shifted in my heart since the first night

we spent together, and now it was on a path of destruction. When he looked at me hungrily, I stared back with a mirrored look. Maybe there was a fine line between hate and passion, but thinking about what we were doing right now, I couldn't process it. I only knew that I wanted to be wrapped up in this man's arms, and I didn't want him to let go.

"Why not?" I asked. "I was so mean to you. But I was in a relationship the entire time we knew each other. She hurt me."

He shifted, so he was no longer on top of me but lying on his side next to me. "I'm sorry she hurt you, but I'm not sorry you aren't with her anymore. I gotta ask you something, though."

"What?"

"She doesn't like that you're bisexual, does she?"

I had a feeling he overheard her ask me if I was straight today. I had to admit, it surprised me that Benny accepted my identity quicker than she did.

I shook my head. "She was fine with me being bi; she just didn't like that it meant I also liked men."

He tucked my hair behind my ear. "You deserve someone who respects you for you. Who respects that no matter who you're with that doesn't change that you're bisexual. I have to admit, I've always been attracted to you. You were this mystery I wanted to unwrap."

I shook my head. "Bullshit."

"Why else would I stare at you so much?"

He had a point there.

He turned off the hockey game and pulled back the comforter while scooping me up effortlessly to tuck me underneath. "Come on. Let's get some sleep."

He got up to check the door was locked and turn off the

lights, then removed his t-shirt before sliding into the bed beside me. His muscular arm wrapped around my waist, and he nuzzled his face into the crook of my neck.

I leaned up to look at him. "Thanks for coming with me today. Even though I didn't want you to, I needed a friend here."

"Oh, are we friends now?"

I elbowed him in the ribs. "Maybe with some benefits?"

"Are these secret benefits? Or ones our friends can know about?"

I paused and mulled it over. I wanted to keep kissing this man; I didn't want to stop. But if he was asking for a trade to another city, this couldn't be serious. I was down for some hot off-season sex, but it had to be a secret fling until my brother got home. Tristan could never know about this.

"Can we keep it to ourselves? For now?" I asked.

He kissed my neck, and I felt him nod into it, but he didn't say anything.

CHAPTER EIGHTEEN

BENNY

I woke to a weight on my arm and soft wisps of breath tickling my chest hair. I slid my eyes open and looked down at Rox curled up against me. Her leg was thrown over my thigh, and her head rested against my chest. Waking up with her wrapped up in my arms after a night of animalistic fucking was a dream come true.

We had sex four times last night; that was a record for me. Watching her come in the bathroom mirror while I fucked her from behind had been especially hot. It was definitely spank bank material I'd save for later.

It didn't take long to realize I had a problem. I couldn't move my arm, and her hand was curled dangerously close to my raging morning wood.

"Stop fucking staring at me," she snarled into my chest.

I kissed the top of her head and pulled her hand to my mouth to kiss the back of it. "Morning, angel," I said.

She lifted her head and glared up at me. "Did you do that so I wouldn't feel your boner? Because I can see it."

This fucking woman.

I tilted her head up and kissed her softly. Her grumbling subsided when I deepened the kiss. Was it possible that I had tamed the grouchy hurricane that was Roxanne Desjardins? Maybe all I had to do was give her multiple orgasms to get her to stop hating me.

"Benny," she sighed when I pulled away from her.

She shifted so she was no longer crushing my arm, and part of me missed the pressure of her curled up in my arms. The other part of me beamed at the way my name came off her lips. Like I could forget how she moaned it in my ear last night when I lifted her up in my arms and pressed her against the shower wall. Banging her against the wall with her legs wrapped around me used to be what I imagined while I was in the shower. I never imagined I'd get the chance to do it with her.

"What are you thinking about?" she asked.

"Fucking you," I answered honestly.

There was a beat of silence, and then she exploded with laughter. "Benny, holy fuck, don't tell me that!"

I shrugged.

"What time do you want to head out?" I asked. We had a long drive back to Philly, but I wanted to go somewhere before we left.

She chewed her lip. "Sooner rather than later, but I need coffee first. Why?"

"I want to take you somewhere."

"Where?"

"Surprise," I said. If I told her I wanted to take her to the rink and get her back on the ice, she might cut me.

She rolled her eyes.

I slapped her ass playfully while she got out of the bed

and stretched. Her glare could have cut glass, but I didn't care. "I'll order breakfast, and then we can go before we head back," I said.

"Okay!" she called from the bathroom.

I didn't realize that after breakfast, she was gonna ride me again until I was spent. Maybe it wasn't just me who couldn't get enough, but I wasn't gonna complain about it.

❄

"No. Absolutely not!" she yelled at me.

She crossed her arms over her chest while she stood outside the rink. I carried her skates in my hands, and I realized I hadn't thought this through because I needed to rent skates for myself.

Rox was still wearing my Bulldogs sweatshirt since it was cold this morning. I liked her in my sweatshirt; it made her seem like she was mine. Even though she'd made it clear this thing between us could only be casual. Rox didn't deserve to be my dirty little secret, but if that's what she wanted, I had to roll with it. Even if I didn't like it.

"Rox, you miss it, right?" I asked.

She nodded solemnly. "So much."

"Then you need to get back on the ice."

"But...today?"

"You can do this," I reassured her.

"Benny, it's too soon. I'm not ready."

"I've got you, okay? I'm not going to let anything bad happen to you."

"I'm scared," she admitted in a small voice.

I hugged her to my chest and stroked her hair. To my surprise, she didn't struggle in my arms but sighed into my chest. I glanced down and saw her eyes were closed. "I'm sorry; I'm being pushy. I love this sport, and I know you love it too, and I want to help you."

She pulled back and fixed me with her signature glare. "I don't think I'm ready."

"You gotta do it sometime," I argued.

"I don't want to get hurt again!"

"Oh, angel, you won't. You miss the game, right?"

"Duh!"

"And being on the ice? Cutting the blades of your skates into the ice?"

She nodded in recognition. She got it. She understood what it was like being on the ice. It was like no one could touch me, like I was flying.

I held out my hand to her. "Then let's get you on the ice. No hockey, just skating. Okay? You can tell me if you really don't want to, and we'll go home right now."

She stared at my hand, and when I thought she was going to knock it away and insult me like normal, she slipped her hand in mine. We walked into the rink together, and I let go of her hand so I could rent a pair of skates. I found her staring at the empty rink with her laces tied up when I joined her.

"You ready to get out on the ice, bad girl?" I asked.

"Stop calling me that," she growled out.

I grabbed her wrist and kissed her tattoo. When I kissed her wrist, she stopped yelling at me. "Enough," I said.

"Don't tell me what to do," she spat.

I raised an eyebrow and licked my lips. "If you're a good girl, I'll give you a beard ride when we get home."

Her face went paler than normal, and I laughed.

I sat next to her on the bench and laced up my skates. She took my offered hand, and we took to the ice together.

She yanked her hand away as she pushed off and sped across the ice. I stood against the boards and watched in awe as she soared across the surface. The grin on her face got wider as her feet crisscrossed across the surface, and she did laps around it. Damn, she was fast. She never looked more beautiful to me than right then while she was racing off across the ice. This was her happy place. I had never seen a smile on her face so big before.

She raced up to me and did an abrupt hockey stop in front of me, spraying ice across my jeans. She had a wicked grin on her face, but I couldn't stay mad at her because her hazel eyes sparkled with joy.

"We come here to skate or what, big guy?" she teased.

I didn't hate it when she called me that; it amused me. I crossed my arms over my chest. "Oh, you think you're funny, huh?"

She stuck her tongue out at me and tore off again. I took my phone out and shot some video of her on the ice so she could see what I saw. Then I put my phone away and raced after her. She was wicked fast, but I knew I could be faster.

I caught up to her and put my arms around her waist. "Hey!" she yelled in protest.

"Rox, you're so fast," I breathed out.

She shrugged.

I smiled at her, loving that she was letting me hold her hand while we cooled down on the ice. "You look great on the ice, like you never left it."

"Dad got us on the ice and in skates as soon as possible."

"You mean you didn't come out of the womb with ice skates on and a hockey stick in your hand?"

She laughed and skated off to the other side of the ice. Watching her skate made me want to help her get back into the game. Back on a team. I wanted to see this hot-headed woman in hockey gear, snipping and chirping at her opponents.

That's how I knew I was fucked when it came to Roxanne Desjardins. I had already fallen for her.

CHAPTER NINETEEN

ROXANNE

I couldn't believe he had man-handled me into getting back on the ice. I hadn't been on my skates in three years, and that wasn't without some unsuccessful coaxing from my twin brother.

In one night, Michael Bennett had brought down all my defenses. I slowed my skating to a crawl while he looped circles around me. The hockey player in me was equally impressed and turned on by his speed on the ice.

Was that weird?

Maybe, but I didn't care.

Slicing my skates into an iced surface was something I learned before I could talk. Alain Desjardins wanted his kids to be in skates as soon as possible, and he beamed when both Tristan and I took to it like we were born for it. Which we were.

Thinking about my dad made my heart hurt. My mom and I didn't always see eye-to-eye, but it stung when she denied who I was. My dad and I had always been close. It was like a knife to my heart when he let my mom tell me bisexuality wasn't real. It would have been nice if my dad wasn't such a teddy bear who agreed with everything my mother said.

Benny's skates scraped the ice next to me, and this time, he sprayed me with ice.

"Hey!" I yelled at him.

He smiled cheekily, and we raced after each other on the ice. I was mad when he said he wanted to take me somewhere today, and it was to an ice rink. It scared me to get back on the ice, but now that I was here, I was glad he'd pushed me. This was my happy place. I never thought I would be here, especially not with the man I'd hated for so many years.

The hockey player in me itched to be barreling down on the breakaway with my stick in hand, chasing after the puck. I missed hockey. Why hadn't I been on skates in three years? Oh, right. I was scared of getting another concussion that could turn into CTE.

I wasn't sure yet, but that drive was hitting me hard. I missed this sport, and I thought I wanted to play again. That thought should have terrified me, but for the first time in years, I was excited to be on the ice.

My skates were stiff from sitting in a box for three years. Before I hung them up, they'd needed to be replaced, but I had been putting it off for as long as possible. Breaking in skates was such a bitch, but if I wanted to play hockey again, I needed to replace my skates. That was a problem for another day, though.

I hadn't felt this happy in a long time. If Benny didn't force the conversation about hockey, I might not be on the ice, contemplating my return to hockey. No matter what happened between us, I could at least thank him for encouraging me not to give up on the sport I loved. God, I loved hockey so much, and the thought of getting back to it filled me with bursts of happiness. I couldn't wait to tell Tristan.

Our chests heaved as we raced against each other. I slowed to a stop and felt Benny's hands slide around my waist. He kissed my neck, and I craned my head to give him more access. Neck kisses were my favorite thing, and he had latched onto that quickly. I didn't know what we were doing, but I wanted to enjoy his mouth on me and think about the consequences later.

"Are you still mad at me?" he asked.

I shook my head and spun around on my skates. "No. Thank you for pushing me. I needed this."

He grinned down at me. "Good."

I reached my hand up and brushed my thumb across the growing stubble on his jaw. "Benny?"

He gripped my waist, pulled me closer, and tilted down to look at me. I craned my head up, and he crushed his lips onto mine. I gripped his unshaven jaw in my hand while we kissed, our breaths labored and our tongues tangling up. He kissed me like he was on the breakaway, about to score the game-winning goal. He kissed me like I was the way to win the Cup. His kisses made me feel like I had already staked my claim on victory, and I never wanted it to stop.

He pulled away and pressed his forehead against mine, his hands still on my hips. "We should go," he said. His eyes told me he wanted to do nothing of the sort.

"I know," I agreed.

"I don't want to," he admitted.

I peered up at him. "Why?"

He ran a hand across my cheek and rubbed his calloused thumb on it gingerly. "I'm afraid this spell between us will break as soon as we cross that border."

I shook my head. "It won't. You got me back on the ice."

"Yeah, so?"

I sighed. "I haven't been on the ice in three years. One look from you, and I crumbled. Whatever's going to happen between us...let's just enjoy it."

He nodded, and then he kissed me again, hot and needy, and now I was pissed at him because I had to sit in his SUV for hours, and I couldn't touch him.

He pulled away reluctantly, and we skated off the ice together. He went to return his rentals, and I unlaced my skates and changed back into my flats. I checked my phone and saw some notifications from Instagram. I smiled at the post Benny had tagged me in. He posted a video of me skating across the ice with a caption reading, 'Look at this beauty go!' with the heart-eye emoji.

A smile turned up on my lips, but then I saw my brother was calling me.

"Hey," I said into the phone.

He cleared his throat. "You got on the ice today?"

He must have seen Benny's post.

Shit.

"Yeah. It felt great," I admitted.

"What made you get back out there?" he asked.

Tristan was concerned when I had that concussion but supportive when I said I was done with hockey for good. Even if he didn't agree with me. Dad retired from hockey because of concussions, and we took them seriously in our family.

"Oh, Benny insisted before we drove back home. It felt good," I said again.

"Wait, where are you?" he asked.

I sighed. "I had to drive up to St. Catharines to get shit from Lisa."

"Shit, Roxie. You okay?"

"Yeah. I'm good."

"Benny went with you? And you didn't murder each other?" he asked with a laugh.

Nope, he'd murdered my vagina with his amazing cock, but I couldn't tell my brother that. I didn't want Benny to lose a limb or some shit. It was why we were keeping this a secret. My brother could never find out.

I sighed. "We don't hate each other anymore."

I could almost see my brother clenching his jaw. "He got you on the ice? Him?"

I laughed and mouthed 'my brother' to Benny as he joined my side again. I followed him outside to his SUV, and he started it up so we could begin the trek back home.

"Yeah, we learned to live with each other. You're right; he's not a bad guy. He helped me out with dealing with Lisa. He's a good man."

I cut my gaze across to the man driving next to me, and he sunk his teeth into his bottom lip, trying not to laugh. Ugh, those lips. I wanted to feel them on mine again.

"Say it again," Tristan demanded.

"What?"

"That I'm right."

"Oh, for fucks's sake! Goodbye, Tristan!" I snapped and hung up on him.

"I'm proud of you," Benny said after a few minutes of silence.

I eyed him carefully. "For what?"

"Getting back out there, facing your fears."

I sighed and grabbed his hand. "Thank you. I don't know if I could have done it without you."

He squeezed my hand. "Sure you could. I hate that we have a long drive home."

I sighed. "Me too."

"But I'm looking forward to you sitting on my face later."

My mouth hung open at his confession, and he barked out a laugh. I squeezed my thighs together and tried not to think dirty thoughts. "Holy shit!"

"Consider it your reward for letting me help you get back on the ice."

"My reward?" I asked.

"Rox, the only time I've ever seen you happier than when you were out there on the ice is when I'm eating your pussy."

"You've only done that once!" I argued.

He smirked. "It was enough to know I need to do it a lot more."

I laughed into my hand as he drove us out to the highway to start the journey back to Philly. I squeezed his thigh and felt a bulge in his pants. "Because you got me on the ice, you'll go down on me when we get home?"

He smirked. "It's a reward for me, too. I love a woman sitting on my face and riding my tongue."

I whimpered and squeezed my thighs together. I was no stranger to facesitting, but the thought of doing that with him made me uncomfortably aroused.

He lifted his hand off the steering wheel and took my hand in his. He kissed the back of my wrist, right on my maple leaf tattoo. I thought that was my spot because it made me melt whenever he kissed it.

Benny was my match in every sense of the word. Having this casual fling with the sexy left-winger was going to be fun. I couldn't believe we got here, but I wouldn't complain about it. I was going to enjoy the ride with Michael Bennett. Especially the one on his face later.

"Pull over at the next rest stop," I said.

"Why?"

"So we can fuck in the backseat! It's gonna be a long drive back to Philly."

"Fuuckkkk, Rox," he groaned, but I noticed he put his foot on the gas a little harder.

❄

I had Benny practically purring while he laid his head on my naked chest, and I ran my fingers through his inky black hair.

"Mmm, that feels so good," he said.

I tried to control my laughter, but my chest vibrated, and he looked up at me with a glare. I ran my hand across his growing beard. "Sorry. I never thought you would be such a cuddly guy."

He kissed his way up my chest until he pressed a quick kiss to my lips. He cradled my face, and I felt like all the air had gotten sucked out of the room when he looked deep into my eyes.

"What's not to love about cuddling?"

I shook my head. "Nothing, I love it too. Men just don't seem into it."

"Way to generalize, Rox."

I rolled my eyes at him and nearly yelped when he rolled us over so I was on top of him. We had spent the last two hours since we got home from Canada tangled up in his sheets, and even though my thighs were killing me, I couldn't stop when it came to this man.

"You're gonna break me," I whined as I straddled his hips.

He grinned up at me. "I don't see you complaining. You're just as bad as me, huh?"

I bent down to kiss him again. "Insatiable." I ran my hand down and felt his cock harden at my touch. "This is mine now."

He went to say something, but his phone buzzed against the bedside table. I had vaguely heard my phone earlier when I had dropped it on the floor before Benny took my clothes off again.

We tried to ignore it, but the buzzing wouldn't stop. I sighed and got off him.

Benny scowled as he scrolled through his phone.

"What's wrong?" I asked.

"Nothing. Noah was asking how you are because you won't answer your phone."

"Oh. He's trying to be a good friend, and I'm ignoring him."

"We can't tell him," Benny said.

I nodded in agreement. "I know. I love Noah, but he'll tell my brother. He'll feel like he has to."

I chewed on my bottom lip and got out of bed. I pulled on my clothes and paused for a moment before I pulled on Benny's Bulldogs sweatshirt again. It still smelled of him, and I had to admit I loved that. Wearing it made me feel like I was wrapped up in his arms. I shouldn't feel that way about him; I was supposed to hate him. If anything, this was supposed to be a summer fling, but my emotions were already getting the better of me. I should have been concerned by how fast they had come on, but I was still too drunk on orgasms to think about it.

"Where are you going?" he asked as he sat up in bed.

I picked up my phone where it had fallen under the bed and scanned all the texts from Noah. He was just asking me if I was okay after seeing my ex-girlfriend. Noah Kennedy was the epitome of niceness, even if he was being a cock-block. I felt like a dick for ignoring him.

"Noah wants to know if we want to watch the game," I said.

Benny nodded and got dressed while I walked out into the living room just in time to hear the knock on the door. I wasn't surprised when I opened it to find Noah and Dinah at the door. Dinah was holding a casserole dish, and I knew her well enough to know it came from one of her brothers. Probably Frankie; he was the one who owned a pizza shop and usually mother henned her.

"Hey, my brother gave me extra lasagna. Did you eat?" she asked.

I wanted to laugh at that. Dinah complained about her Italian family with all their 'hey, did you eat yet?' BS, but she did the same thing and didn't realize it.

I let them in and shook my head. "Not yet. It was a long drive back today."

"You haven't killed each other yet?" Noah asked as he took off his shoes and slumped on the couch.

"Nah!" Benny said as he walked into the room, now clothed. "I think feeding her helped."

Dinah barked out a laugh, and I helped her find plates to dole out the food.

"Thanks for bringing this, D," I said to her.

She nodded and stared at my face for a little too long. "Sure. I figured you'd both be exhausted after the drive."

I nodded.

We were exhausted, but not for the reason she was implying. It was because we couldn't stop fucking, no matter how much we tried. Okay, we didn't try to stop at all. We didn't want to.

"How are you?" she asked.

I spied Noah and Benny on the couch with eyes fixed on the hockey game on the TV. I imagined they were having a completely different conversation. I felt like I was being interrogated by Dinah. The tiny woman could be scary sometimes. I had to remind myself to school my features so my friends couldn't tell that Benny's cock had been down my throat earlier.

"Good," I said.

She squeezed my arm. "Sorry. I would have gone with you."

I shook my head. "You weren't back from Winnipeg yet."

"Still, I would have gone with you for moral support."

"It's okay. Benny went with me, and he scared her off."

I handed Benny a plate, and he took it while I sat in the armchair and Dinah pressed herself next to Noah. She was so tiny next to him, but they looked so cute together.

"What do you mean by that?" Noah asked around a mouthful of food.

"It was just a ploy to get her to come back," Benny said.

"He pretended to be my boyfriend so she would lay off. And then she got really biphobic about it, so I'm glad I'm done with her," I explained and shoved pasta into my face.

Dinah cocked an eyebrow at me, and I felt uncomfortable at the way she stared at me. Was it all over my face that Benny had given me countless orgasms and I was starving for more?

"This is weird," she finally said.

"What is?" I grumbled.

"You two not trying to claw each other's eyes out," Noah supplied.

Benny shrugged. "We learned to live together."

"But not for long," I pointed out.

"What do you mean?" Dinah asked.

"Oh, I found a place."

"Oh, the place in Fishtown?" she asked. I guessed Fi had told her. I hadn't realized how close they were.

I nodded. "Yeah, it's a decent size and within my budget, so it will be perfect."

Dinah nodded, but she was still studying Benny and me, and I felt uncomfortable. Could she tell? I checked Benny's face to see if my lipstick was on him, but there was no evidence of that.

Noah kicked my foot and startled me. "I saw you got on the ice."

I nodded.

"That's great!" Noah said with a big smile. "T said you haven't been on in years."

I nodded. "I'm still scared about that concussion I got during University."

"Well, you looked good out there," Noah said.

"I think she's the fastest skater I've ever seen," Benny said.

Dinah fixed her studious gaze on Benny like she was trying to suss something out.

"No way she's faster than me!" Noah argued.

"Hell yeah, I am!" I teased. "I'll leave you in my dust, Kennedy!"

Dinah laughed at that and shook her head. "You hockey players."

"Aw, lovey. You love us," Noah said and kissed her cheek.

They left after the game because Dinah and I both had to be up early since we had day jobs. I took a shower, and it surprised me to find Benny sitting on Tristan's bed when I got out.

"What's up?" I asked.

"Do you think Dinah knows?" he asked.

"I think she suspects something. We have to be careful," I told him as I dropped my towel and changed into clean pajamas.

He watched me while I brushed my hair out.

"Rox?"

"Hmm?"

"I like us not fighting."

I gave him a small smile. It felt weird not having the urge to punch him in the face, but I liked the shift between us. It was a welcome change. "Me too."

"Not sorry it took me giving you countless orgasms to change that."

"Ass!" I shrieked and threw a pillow at his head, but I liked the way he smirked at me.

"C'mere you," he demanded.

Before I knew it, I was in his arms again, and the idea of me sleeping in my brother's bed was long forgotten.

This man was bad news, but I would enjoy every minute of our secret affair. Even if I was sure it would break my heart in the process. I had to remind my heart that he wasn't sticking around. I might enjoy all the orgasms he gave me, and we might have overcome our past issues, but I couldn't fall in love with him.

CHAPTER TWENTY

BENNY

I ran my fingers through Rox's hair as she lay naked and spent across my chest. Something had shifted between us since we got back from Canada. I thought the fire would have died out, but it was weeks later, and we still couldn't control the need to constantly be wrapped up in each other's arms. It was getting harder to pretend I hadn't caught feelings for this feisty woman. Especially when the little minx had woken me up this morning for sex.

"What did I do to deserve morning sex?" I asked her as I kissed the top of her head.

She grinned up at me. "To thank you for last night." She nuzzled her nose across my neck and laid a soft kiss against my skin. "It was so nice. No one's ever done that for me before."

Last night I told everyone I was busy, set my phone to Do Not Disturb, and spent the night satisfying my angel. She had been having a stressful week at work, so I wanted to help her relax. It was a total boyfriend move, even though she had made it clear I was one hundred percent not her boyfriend. If this was a casual affair with a timestamp, I would take whatever I got from her. Even if it broke my heart. And it would. Because I was pretty sure I was in love with Roxanne Desjardins. Maybe I always had been.

"I thought you would be too sore," I said.

She kissed my neck again, which didn't help with the guy downstairs, thinking it was time to go again. My dick was insatiable for her. It always wanted to be buried deep inside her. How was I so horny again?

"That's what lube's for," she whispered in my ear. She nipped at my skin, and her hand traveled down my abs.

"Rox," I warned.

"What?"

"Angel, I don't think I have anything left in the tank."

She cackled. "Oh, did I wear you out?"

I groaned and gave her a knowing look. "You know you did."

She laughed into my skin.

I curled around her, my head in the crook of her neck. She stroked my hair, and I closed my eyes in contentment as her fingers trailed down so she could trace the tattoo on my arm.

"This is a Day of the Dead skull, right?" she asked.

"Yeah, it's a sugar skull—a Calavera," I said.

Her deft fingers traced across the lines of colorful ink. "It's beautiful."

"I'm proud of my Mexican heritage. I'm proud of who I am and where I come from. It's important for me to remember that."

"I love that," she said while she traced the lines on my arm. "This is good. The artist knew what he was doing."

"Dinah's brother-in-law Alex did it. He's also a Mexican guy with a white dad, so it felt like fate to have him do it. He knows how to tattoo on darker skin tones, which is why I went to him. I've sent Hallsy his way too."

"Oh! Her brother Eddie's husband?"

I nodded. "Yeah."

"I should check out the shop."

"You should. Alex's sister does a lot of flower tattoos; I didn't meet her, though."

I shifted our positions, so her back was against my chest, and I cradled her in my arms. My hand traced across the white flower on her shoulder blade and then over to the cherry blossom tattoo on the other one. I pressed a kiss onto her tattoos and smiled when she let out a girlish giggle. "You want to get another tattoo?"

"Yeah. Maybe something big on my thigh."

I ran a hand down her thigh slowly. "What of?"

She shrugged. "Not sure yet. I saw this one of different-sized blue snowflakes down a woman's leg."

"Sexy," I purred into her neck.

"Mmm," she moaned in response.

"I could kiss all down your leg, tormenting you until I gave you what you wanted," I teased.

"Mmm, what do I want?"

"You know, you little vixen. You want my tongue on your clit."

Instead of leaning back into me or kissing me again, she slid out of my arms and stretched her arms over her head.

"Hey, where are you going?" I asked while she put her pajamas back on.

I smiled when she pulled my Bulldogs sweatshirt over her head. I felt like I wasn't getting my sweatshirt back, but I was okay with that. The possessive part of me enjoyed seeing her wearing it like it proved she was mine even when she wasn't.

"I need coffee," she explained.

I leaned back against my pillow. "Make me some?"

"Of course, love."

I pretended not to notice her letting that pet name slip. I switched my phone off Do Not Disturb and checked my messages. My stomach fell when I saw a couple of texts from my sister, fearing the worst, but it was just photos of my nephews at their first Red Sox game. I had already mentioned to my agent that if the Bulldogs were looking to trade me, my first choice would be Boston. Now I wasn't sure I wanted to leave Philly. Not when I spent all my time wrapped up in the woman who used to be my enemy.

Rox came back into the room and held out a cup of coffee to me. I sat up and took it from her as she slid into the bed next to me with her own cup. I put my arm around her shoulders and squeezed her into my side. She fit perfectly there, like it was made just for her.

She glanced over at my phone and saw the photos. "Who are they?"

"My nephews."

"Oh, right, you mentioned your sister had kids."

"My sister's a therapist for at-risk kids, and she kept seeing all these kids in dangerous situations. They ended up fostering the twins before they could adopt them."

"What are their names?" she asked and took a sip of her drink.

"Carlos and Miguel," I said and pointed them out.

We drank our coffee in silence for a couple of minutes.

"Do you want children?" she asked.

I wrenched my head to look at her in shock. "Is there something you need to tell me?"

Horror etched across her face. "Oh God, no! We always use condoms, and I got back on the pill to be sure. I don't want kids."

I breathed a sigh of relief. "Oh, okay. Way to give a guy a heart attack." Then I frowned, remembering that her week had been stressful because she had been complaining about headaches. "Wait, is that why you've been having headaches?"

She took a sip of coffee, so she didn't have to answer.

"Angel, come on."

"Yes," she answered bitterly.

"Hey, I'm cool with using condoms. You don't have to be on the pill if it makes you sick like that. I don't want kids either."

She shook her head. "Benny, I really don't want kids. I'd rather be double protected."

"What about an IUD?" I asked.

She shook her head in horror. "No way! I had one for a year and had to get it taken out. The side effects were worse for me."

"Angel, why didn't you say anything?"

She waved me off. "It's fine. Again, I don't want kids."

"Neither do I, but I don't want you to suffer because of the pill."

"Is that why you and your ex broke up? Because you wanted different things?" she asked, changing the subject. I let her, even though I would press her about this later. I didn't like her being in pain because she didn't want kids. I was always careful. Always.

I sighed. "The whole kids and marriage thing isn't for me."

"Why not?"

"Look, my grandparents and my sister have great

marriages, but I grew up watching my asshole Dad treat my mom like garbage, and she just took it."

She set her coffee down on the bedside table and crawled into my lap. Her hands reached up and framed my face. "Hey. You're not him, okay?"

I kissed her hand and ran my hands down her curvy body. I liked her straddling me like this, but I had to tell my dick to focus. This was a serious conversation, not playtime.

"I don't want to be him. He's a dick, and he cheated on my mom all my life."

"Michael, you're not him. I see that now." She pressed a hand to my chest. "I see you."

Something hit me right in the chest at her calling me by my first name instead of my hockey nickname. I took my free hand and kissed her tattooed wrist. "I see you too, bad girl."

She glared at me. "Ass! We were having a moment."

"Still are, angel," I said, and I pressed my lips to her wrist again.

"Truth be told, I don't want to get married either."

"Why not? I thought all chicks wanted that."

She made a face. "Nah. Not for me."

"No?"

"I don't see the point. It's just a piece of paper. Why do I have to prove to people my love is strong with an antiquated institution?"

I laughed. "Please tell that to my grandparents. They constantly harp on me about settling down and having babies."

She made a face. "Hard pass."

She slid off my lap to grab her coffee again. She leaned her head on my shoulder, and it was in these quiet moments with her where we unraveled our souls to each other that I knew I was done for. I was falling deeper and deeper in love with her as the days passed.

This thing between us wasn't just a casual fling, we were practically dating, and it was getting on my nerves that it could only be behind closed doors. The fact she wanted the same thing as me made me want to make her mine even more. I didn't know how to prove to her that we should give it a shot, though. I did know I craved learning more about this feisty woman.

"How did you know?" I asked her.

"Know what, love?" she asked again, that pet name making me grin because I didn't think she noticed she did it.

"Don't get mad at me," I forewarned. She opened her mouth to protest, but I put a finger to her lips. "How did you know you were bisexual?"

She laughed and batted my hand away. "Oh. What brought that up?"

"I want to know more about you."

She side-eyed me suspiciously. I wasn't sure why I wanted to know the story. I loved hearing her bare her soul to me. Telling me those dark secrets that I was sure she didn't tell anyone else.

"I think if you'd asked me before, I would tell you the story about my friend Natalie kissing me on a dare, and it was this big epiphany, but that wasn't the case."

"Oh?" I asked and quirked up an eyebrow.

"That was when I put all the pieces together. A couple of months before, I watched Mulholland Drive with my boyfriend. There's a lesbian sex scene in it, and I remember feeling uncomfortable watching it. I knew I wasn't homophobic, but I pushed that feeling away, and when Natalie kissed me that night, it all clicked. It was confusing because I thought I was gay."

"So, how did you know you weren't?"

"I went to a hockey party with Tristan, and one of his teammates started flirting with me, and I thought, 'damn he's got some nice forearms.'"

"Forearms? Is that what women are interested in?" I asked with a laugh and flexed my muscles.

She laughed. "I like a muscular back. And beards. Ugh, men in red plaid too—it's my weakness."

"I think you just described the Brawny Man."

"Don't kink shame me!"

I grabbed her hand and kissed her wrist gently. "You didn't have to tell me that, but I'm glad you did."

She smiled at me. "I haven't told anyone that. Not even Tristan."

I rubbed my thumb over her tattoo. "Thank you for trusting me with it."

My phone vibrated on the bedside table, and I cringed because I knew it was either Noah or Riley asking me where the fuck I was. I was late for a training session with them. It hadn't been the first time either, and my teammates were getting suspicious. I wasn't sure what excuse I would use this time. But I didn't care—not when I got to have these intimate moments with Rox. When I lay in bed with her, she made me want to never leave. So, I didn't give a shit how much Riley and Noah chirped me for being late.

Rox nodded at my phone, which went off a few more times while I sipped on my coffee. "Do you have somewhere you need to be?"

I chugged the rest of my coffee and got out of bed. "Yeah. I have to get going. I was supposed to meet Riley and Noah, and I'm late."

She nodded and got up, too. "I better get started on my day, too. I'm supposed to meet Dinah and Fi for brunch."

I kissed her goodbye, which seemed oddly relationship-y, and when I was out the door two seconds later, I realized that was what we were doing. She'd just told me about discovering her sexuality because I was curious. Instead of glaring at me, she revealed the most personal story about herself. If this wasn't a relationship, she wouldn't have told me that. If we were just fuck buddies, she would have kicked me out of bed and told me to fuck off.

The old Rox sure as shit wouldn't be cuddling in bed with me and telling me all her secrets. The old Rox would have told me to go fuck myself gently with a chainsaw for asking her that question.

I realized that somewhere along the way, we'd fallen into something we hadn't been expecting. We were in a relationship, but she didn't want to admit it. I told myself I wouldn't catch feelings, but I think I'd had feelings for this woman since the day I met her. And I was so totally screwed.

CHAPTER TWENTY-ONE

ROXANNE

"Can I have it, please!" I begged Fi, grilling her about the romance book she was working on.

Since Benny let it slip that Fi was writing a romance book, I had been hounding her about it. She normally wrote young adult sci-fi/fantasy, so this was her trying something new. I was all for it.

Dinah and Fi had been begging me to hang out, and I had been a shitty friend lately, but I couldn't tell them why. I couldn't tell them the reason I was always so tired and didn't want to hang out was because I was too busy playing house with the man I used to think of as my sworn enemy. After weeks of skirting their invites, I finally caved and met them for brunch.

Fi laughed and took a sip of her water. "Not yet!"

"Ugh, you're no fun. I love romance books."

I smirked to myself, thinking about the enemies-to-lovers hockey romance I was reading the other night. Even if I eventually told these two about me and Benny, I would never admit to them that sometimes I read him the steamy parts. He usually laughed, and then we got so riled up that we had to create our own steamy scenes.

I'd come a long way from wanting to straight-up murder Michael Bennett. Last night, he told everyone he was busy so we could spend all night in bed together. I didn't think any of my past partners gave themselves over to me like that. I worried I was getting too attached to him and that I wanted something real with him.

I kept thinking about what he said about asking for a trade to Boston, and I knew I had to steel my heart for the inevitable. I couldn't get attached to someone who was going to leave and break my heart. I had to pretend these feelings bubbling up inside me weren't real. I had to shove them down.

I had to tell my heart to stop getting big silly ideas whenever Benny was around. I couldn't help that it flipped over inside my chest every time he looked at me. I thought Lisa was going to be my forever; I thought she was my soulmate, but I had been wrong about her. What if my feelings for Benny were just lust? I couldn't fall in love with Benny! I spent months couch surfing and trying to figure out my next step after Lisa broke my heart. I wasn't sure I could handle it again. Maybe I shouldn't have slept with Benny; it would just get complicated when my brother got home.

"What other romance authors do you like?" Fi asked.

"Oh! I like Ruby Walker. I think she's local."

"She is!" Fi exclaimed. "We've kinda become friends."

Dinah nodded. "Aren't she and Jonesy a thing?"

Jonesy was Riley's defensive partner. He was a hot bearded guy with sleeve tattoos, so I saw the appeal.

Fi bit her lip. "I think they're just fuck buddies. Ruby doesn't do relationships since her divorce."

Dinah frowned. "Oh, too bad. They're cute together." Her gaze shifted to me like she was waiting for me to say something.

"What?" I asked and took another sip of my coffee.

"So, you and Benny aren't fighting anymore..." Dinah said and let her unspoken question hang in the air.

"Nope. It's been kind of peaceful," I told her coyly with a shrug.

It was getting harder to not admit my feelings about him to my friends. It was hard not to smile at him when he looked at me, too. I wondered if they noticed all the heated looks he threw my way when he thought no one was looking. If I knew anything about the two authors in front of me, they noticed. Which was why they were grilling me.

Dinah crossed her arms. "Uh-huh. Hey, do you know if Benny has a new girlfriend?"

"Um...no idea. Why?"

She smirked at me. "You know, Noah swore he heard someone having very loud sex in Benny's condo this morning."

"How loud, Dinah?" Fi asked, and they both smirked.

"So loud I could hear them screaming their orgasms while Noah and I were making coffee."

I froze.

Shit.

I was very loud this morning. Like so loud, I was practically screaming his name while I rode him and he fingered my clit. Fuck, did he moan my name? I couldn't remember.

"Well, no girlfriend. Not that I'm aware of," I lied.

Fi grinned. "Are you sure about that?"

I changed the subject. "Hey, Dinah, I heard your brother opened his new shop."

"Oh, yeah." she held up her wrist where she had a tiny black quill pen inked. It was cute, and it suited the tiny woman. "You looking to get another tattoo?"

"Maybe. I haven't decided yet. I have three tattoos right now."

Fi cocked her head. "You have other tattoos?"

I nodded and pulled out my phone to show her the photos of my tattoos. I didn't even think about it when I handed over my phone. She took my phone and scrolled past to the next photo. "Oh, these are really pretty," she said. Her finger scrolled again, and then her eyes widened. "Oh! I don't think you wanted me to see this photo."

I frowned and wracked my brain for any risque photos I had on my phone that would have caused her shocked reaction. I chewed my bottom lip in concern but saw D's eyes widen as she looked over Fi's shoulder.

The tiny woman fixed me with a wicked grin. "I knew it!" she exclaimed. "You're such a fucking liar!"

Fi grinned too as she handed me back my phone, and that's when I saw it. The photo of Benny and me kissing in that hotel room in St. Catharines. I was wearing his Bulldogs sweatshirt like I belonged to him. The sweatshirt I never wanted to give back because it smelled like him and made me feel like I was his.

Fuck, I am so busted.

"Woman, explain!" Fi demanded.

"Rox?" Dinah asked with a hint of concern in her voice. "Why did you keep this a secret? We love you and have been waiting for you two to get your heads out of your asses for years."

"Is it because of your brother? Just talk to him. It'll be okay," Fi said.

I shook my head slowly, and then I burst into tears because I couldn't keep my emotions in check anymore.

"Oh, honey..." Fi cooed, and both women came around to my side of the table and hugged me tightly. Fi stroked my hair. "Honey, tell us what's wrong."

"What did he do?" Dinah snapped.

This tiny girl was fierce, and I loved that she immediately assumed Benny did something wrong and needed to die.

"Nothing," I blubbered and wiped my tears away. "I asked him to keep it a secret."

"Why?" Dinah asked.

"I can't have anything serious with him when he's going to ask for a trade to Boston."

"Motherfucker, what?" Dinah seethed.

"Why? I thought he liked Philly," Fi commented, confused.

I nodded. "He does, but he feels guilty being away from his family. I was so wrong about him for so long. That man's so good and kind, and I'm such a raging bitch."

Dinah stroked my hair. "Oh, honey, you're not. You're fierce, and you don't take anyone's shit. That's why I like you."

"Why don't you talk with Benny?" Fi suggested.

I shook my head. "I can't stand in the way when he wants to be with his family. It can only be a casual thing between us. It's just sex."

Dinah grinned. "Sounded like good sex, though. By the way, if you're trying to have secret sexy times with someone, maybe tell him to not scream your name so loud?"

I laughed. "Shut up. That's not the point."

"Also, Noah told me he had the flimsiest excuse for being late for training today."

I groaned. "When did he even tell you that?"

She scrolled through her phone. "When he got to the practice facility. They're doing strength training today, so he has his phone."

"Christ, Dinah, do you tell each other everything?" I asked.

"Yes," she said.

"Really?" I asked in surprise.

"I really hurt Noah when I broke up with him, and he made me promise that if I ever got scared about our relationship again to talk to him first. We're open with each other," Dinah explained.

"Dinah, I worried you two wouldn't last. You really hurt Noah."

"I know."

"But I love you two, and I want you to last," I added.

The petite woman beamed. "I don't want to lose my best friend again."

A pang of jealousy reached up and squeezed my heart because I wanted what Dinah and Fi had with their men. I wanted that love. It didn't have to be with Benny, but I wanted someone who wouldn't cheat on me or leave me for a different city. Was that too much to ask?

"I want what you both have. I want someone to love me," I said and wiped the tears from my eyes.

"Oh, honey." Fi sighed and pushed my hair behind my ear. "Do you love him? Do you think he doesn't feel the same way?"

I stared at her, but then I answered her honestly. "I don't know, but I know I can't let myself have feelings for him if he's not gonna be here next year."

"Okay, fuck it. We're going out and getting drunk tonight, just the three of us. Let's go, you're putting on something nice, and we're gonna have a girls' night." Fi didn't ask; she demanded it.

Dinah shrugged. "This is what Fi does. She gets ya real drunk, and you figure out what you want."

Fi laughed. "Hey, it worked with you when you broke up with Noah!"

I remembered Noah distraught when Dinah broke up with him. I had come into town to make sure he was okay. Tristan had asked me to come, partly because he was worried about me but partly because he couldn't get Noah out of his funk. Noah was a sensitive guy, and he had been a miserable shit. I didn't know that Fi helped Noah and Dinah figure things out. It made me like her even more. She was a good friend, and I didn't deserve either of them.

"I haven't told Tristan. I tell him everything, but he knows I'm holding back something, and it hurts so much," I admitted.

They both hugged me tightly. "Rox, we're gonna figure it out," Fi reassured me.

"If not, I might murder your boyfriend," Dinah said with a wicked grin.

Oh my God. Dinah Lace was something else, and I loved this woman for it.

"He's not my boyfriend," I argued.

Fi raised a red eyebrow. "Hey, D, you ever have a picture of you and your friends with benefits looking cozy and kissing on your phone?"

Dinah shook her head.

I glared at her. "You've never had a friend with benefits before, so you don't count."

"But I have," Fi argued. "And I've never had one look at

me like that or take a freaking selfie of us kissing. Hey, can you send that to me? I think I should use it for the cover of my book."

"Shut up!" I argued, but I smiled. Leave it to these women to cheer me up when my heart was breaking in two.

"So what were you really doing last night?" Fi asked with a raised eyebrow.

"Fucking all night long," I answered honestly.

They both laughed at my bluntness

"He knew I had a shitty week at work."

The two exchanged looks. Dinah cleared her throat. "He knew you had a terrible week, so he ignored everyone else to make you feel good?"

"What? That's not weird, right?"

Fi shook her head. "Not weird...but I don't think that's something you do for someone you're only sleeping with."

"That's a boyfriend move," Dinah agreed.

"Husband move," Fi corrected.

I put my head in my hands. Now I was even more confused.

Dinah peered at me for a second. "But it explains why you are always so 'tired' and keep avoiding us."

I groaned. "I'm sorry. I'm a shitty friend."

"Yeah, she's too tired because Benny is dicking her down too much!" Fi joked.

"Actually..." I trailed off and smirked when they both looked way too interested in what I was about to say. "I think I wear him out."

Dinah cackled. "Get it, girl!"

I took a sip of my coffee and grinned at her over the rim. "Oh, I do."

They cackled with laughter. I felt a weight lift from my shoulders now that I'd finally told them what was going on, but I still was unsure where that left me. I loved spending time with Benny, but I knew we had an expiration date, one that was quickly closing in on us. This was all gonna end soon, and then I would be back to square one, trying to start over in a new city with a broken heart.

CHAPTER TWENTY-TWO

BENNY

When I got home after training with Riley and Noah, Rox wasn't home. I figured she was still out with the girls. I had to admit; I was a little disappointed she wasn't home yet. I kind of wanted another night-in with her cuddled up in my bed. How was I whipped by a chick who wasn't even my girlfriend? I flopped down on the bed and noticed my sweatshirt was lying on her side of the bed.

Fuck, she had her own side of the bed. Of course she did because she hadn't slept in TJ's room since before we went to Canada.

We were practically dating, and I couldn't stand all this hiding. I was a sensitive guy; I fell in love hard and a lot, but I felt like my heart was already broken because she didn't want what I wanted.

I wasn't wallowing in self-pity for long before Riley hit me up again.

RILEY: *Bar tonight.*

ME: *Do I have a choice?*
RILEY: *Nah.*
ME: *Eileen's?*
RILEY: *You know it.*

When I got to Eileen's, it wasn't just to meet Riley. He waved me over to a table in the back, where he sat with Noah, Dinah, Fi, and Rox. The only open seat was next to Rox. When our gazes met, something in her eyes didn't sit right with me. There was a sadness there that I didn't understand. It pierced my heart because I wanted to take that sadness away from her.

The server came over to take our orders, and I mumbled out my choice.

Dinah and Fi were in a deep conversation about their writing, and Noah and Riley were arguing about a call in the hockey game.

I put a hand on Rox's thigh and leaned into her ear. "Are you okay?" I asked.

She nodded, but she was lying.

"You sure?" I asked into her ear.

"I'm fine," she snapped a little too loudly, and that got us a double raised eyebrow look from my teammates.

What did I do to piss her off?

I pulled my hand off her thigh, but she yanked it back and threaded her fingers between mine underneath the table.

Okay, what is going on?

I rested my hand on her bare thigh and noticed she was wearing the red dress with the white flowers that I loved. It hugged all her curves in the right places, like someone made the dress specifically for her. She was the only woman I noticed in the bar, and I wanted to kiss her so badly. I wanted to show everyone how much she meant to me. But that wasn't a part of our deal.

I took a sip of my beer and noticed Fi giving me a death glare.

After we ate, Riley bet me he could beat me at pool. I took that bet because he sucked at pool. Rox released my hand from underneath the table so I could stand up, and Noah joined us over at the pool table. I felt like this was a setup for them to grill me about why I was late for training today.

I lined up the balls and broke. I hit a striped ball into the back left pocket.

"You gonna tell us what's going on with you and Rox?" Riley asked.

I gritted my teeth. "Nothing. You saw how she snapped at me."

"Dude, I heard you fucking this morning," Noah announced.

I stared at him while Riley took his shot. "How do you know that was me? Could have been her."

Riley barked out a laugh. "Okay, she definitely wouldn't fuck in her brother's bed. Also, conveniently you said you were 'busy' last night, and when Fi asked Rox if she wanted to hang out, she was also 'busy.' We put two-and-two together, bud!"

"And I heard you screaming her name this morning," Noah added with a grin.

FUCK!

Is that why Rox is so mad?

I hazarded a glance at the table behind us, but Rox was laughing with the girls like nothing was wrong. Was she just in a weird mood? Then why did Fi give me that death glare? What was that about?

"Don't know what you're talking about, man," I lied.

Noah sighed and seemed to weigh his words. "Is the lying because of TJ?"

"Still don't know what you're talking about. Rox and I are just friends."

Riley narrowed his eyes at me. "A couple of weeks ago, you were at each other's throats. Don't think I didn't notice you holding hands under the table."

"Like two sneaky teenagers!" Noah teased.

I ignored him and took my next shot. I wouldn't dignify that with an answer. I looked up after I missed my shot and saw Fi sauntering over to us.

She sidled up to her husband. "Hey, baby. Can I borrow Benny for a second?" she asked.

Riley gave her a quick kiss. "Of course, sweetheart."

Fi's nails dug into my arm as she pulled me out of earshot. "You need to go talk to your girl," she ordered.

"What?"

She narrowed her eyes at me. "She seems to have it in her head that you're gonna ask for a trade to Boston. You need to tell her that's not happening. And for fuck's sake, Benny, tell her you love her already."

I sighed.

Fuck.

Boston.

Of course.

She didn't want anyone to know we were together because she thought I wasn't sticking around. That I was gonna leave her.

I'd asked my agent to tell the team Boston was on my list of places I was open to going to *if* they wanted to trade me. I didn't ask for a trade but wanted the option to be near my family if it happened; my contract didn't have a no-trade clause, so if they wanted, they could send me across the country. Or even up to Canada. I didn't have a choice in the matter, but if they were sending me anywhere, I wanted to be close to my family. But my agent said the team wanted to keep me until my contract was up, so I wasn't going anywhere.

Besides, I didn't want to move back to Boston anymore. I didn't want to leave the woman I loved, even if she didn't know I loved her yet.

"Wait...did she tell you about us?" I asked.

Fi laughed. "Nope. She gave me her phone to look at pictures of her tattoos, and I saw a picture of you two."

"Oh."

"Kissing," she elaborated.

"Oh," I breathed out. She saw *that* photo.

Fi put her hand on my shoulder. "Benny, talk to her. She's upset because she thinks you're gonna leave her next year, so she doesn't see the point in letting you into her heart."

I hung my head. "I knew she was holding back."

"That's why she didn't want you to tell anyone."

I ran a hand through my hair and squinted at the goofy grin on Fi's face. "What?"

"You two have been really obvious."

"Really?"

I thought we had been so careful about everything. Sometimes I even pushed her buttons on purpose so nothing would seem amiss.

She nodded. "D figured it out the night you got back from Canada. She said you looked at Rox with stars in your eyes."

"What?"

"You look at Rox the same way Noah looks at Dinah and Riley looks at me. Like she should be worshipped."

"No, I don't," I grumbled.

Fi laughed. "Okay, but go talk to your lady because I had to dry her tears at brunch today."

I frowned. "What?"

Fi shoved me toward where Rox sat. "Go, big guy!"

I glared at her but did as she asked. I saw Dinah squeeze Rox's shoulder and then walk over to join Noah, who took my place playing pool with Riley. Rox glanced up at my approach, and she gave me a fake smile that crushed me.

I took the seat next to her. "Angel, talk to me. What's bothering you?"

She sighed. "Fi and Dinah found out about us."

"Yeah, Fi just told me, but that's not what's bothering you."

"I really like you, okay? You, of all people! I thought I would hate you forever, but I misjudged you unfairly. You're such a better person than me."

"Roxanne—"

"I'm an asshole, Benny. I've been a raging bitch to you because of one mistake you made three years ago. I'm a bad person. I deserve this."

"Rox, what are you talking about?"

She squeezed her eyes shut, and when she opened them, my chest felt heavy when I saw the tears she was trying so hard to keep in. "This has a time limit, so I didn't want to get attached to you...but I'm afraid I already have."

I pushed her hair behind her ear, and my hand lingered on her face. Her eyes were wet with tears, and it made my chest ache that I had done that to her. "First, you're not a bad person. I like that you're feisty."

She shook her head, but I put a finger on her lips to silence her before she tried to argue with me again.

"Second, why do you think there's a time limit?"

"Because you told me you asked for a trade to Boston. What's the point of telling everyone we're together if it's all gonna end anyway?"

I held her face in my hands, and she tried to look away. "Hey, look at me. I don't want to go to Boston."

"But, you—"

"I want to stay here and be with you. I don't want to hide how I feel about you from everyone. I want to hold your hand in public and tell all my friends that you're my girl. That I got to tame Roxanne Desjardins."

She glared. "You didn't tame me."

I chuckled. "Okay, you keep telling yourself that."

"Don't be a dick!"

"I love spending time with you. Rox, I don't do casual. I'm an all-or-nothing type of guy, and I think you have enchanted me since the moment I met you."

Her mouth formed a little 'o' in surprise.

"Why do you think I asked if those were real?" I asked and gestured to her ample chest. "Here was this beautiful woman standing in front of me, and my brain was like, 'hey, say what you're thinking to this hottie.' I'm sorry for saying all the wrong things to you over the years."

She grinned at me. "Not your best moment."

"I like you a lot, probably have for a long time, but you hated my guts for so long—"

She cut me off by leaning into me and pressing her lips to mine. I smiled into the kiss and slid my hands into her hair.

When we parted, she was all smiles again. "I think I felt

it that night in Canada. You were breaking down all my defenses."

"Really?"

She nodded. "You were gonna start a fight with that drunk guy at the bar because you always saw me for me. You never cared that I didn't have a flat stomach or—"

I cut her off again with another kiss. "I told you," I growled, "I'll never stop loving your curves. I thought you were mad at me about that, though."

"I was. I worried about it affecting your career."

"What do you mean?"

"Benny, you're a Mexican guy who plays hockey. The league talks a big game about hockey being for everyone, but the media criticizes players of color more than white players. I didn't want any heat to come back on you because of me."

I cupped her face in my hands again. "I don't give a fuck; I would have fought that guy for being an asshole. But you were really only mad because you care about my career?"

She nodded. "I didn't want to cause any fallout. But it was nice that you wanted to stand up for me, even though I've been awful to you. I don't give a shit about what drunk jerk-offs say about me, but you did, and you wanted him to apologize."

"I'm always gonna fight for you."

She bit her lip. "But Benny..."

"What, angel?"

"What about your family?"

"What about them?"

She cupped my bearded jaw in her small hands. "I love that you care about your family so much that you want to be closer to them. I can't stand in the way. If you want to go to Boston…I don't know. We'll figure it out."

"Angel, my family has specifically told me not to ask for a trade. They think it would jeopardize my career and my happiness."

"But—"

"Hush. I'm not going anywhere."

She glared at me. "Did you just freaking hush me?"

"Yeah, I did." I gave her a cocky grin. "What are you gonna do about it?"

She gave me a wicked grin. "I think someone wants to be punished."

I arched an eyebrow at her and licked my lips. "How about…I let you ride my beard tonight?"

She ran a hand across said beard. "I think I like that plan."

I covered her hand with mine and kissed the tattoo on her wrist. "I knew you would, bad girl. Let's get out of here."

"Please. I want to spend another night wrapped up with my super hot hockey-playing boyfriend."

I grinned at her. "Well, good because I want to be wrapped up with my even sexier hockey-playing girlfriend."

Her smile was a thousand-watt, and I wanted to tattoo the image of that onto my brain so I would never forget it.

CHAPTER TWENTY-THREE

ROXANNE

"Come on, girl, show me what you got," Benny coaxed from his spot three stick-lengths away.

I leveled my stick onto the ice. I couldn't believe I was not only back on the ice, but my new boyfriend was making me run through shooting drills at the practice arena. The big guy sure was pushy.

When he woke me up this morning and said he had a surprise for me, I thought it meant more 'YAY! We told each other how we feel' sex. But nope—Benny was determined to get me hockey ready. He had even printed out a list of adult leagues he wanted me to consider joining in the fall. Most were on a weekend or night-time schedule since most of the players did it just for fun.

I'd rather be spending my Sunday afternoon lounging in bed with him, but it was romantic how supportive he was about me playing hockey again. I didn't realize how much I had missed hockey until he pushed the conversation with me and made me get on the ice in Canada.

But I hadn't imagined that today, I would run through fricking one-touch and breakout drills with him. I was rusty and getting testy, which he knew.

How could I have ever hated this kind, patient man?

I was such a bitch.

We ran through more drills until I got annoyed and iced the puck in anger. "Benny! I'm not trying to make it into the pros; I'm just trying to shake off the dust to play in a fucking beer league," I screeched at him.

He skated over to me but was laughing. "Will you calm your tits? I'm trying to help!"

I jabbed him with my stick. "You're annoying me."

"C'mere you," he ordered and skated closer to me.

"No!"

He smirked at me and wrapped me in his massive arms. "You're so feisty. You're gonna be a real scrapper when you get back out there."

I glared again, but I couldn't stay mad at him when I looked up into his dark eyes. He lifted my chin up and kissed me. "Better?" he asked.

I nodded. "Fine. But I think I'm a little hangry. Sorry."

"Let's get out of here so I can feed ya, bad girl."

I glared again.

He pulled away and skated off to clean up the cones and pucks we had set up at the practice arena. I couldn't believe he had arranged ice time for me. My heart soared at his kindness, even if I was being a raging bitch. My anger was a little warranted, though.

After easing me into some warm-up laps and stretches, he made me skate lines. I totally left him in my dust by outskating him. Unlike the other hockey players I had dated over the years, Benny didn't get mad about it. Instead, he looked gleeful. I forgot what it was like to skate beside someone who wanted you to succeed.

I helped him with the clean-up, and I was all smiles when we got back to the condo and he put food in front of me.

"I'm sorry. I think I'm PMSing, so I'm being a raging bitch."

He kissed my cheek. "You're just hangry."

After we ate, we aired out our equipment on the floor of Tristan's room and sprayed deodorizer in the room before getting a shower together. To 'save water,' Benny said, but it was just so he could make my tits nice and shiny. We were insatiable, and I loved every minute of it.

We settled onto the couch to catch the tail-end of one of the afternoon hockey games. Benny put his arm around my shoulder, and I snuggled down into his chest.

He kissed the top of my head. "I love cuddling."

I laughed. "You so are a soft boy."

He grumbled.

I leaned up to kiss him. "It's a good thing, love. It's cute. I feel like this is my spot, right here," I said and pulled away to press my hand onto his chest, right on his heart. "It's like I belong here."

He smiled at that. "I like you there."

"Thank you."

"For what?" he asked.

"For forcing me to do drills today," I grumbled. "I'm rusty."

"Ha!" he cheered and fist-pumped. "I knew you would be happy about it. Eventually."

"Do you really think I could play again?"

"Yeah! You left me in your dust today. Have you looked at any of the leagues yet?"

I shook my head.

"Dinah's brother Eddie has one. I put it at the top of the list."

"I didn't realize Eddie played. I'll check that one out first."

We settled into each other, and I relaxed into his arms. He pulled his phone out of his pocket and changed his background to one of the photos he took of us in Canada. I smiled at the small move. Last night, I changed mine too. I loved those photos of us, and I was glad we could share more of those moments together.

I never thought I would be relaxing in his arms. I thought Benny and I would circle around each other and fight forever. I knew a lot of the animosity between us had been because of me. I could be a fickle asshole, and when someone crossed me, I held onto that.

"I'm sorry," I whispered.

He nosed across my neck. "For what, angel?"

I smiled at the pet name. That was growing on me, even if he made a joke about me being a demon the first time he called me it. In retrospect, it made me laugh.

"For the way I treated you in the past. I wasn't fair to you," I said.

"Please stop apologizing. It was my fault too."

"Still, it wasn't right."

"Angel—"

"I'm sorry."

"Jesus, have you been hanging out with Noah too much? Stop apologizing! It's in the past."

I nodded, and he wrapped his arms around me tighter, pulling me into his lap. I closed my eyes and snuggled further into him. I loved the feel of this big man and how he made me feel so secure and loved.

"Benny?"

"Hmm?"

"How are we gonna tell my brother?"

He sighed. "Fuck."

"Yeah..."

"I want to tell him in person."

"Okay. Over a drink, maybe?" I suggested.

"Definitely. Maybe three. Don't worry, though. Nothing's gonna keep us apart. I don't care what your brother thinks. You're mine, and I'm yours."

This man... I was pretty sure I loved him right then. "Damn right, you're mine. I own you," I said.

He grinned and held me closer. "I think you always did. Even when you screamed that you hated me."

"You always screamed right back at me."

"Every time, I thought, 'What if I pushed her up against the wall and shoved my tongue in her mouth? That would shut her up.' But I never thought I would actually do it."

I laughed. "You should have done it sooner."

His laughter rumbled again in his broad chest. "Hey, do you want to go out and buy new hockey gear?"

I lifted my head up. "Wow, you say the sexiest things to me."

He chuckled.

"No, I'm serious!"

"Really?"

I nodded vigorously. "You encouraging me to play hockey again and compiling a list of leagues for me to join is romantic to me. It shows you really care and want the best for me."

He grinned. "I've never seen you happier than when you're on the ice. You deserve that, and I want to give that to you. Even if you lob a puck down the ice and want to throw your stick at me."

"I mean, sometimes I want to drop the gloves too."

He pinched my side. "Brat."

"You like it," I said while pressing small kisses on his neck. I arched my eyebrow when I felt exactly how much he liked it from the bulge in his pants. "You love getting me all riled up."

"Angel?" he asked.

I pulled back and wound my hands around the back of his neck. "Hmm?"

His gaze was ablaze with passion. "You better get your ass in my bed right now," he growled.

"Fucking make me," I goaded.

I yelped when he stood up and carried me into his bedroom. He might have been a soft, sensitive boy, but he knew when I wanted an aggressive man in the bedroom.

CHAPTER TWENTY-FOUR

BENNY

Riley and I leaned against the boards in front of the bench as we watched Rox and Noah doing one-on-one plays down the other end of the ice.

It had been a couple of days since Rox and I told each other how we felt, and when we weren't spending time between my sheets, we were on the ice together. Riley and Noah had been bugging me about skipping out on training sessions with them, so I ended up recruiting them to help Rox get hockey ready.

"I think I need to get her new skates," I said.

Riley winced.

Every player knew that breaking in a fresh pair of skates was the absolute worst. We waited until the absolute last minute to replace them, preferring to wear the same ones for three years straight. Breaking in a new boot was a pain in the ass, and you always felt for another player when they were going through it.

When we went to buy new gear the other day, Rox had

mentioned her boots were falling apart, and it was probably time to get a new pair. I hadn't pressed her on it because it sucked having to break in a new boot. I also wondered if part of her hesitation had to do with the expense. Hockey gear wasn't cheap, and even though she worked for the team, her salary was nowhere near mine. Because of that, I had offered to help pay for her gear, but being the stubborn woman she was, she refused. But her birthday was coming up, and an idea had percolated in my brain.

"Would it be weird if I bought her skates for her birthday?" I asked Riley.

He chewed on his lip. "Nah. It shows you want what's best for her, even if she doesn't want to do it. Don't envy her having to break in new skates, though."

I nodded. "I know, but she'll wear that old pair until they literally fall off on the ice."

Riley smirked. "That sounds familiar."

TJ had to replace his skates last season, and he still hadn't stopped complaining about it. The Desjardins Twins had way more in common than I ever realized.

I turned my attention back to watching Rox and Noah on the ice together. Rox deked a shot and got the wrap-around goal. Noah never saw it coming, and pride swelled in my chest at watching her. In a flash, Noah got the better of her by getting possession of the puck from her. She flew across the ice, tearing after Noah at the other end. I loved watching her play her two-hundred-foot game. She was more skilled at this sport than some of our fourth-liners. She tried to get the puck out from underneath Noah, but he toe-dragged it and directed it into the net before she could stop it.

"She can buy her own pair. Why do you want to do it?" Riley asked.

"I'm afraid she's not gonna follow through with playing hockey again if she doesn't replace them."

Riley raised an eyebrow. "What do you mean?"

"She had a severe concussion in college and hung up her skates for a while. I think if I buy her new ones, it will force her to get back on the ice."

"She's on the ice right now."

"No, like on a team."

"You think she should try out for one of the PHF teams, don't you?"

I nodded. I gave her some beer league teams to look up, but she looked ready to be on the ice with players of her caliber.

"Wow. You love her, don't ya?" Riley asked with a smirk.

"You think that because I know she's better than beer league?"

He nodded. "Yeah, bro. When you love someone, you want them to be the best they can be. You cheer on the sidelines for them and let them complain when things get hard. Like how I do for Fi with her writing. You're doing that for Rox."

"You think I fell too fast?"

Rox and I had only been sneaking around for a couple of weeks. A part of me felt like my feelings for her came on too soon. The other part of me worried she'd realize she still hated my freaking guts and dump me. I dreaded that the most because I never wanted to go back to a time when she hated me. The only time I enjoyed fighting with her now was in bed.

Riley laughed. "I think it's about damn time! You've been in love with that feisty woman for years. You were both just too stubborn to realize it. Have you told TJ yet?"

I shook my head.

I wasn't looking forward to that. The code was such bullshit. Rox was her own person and could make her own decisions about who she wanted to date. However, TJ was also my teammate and my roommate, and I wasn't trying to piss him off. I wanted to sit him down and tell him I loved his sister and that I wanted to make this work. It wasn't a conversation you did via text. It was one you did after several drinks.

"I don't envy you," Riley admitted.

"I'm not afraid of TJ."

"Yeah, but dude...the code."

"Is bullshit."

"I don't disagree, but you know how he feels about it."

I rolled my eyes.

TJ had made it clear Rox was off-limits several times. In the past, it hadn't been an issue because it wasn't like anything was gonna happen between me and Rox. Now I had to figure out how to break the news to him that while he was playing in the World Hockey Championship, I'd been banging his sister.

I watched Noah check Rox into the boards and swipe the puck from her. I might have been annoyed with Noah for doing that if Rox didn't give it right back to him. Rox and TJ had a similar style of play. She was good at getting under your skin and was scrappy as hell.

"Come on, girl, you gonna let him beat you?" I yelled.

"Oy! Fuck you, Bennett!" she yelled back.

I removed my gloves and reached behind me on the bench to grab my phone. I recorded her for a couple minutes, so I could play it back to her later and show her she belonged on the ice again. I wished she saw her potential. She hadn't contacted any of the leagues I had researched for her. I thought she was still scared of concussions and not being healthy.

I wished women had better options in professional sports. It was unfair. Some of them had a harder shot than us, but yet they weren't getting paid millions like I was.

Riley nudged me. "How long were you two sneaking around?"

"Come on, not this again."

He poked me with his stick. I put my phone behind the bench and put my gloves back on. "Remember how I had to rescue her from that awful date?" I asked.

"No shit? I knew it."

"Well, kinda. We thought it was a one-time thing, but..."

"But what?"

"That shit with her ex happened, and she was so upset. I had to drive up to Canada with her. Then she had me pretend to be her boyfriend in front of her ex."

"Oh, fake dating. That's the trope Fi is going for in her romance book."

I laughed. "Yeah, that's always a good one."

Riley cocked an eyebrow. "How would you know?"

"Listen, my lady likes to read romance books, and I'm very supportive of it."

Riley smiled. "Yeah, I liked all the 'research' Fi needed to do for writing one, too. It's definitely a departure from her young adult sci-fi stuff."

I rolled my eyes. "Yeah, I heard a lot of that 'research' when I stayed with you. Why do you think I fucked off to Boston when our season was done?"

Riley shook his head at me. "So why did you and Rox keep it a secret?"

"That's what she wanted."

"Why?"

"Your wife put it in perspective for me. I thought it was because of TJ, but it's because I told her I was thinking of asking for a trade. She didn't want to get attached if I was gonna leave her."

Riley furrowed his brow at me. "You didn't ask for one, though, right?"

I shrugged. "Steve gave the team my list of places I'm willing to go, and Boston is at the top of it."

"Benny!" Riley scolded. "You know if the press gets wind of that, they'll have a field day."

"Nobody's gonna find out." Riley gave me an unsure look, but I shrugged. "Doesn't matter now. Rox and I worked everything out."

"You have been a little mopey lately, but I couldn't figure out why."

I nodded. "You know I go all in."

He raised an eyebrow. "You? No?"

I glared at him.

He rolled his eyes at me. "Does she know you talked to Steve?"

I shook my head. "Nah."

"Dude, make sure she knows."

"Why?"

He raised a blonde eyebrow at me and then looked across the ice at my girlfriend checking Noah into the boards. "Because if she finds out you gave the Bulldogs a list of teams you'd be open to going to, that's basically you asking for a trade, and she'll go ballistic."

"But I didn't," I argued.

He narrowed his eyes at me. It seemed like he wanted to say something else, but he held his tongue.

Noah and Rox ran through plays together while Riley and I skated to the other zone. Riley was a defenseman, so we didn't skate on the same line together, but he was perceptive in terms of what our team needed to work on.

During the off-season, I stayed off the ice for a while, preferring to stick to cardio and weight training to keep in shape. Couldn't say the same for Riley and Noah—those two never left the ice. It was why they didn't even flinch when I asked them to help me get Rox back into playing shape. I knew working all day long and then coming home for a quick dinner before getting out on the ice was tough for her, but the smile on her face told me it was worth it.

I skated over to the bench where Rox was standing with her helmet off and fixing her sweaty hair. I wrapped my gloved hands around her waist from behind her, and she smiled up at me. I kissed her cheek. "You're looking good out there," I said into her ear.

"Thank you for pushing me. I missed this," she said.

Riley and Noah skated over and sprayed us with ice. "Aw, you two are so disgustingly sweet!" Riley teased.

Rox and I gave him matching middle fingers, and we laughed while she reached up and pulled me down to kiss her hard in front of my teammates. They both catcalled us, but I knew these two fuckers were just as in love with their women as I was in love with Rox.

When I pulled away, she gave me a wicked grin. "Want to cream these two assholes?" she asked.

"You say the sexiest things to me."

CHAPTER TWENTY-FIVE

ROXANNE

I groaned at the sound of my alarm going off. I hit snooze and then turned in bed to snuggle down into Benny's chest. It was the morning of my twenty-fifth birthday and an entire week since Benny and I made our relationship official. The World Championship in Russia had ended last week, but Tristan was taking a well-deserved vacation. He had been coy about it, so I didn't know when he would return home. As soon as he did, shit would hit the fan. I was dreading telling my brother I was dating his teammate and that I had kept it from him. He was my twin; Tristan knew when I was keeping something from him.

Benny pulled me closer to him, and I smiled as I laid my head on his chest and listened to his heartbeat. "Happy birthday, angel," he said into my hair.

"Mmm. I wish I didn't have to go to work today," I groaned and rolled over onto my back.

He leaned over and kissed me hard on the mouth. I gave in to it, even though I shouldn't have, because I had to get up and get ready for work. He threaded his hand through my hair and pulled me closer to deepen the kiss. I opened my mouth to him and let his tongue slide over mine. He distracted me enough that I didn't even notice his other hand inching the tank top up my stomach until he pulled away so he could pull it over my head.

"Hey! I have to get up for work," I said and tried to push him away.

He pinned my arms above my head in an aggressive move he knew got me all hot and bothered. He kissed my neck and moved down my chest until he was pulling the bud of my nipple taut into his mouth. I arched into him while he licked and sucked at my skin until I moaned in pleasure. I whined when his lips moved away to trail tiny kisses down my stomach. He stopped at the hem of my panties and looked up at me with a devilish smile while he toyed with the fabric.

"Love," I whined, "I don't have time."

He slipped my underwear off and continued to kiss his way down the length of my body until he was placing soft kisses on the inside of my thighs.

"I'll be quick," he promised.

He was never quick. Much to my surprise, going down on me was like an art form for him. He liked to savor me and lick me through at least two orgasms before he was satisfied. Which I loved, but not so much when I had already hit snooze on my alarm twice, and I was running late.

He bent his head to my mound and parted my slick folds with his tongue. I didn't have time for this, but when he pulled my clit into his mouth, I lost my will to argue. Benny made it his job to please me. I never would have thought Benny would love eating pussy as much as he did. Then again, I had seriously misjudged him for several years.

I didn't mind being proven wrong if it meant his head was regularly between my legs.

I clutched his hair in my hands while he pinned me beneath him so he could get his fill of me. He curled his fingers up inside me, pressing into that spot deep inside while his magical tongue worked over my clit. Seriously, how was he so good at this? I closed my eyes as the pleasure coursed through me, and I thrusted my hips up against his face.

"That's it, angel. Fuck my face."

I gripped his hair harder. "Michael," I moaned.

Benny loved it when I moaned his first name.

"Good girl."

"I'm not a good girl!" I snapped.

He chuckled into me, his fingers still pumping inside while he gave me a mischievous grin. "No, you're my bad girl, huh?"

I nodded and tried to push his head back down. "Yeah, now get back down there and punish me with your tongue some more."

He grinned while he slipped a third finger inside and wrapped his lips around my clit, giving it a long, hard suck. That pushed me over the edge, and I rode my orgasm out on his tongue, writhing and crying out his name as I came.

He had the biggest grin on his face when he lifted his head up from between my legs and wiped my cum off his beard. I let go of his hair and moaned again when he lifted his fingers to his mouth and seductively licked them clean.

"Oh God, that's so hot," I breathed. "I want you to be inside of me so bad right now, but I don't have time for sex this morning."

He kissed his way back up my body. "Bad girls have to wait. You can have the rest of me when you get home."

"You're evil, you know."

He winked, and I ran to get the quickest shower known to man. I shouldn't have liked it when he called me a bad girl in bed, but goddamn did he do things I never realized were my motherfucking jam. I dressed in a flash and ran around the room, searching for my phone. He laid in bed with a smile on his face and held his hand out to me to hand me my phone.

I kissed him quickly. "I'm sorry I have to go."

"Hey, your dad keeps calling you," he said and gripped my hand so I couldn't let him go.

I made a face. "I don't want to talk to him; he can leave a message. I'm sorry, love, I need to go. I have a meeting at ten I can't miss."

I kissed him once more and flew out the door, practically running to my car. Miraculously, I wasn't late to work, but I drove there in a dreamlike state after getting pleasured by my boyfriend first thing in the morning.

It was still strange that Michael Bennett, the man I'd vowed to hate until the end of time, was my boyfriend. He was patient and kind but also knew when to be aggressive with me. When we weren't spending all of our time horizontally on his bed, we were on the ice, training to get me back into playing shape. It made my heart sing that he wanted me to get back to playing hockey.

I was in a daze when I walked into the office. Quinn quirked her head at me in confusion as she stood outside of my office. I felt the blush color my face, and I thought maybe she could tell my cheery mood was from sexual satisfaction. I hoped not. That would be embarrassing.

"What's that look for?" she asked.

"Nothing!" I protested.

"Oh, you got a delivery this morning," she said.

"Is that why you're being a creep and lurking outside my office?" I asked.

"She's nosy!" Maxine chimed in from her cubicle. "Who's it from?"

I shrugged. "I don't even know what it is!"

I walked into my office, flicked the light switch on, and saw a vase of cherry blossom branches on my desk. Those were my favorite flowers, so much I had a cherry blossom tattoo on one of my shoulder blades. Quinn grinned and followed me into my office. I snatched the card up before she could read it.

For my angel. Happy birthday.
Love, Michael

I pressed the note to my chest and felt myself getting misty eyed. No one had ever bought me flowers before. How did I get so lucky with this guy? First, he pushed me to play the sport I loved, and now, he was sending me flowers. My heart flipped over in my chest in happiness.

"Oh my God, are you crying?" Quinn asked with a laugh.

"No," I lied and wiped my eyes. "No one's sent me flowers before. Oh God, he's so sweet."

She snatched the card out of my hand. "I didn't know it was your birthday. Michael, huh? Wait..." Her eyes widened when she saw me take out my phone. She must have seen my lock screen photo of me and Benny kissing. She got up and shut my office door suddenly. "Oh my God, are you dating Michael Bennett?" she asked, pointing at my phone.

I bit my lip. "Um...is that against the rules?"

She shook her head. "The GM's my husband, remember?"

"Oh, right."

"Is that who you've been seeing?" she asked incredulously, but she looked giddy.

"Wait, you knew I was seeing someone?"

She rolled her eyes. "Yeah, since you got back from Canada, you race out of here on time. It wasn't that hard to figure out. Plus, you rolled in this morning looking like someone had well fucked you."

I laughed and closed my eyes. "Is it that obvious?"

She cackled. "Get it, girl! So what's the deal? Why didn't you say anything?"

I chewed on my bottom lip. "Um...it's kind of been casual for a while. We've only been officially dating for about a week."

"He went with you to Canada."

"Yup."

She laughed. "Damn, girl. Does your brother know yet?"

I groaned and shook my head. "We want to tell him in person, over drinks."

She smiled at me. "Good plan. By the way, you look so cute together in that photo."

I beamed. "I know."

"Ha! So modest."

❄

I spent the morning in meetings and didn't look at my phone until lunch. I had a bunch of messages and even a voicemail from my mom. It wasn't odd for my mom to call me or leave me a voicemail. I just always deleted them without listening to them. She'd said what she needed to say all those years ago.

I scrolled through the texts from Benny first.

BENNY: *How's your day?*

ME: *You sent me flowers?*

BENNY: *Did you like them? I know they're your favorite.*

ME: *I LOVED them. No one has ever sent me flowers. How did you know?*

BENNY: *Rox, you have a cherry blossom tattoo. It doesn't take a genius to figure it out.*

He was wrong; it took a genius because no one I had dated before him ever bought me flowers. Come to think of it, none of my previous partners even asked me what my favorite flower was. Benny didn't have to ask; he just knew.

I flipped over to the texts from my brother.

TRISTAN: *Yo, slut! Happy birthday!*

ME: *Hoe! Happy Birthday! I saw you won gold! When are you coming home?*

TRISTAN: *Soon!*

ME: *So vague!*

TRISTAN: *Who sent you flowers?*

Shit. I forgot I got so emotional this morning that I snapped a quick thing on my Instagram. I didn't think he looked at them.

ME: *I'll tell you when you get back...but I'm seeing someone right now.*

I responded to a couple of messages that were basic birthday wishes while I tried to decide what to do for lunch. My office phone rang, and I saw it was our receptionist, Cindy. I picked it up. "Hey, Cindy, what's up?"

"Um...you have a visitor who wants to see you?"

"I do?" I asked. I put the phone on speaker and checked my calendar. "I don't have anything on my calendar."

"Um...yeah. It's your dad."

I hung up. I told Quinn I needed to run an errand and

went to Cindy's desk in the front. Sure enough, there was my dad standing there in all his six-foot-two glory with his shock of salt and pepper hair.

"Dad?" I asked, not believing what I was seeing.

When he saw me, he didn't say anything but pulled me into a great big bear hug. "Roxie girl!"

I turned to Cindy. "I'm gonna run out for lunch. Call me if you need anything. I don't have any meetings for the rest of the day."

I drug my dad outside. "What are you doing here?" I seethed.

His face hardened, and his hazel eyes bored into me. "You don't answer my calls. I had to find out from Natalie that you moved to The States," he said.

I clenched my hands into fists and tried to calm down. I failed. "Why do you even care?" I yelled back at him.

"Look, can we go somewhere to talk?" he asked.

"Fine."

I made my dad get into my car, and we drove to a nearby sandwich place I loved. I had no idea why he was here. We ordered food and ate in a terse silence for a few minutes.

"Roxie, I didn't agree with what your mother said all those years ago," he said as he put down his sandwich.

I mimicked his action and wiped my mouth with a napkin before I spoke. "She told me I was being selfish and had to choose."

He sighed. "I know, and it wasn't right. It wasn't right that Tristan was put in the middle of it either."

"I never asked him to pick a side."

"I know."

"So, why are you here? Why now? It's been years."

"Someone asked me about my daughter, who was couch

surfing because her partner kicked her out. I had no idea, and you wouldn't answer your phone. I finally called Nat, who told me the truth. You know, you could have come to us for help."

I held up my hands. "Did you really expect me to come to you for help?"

He ran his hands through his hair in frustration. "I hated leaving things like we did. I'm not saying I understand being bisexual, but I love you, and I want you to be happy."

"What about Mom?"

"She wants to make amends, too. She knows she was wrong. It took her a long time to figure that out."

Is that what the voicemail was about? Is that why she called me on occasion? I just always thought it was so she could berate me some more that my sexuality wasn't real.

"Then why isn't she here? What caused her to change her mind?"

Dad ran a shaky hand through his hair. "Roxie, when you had that concussion..."

A year after I came out, I had that nasty spill on the ice. It was my last year of university, and I hadn't spoken to my parents in an entire year. I blocked out a lot of what happened when I healed from the concussion, but I vaguely remembered having a screaming match with my mother when she tried to visit me in the hospital.

I stared at him. "Dad, that was three years ago."

"You told your mother to go to hell and have ignored us anytime either of us calls you. We've spent three years trying to win you back."

I clenched my teeth and tried not to yell at him. "You both said what you needed to say, that who I was wasn't acceptable to you."

Dad's face fell, and he put a meaty hand on top of mine, but I pulled mine back as if his touch was fire.

"Roxie, we both messed up, but we love and miss you."

"She'll accept me now that I'm dating a man," I muttered to myself.

I was sure she would think me being with Benny meant I had 'chosen' to be straight. Even if my relationship made me look 'straight-passing,' it didn't change that I was always gonna be bisexual. I didn't think she would ever understand that.

Dad furrowed his brow at me. "What's that?"

"I'm dating someone new."

"Oh, that's good. What's her name? Is she good to you? What does she do?"

"Dad! Stop!" I picked up my sandwich and took another bite to calm my nerves. "It's a man. I'm dating a man again."

He narrowed his eyes. "Okay, those questions again, but now I want to see a copy of his 401K and his—"

"DAD!"

He gave me that cocky grin that I knew we shared. Jerk.

"You gonna tell me about him?" he asked.

"I haven't told Tristan yet."

"Okay..." He trailed off, and then the realization hit him. "Fuck, Roxie, a hockey player?"

"Dad, you were a hockey player. Tristan's a hockey player."

He shook his head in disbelief. "Christ, I was hoping to keep you away from that life. It's hard on spouses. All right, tell me who it is. I assume he plays for the Bulldogs."

"Michael Bennett," I said through my hands.

"Tristan said you hate each other."

"Yeah...turns out not really."

He nodded. "Tristan's been in Russia."

"Uh-huh."

"And you've been living together," he stated the obvious again.

"Dad, he got me back on the ice."

"Tristan told me."

"I don't want to play professionally again, but he's been helping me get back into hockey form, see if I can join a rec league or something next fall. I'm still scared to play again, though."

Dad laid a hand on mine again. I didn't pull away. "You can get back out there."

I nodded. "I know, and that's what Benny's been trying to tell me. But you know us, Desjardins. We're stubborn."

"He's good to you?"

My face hurt from the size of the smile formed across my lips. "Yeah, he is. He's patient and sweet...he's a lot like you. You'd like him."

"I've met him, and I do like him. Roxie girl, if you're happy, I'm glad for you. Men, women, genderfluid, nonbinary, I want you to find someone who makes you happy."

I was floored. Obviously, Dad had done some research. When I came out, Dad just stared blankly at me and said nothing. I had always assumed that meant he felt the same way as Mom. It never occurred to me that it took my dad some time to process the news.

"Dad, you know what nonbinary and genderfluid are?" I asked.

He steepled his hands in front of his face. "Look, I did a lot of research, okay? I wanted to understand you, understand what it meant for you to be bisexual."

"I'm still bisexual just because Benny's a man."

He held up a hand to me. "I wasn't trying to say that. I

get that. I wanted you to know that I love you, no matter what. It was killing me that we weren't speaking."

I wiped a tear from my eye. "Dad..."

"Aw, Roxie, don't cry," he said and handed me a napkin.

I dabbed my eyes and checked my watch. "I got to get back to work."

"I should have told you I supported you then. It was just a shock, and I didn't know what it all meant. Then you wouldn't return any of my calls."

"Do you blame me after the way Mom reacted?"

He shook his head with a sigh. "No, but I want us to be a family again. I don't want this wedge between you and your mother. And neither does she."

I shook my head as tears continued to fall, and Dad shoved more napkins at me. "Mom has never really gotten me. I'm used to that. But it hurt when she denied who I am."

"I know, and she knows she messed up. I want you to know that I'm sorry about everything, and I'm really proud of you."

"Dad!" I cried and then collapsed into more tears.

What a weird birthday.

CHAPTER TWENTY-SIX

BENNY

I looked over my shoulder at the sound of the door opening, and I smiled when Roxanne walked over to me. She jumped into my arms and wrapped her legs around my waist while she buried her face in my neck. I laughed and squeezed her ass.

"Whoa, there."

She lifted her head up and took my face in her hands to pull me into a tender kiss. "Hi," she said sheepishly with a seductive smile. She dug her heels into my back.

"Damn, girl, you didn't even take your shoes off?" I asked with a laugh.

She leaned her head back, and I took that as my opportunity to kiss the hollow of her throat. She purred under my touch, but I dropped her off on the kitchen counter. I kissed her nose and turned back to making dinner. I loved cooking for her, especially since come hockey season, I wouldn't be able to do it as much. Plus, she wasn't too bad in the kitchen either, and it was nice to cook beside her every night. All of that would change once TJ got back from Russia, but I didn't want to think about that yet.

"How was work?" I asked.

"Oh, I had a weird day. My dad showed up."

I flipped the chicken in the grill pan and checked on the rice. I looked back at her with a raised eyebrow. "I'm sorry, what?"

She nodded and hopped down from off the counter. She went to the front door to kick off her shoes and shed her cardigan. She came back into the kitchen and poured herself a shot of vodka. I watched, amused, as she knocked it back.

"Don't drink too much, angel. I want you to be awake later."

"I'm taking advantage of you being around now because I know I'll be dating my vibrator when the season starts," she joked with a smile.

"I'm gonna miss you so much when I'm on the road. There's always video chat sex, though," I said with a wink.

"Who are we kidding? You'll be sick of me by the time training camp starts."

"Never."

"What do you need me to do to help with dinner?" she asked.

"Nothing. You sit that gorgeous ass down and let me cook you dinner."

"What's for dinner?"

"Chicken, rice, and vegetables. Not that exciting, but I know you're serious about eating healthy and training."

She beamed at me. "Thank you for remembering."

We ate dinner in front of the TV and watched the rest of the Boston hockey game. I had my arm around her as she snuggled into my chest.

"Thanks for dinner," she said.

"Of course. Did you like the flowers? I knew you liked cherry blossoms, but I wasn't sure if I should get something else."

"I loved them; it was really thoughtful."

I smiled. "I'm glad. Hey, wait, before I kiss you into submission—" She cut me off with a playful slap to the arm. "I have something for you."

"Oh, you didn't have to get me a gift. The flowers and dinner were enough."

I shook my head and went into my room to fetch her gift. I knew she didn't care about cards, so I didn't get her one. I handed her the box and watched her tear the wrapping off. She put her hands to her chest and looked at me in surprise.

"Oh, you didn't!" she scolded, but her grin was big. She flipped the box open and took out the brand new skates. "Fuck, these are gonna be a bitch to break in."

I laughed. "I know, but your skates are garbage. You needed new ones, and I knew you wouldn't get them until you absolutely had to."

"Thank you for this. Even though it sucks that I have to break new boots in, I know you bought them for me because you want me to get back on the ice. I'm gonna do it, though. I'm going to play hockey again."

I kissed her cheek. "You will. I have faith in you."

She placed the box of skates on the coffee table and kissed me hard. I melted into it and pulled her into my lap. I kissed her neck and massaged her tits through her shirt.

"Mmm, love when you do that," she moaned.

"I'd like it better if your shirt was off," I whispered huskily against her skin.

"Who told you I wanted it on?"

I flipped off the TV, and she dragged me by the hand into my bedroom. Once inside my bedroom, she pulled her shirt over her head. She wore a bra so lacy it was practically see-through, and her tits spilled out of it, teasing at what lay underneath the restrictive garment.

Fuck me, this woman was a goddess. I reached behind me and stripped myself of my shirt. Her hand ran down my chest slowly, like she was torturing me until she reached the top of my jeans.

"Angel," I groaned.

"What's wrong, love?" she purred as she unbuttoned my jeans and slid the zipper down. She rubbed me through the thin material of my boxers.

"You're killing me!"

She laughed, but then she turned around and slid her skirt down over her hips. My mouth watered as I saw the skimpy piece of clothing she wore underneath her skirt. Her cheeks were bare for me to see in a sexy thong I had never seen her wear before.

"You like?" she asked. She bent over the bed so I could get a good look.

I slid my pants and boxers down around my ankles and stepped out of them. "Oh, fuck, you're trying to give me a heart attack. I've never seen you wear something like that."

She turned back around to face me. "Special occasion."

"You got dressed in a huff this morning."

She dragged her finger down my face and ran her thumb across my bottom lip. "I knew I was getting some later and that you'd like it. I thought I owed you after what this sweet mouth of yours did this morning."

My dick throbbed painfully at her words. I trailed my finger down her gorgeous curvy body until I landed on the hem of her bra and pulled her closer. I undid the front clasp of her bra and watched the material pop-open to release those enormous globes. She shimmied out of the bra and let it fall down her back. My hand traveled down her body to finger the thin string of her thong. I reached around behind her to feel her naked ass in my hands. Then I ripped the material down her legs and pushed her onto the bed.

She laughed. "Shit, I should wear those more often."

I stretched out on the bed beside her, and we kissed each other slowly. Her hands rubbed across my beard when I pulled away. "I love your beard. I'm so glad you grew it back out."

"Yeah?" I asked and buried my face in her chest, rubbing it across her pale white skin.

She giggled. "I love when you do that and how it feels on my thighs."

"You love riding my beard."

"Duh!"

I pressed tiny kisses across her chest and watched her squirm because I wasn't giving her the satisfaction she wanted. I leisurely flicked my tongue across one of her nipples, taking the sweet hard nub into my mouth and massaging the other one with my hand. I slid down her body, giving her teasing little kisses as I did.

"What are you doing?" she asked.

I spread her legs and threw them over my shoulders. "What does it look like?"

I dipped my head to kiss her teasingly before darting my tongue out across her glistening slit. I glided my tongue across her clit, focusing on her pleasure even though I felt like my dick was about to explode. I swirled my tongue around her clit and sucked until her legs quivered and she moaned my name.

I slipped her legs off my shoulders and wiped my beard

off with a tissue from the bedside table. I laid back on the bed beside her and stroked a hand on her hip. Her hazel eyes popped open, and she gave me a satisfied smirk while she reached down and stroked me.

"Rox, please stop. I'm gonna come too soon," I told her and tried to push her away.

"That's okay," she said and bent over my lap to take it in her mouth.

I watched as her plum-colored lipstick smeared across my dick as she bobbed up and down on it. I leaned back and moaned as she reintroduced her hand at the same time. I reached down to hold back her hair so I could watch her. She pulled off for a moment and licked around the head and down the length of my shaft. I groaned, and she gave me a brief smile before taking me back into her mouth.

"Angel..." I moaned and gripped her hair tightly.

She ignored me and moaned as she took me deeper into her mouth. She sucked until I spilled my cum down her throat.

She popped up to lie back on the bed and wiped her lips. I leaned over and kissed her. "I'm gonna need a minute," I admitted.

She laughed. "I realized. You think you can handle this tonight?" She shimmied in her place on the bed, her tits jiggling around, and I laughed.

"Oh, I think so. Give me some time to recover. But, Rox, fuck, that was so good."

"I felt bad. You went down on me twice today."

I smiled at her. "Yeah, but it's your birthday. And it's my job to pleasure you as much as possible."

I laughed as she fanned herself. "Damn, you make me so horny. Do you think if we hadn't spent three years hating each other, we would fuck like rabbits all the time?"

I caressed her face. "I want to be inside you at all times, every day. I don't think it would have mattered when we got together, we would still be this horny."

She tipped back her head and barked out a laugh. "I love that I get to call you my boyfriend now. I can't believe it's only been a week!"

I laughed. "It's been longer than a week."

"Yeah, but I thought it was just sex for you then."

I laid on my side and caressed her face. "Roxanne, it was never just sex for me. I knew it was always going to end up with you and me against the world."

"Aw, when did you know?"

"That night in Canada."

"Really?"

I nodded and nuzzled into her neck. "I loved the passion between us and how you goaded me but melted into my kisses. I knew I wanted to have something more with you. I just didn't want to scare you away."

"I wish you'd told me sooner," she said in a small voice. "I didn't want to get attached if I knew you were leaving."

"We're here now; that's what matters," I reassured her. I pressed my forehead against hers and gave her a small kiss. "I'm never gonna stop fighting for you, fighting for us."

She beamed and kissed me again. It didn't take long for me to get hard again, especially when she stroked me while I made her come again with my fingers. We were like horny teenagers, but I didn't care. My dick wanted to be buried inside her pussy all the time.

It surprised me when she got on all fours. Doggy-style was my favorite position, and we did it a lot, but I was under the assumption she didn't like it.

"Oh, yeah?" I asked.

"It feels so good when you grab my hips and fucking rail me."

I chuckled behind her while I rolled a condom on, lubed up, and lined myself up with her entrance. "You want to get railed tonight?"

"Uh-huh."

I slid into her slowly. I ran my hands down her back and got into a steady rhythm. I kissed her neck. "I'm going to hit that g-spot good tonight," I said into her ear.

"Please," she begged.

I quickened my pace, pumping into her hard and fast while I gripped onto her hips. The reason she liked this position was the same reason I liked it. She clutched the bedsheets and moaned until she froze suddenly and made me stop.

"Did you hear something?" she asked and looked back at me over her shoulder.

"Rox, it's nothing."

She chewed her lip but then turned back to face the headboard. She ground her ass back into me, and I continued thrusting into her. I slapped her ass, and that seemed to make her moan louder.

"You need a good spanking, you bad girl," I growled at her.

"Benny, shut up and fuck me hard!" she snapped back at me.

I loved how aggressive she got when we did it doggy-style. It was so hot. She unraveled underneath me as I pounded into her from behind and gripped her hair in my fist.

"You love it rough."

She nodded into the bed, and her hands clutched at the headboard. "Punish me for being a bad girl."

I grinned at her demand while I gripped her hair tighter. "Oh, I will. *So* bad."

"Benny," she panted.

"What?"

"Please," she begged.

"Please what, angel?"

"Make me come."

I slowed to a stop and pulled out.

"Why did you stop? I was so close," she whined.

I chuckled and flipped her over onto her back. "I want to change positions," I explained.

Those wild hazel eyes looked up at me with desire.

I ran my hand down her face and rubbed my thumb across her bottom lip. "You're so beautiful. I want to see your face when I make you come all over my dick."

Her face softened. "God, that's so sweet. And so dirty."

I grinned and pushed her legs apart gently, lowering myself in-between them and sliding home again. "You love it."

"I do," she admitted.

"Come with me," I demanded as I quickened my pace, and she wrapped her legs around my waist.

She clutched at my back and dug her fingernails into me. I loved the pleasure and pain she brought to the bedroom. I loved that she made me feel alive like no woman had ever made me feel before. Roxanne Desjardins was a challenging woman, but she was mine, and I wouldn't let her go.

"Angel..." I sighed and kissed her neck.

"Hmm?"

"I love you," I moaned.

She pushed me off so she could look me in the eye.

Instead of the loving look she had been giving me, she looked pissed off. "You what?" she screeched.

"I love you," I repeated. "I can't believe I haven't said it before, but I do."

"It's too soon."

"Is it? We've been going behind our friends' backs for weeks. Do you think I didn't fall in love with you before we made this official?"

"It doesn't count if you say it during sex!" she complained, but she bucked her hips to meet my thrusts.

I pressed my hand against our connection, giving her feather-light touches across her clit while I rolled my hips against her, pressing deeper inside her. Maybe it was the wrong time to say it to her, but in that moment of passion, I wanted to see her face and tell her what I felt, what I'd wanted to tell her for weeks.

"I love you, Roxanne Desjardins, and I'm never letting you go."

She reached up to cup my face in her hands, and her thumb caressed my beard. "Benny, you don't mean that."

"I do. I love you. Now be a good girl and come for me."

Her eyes flashed in anger, but then her eyes squeezed shut as I hit her spot, and she unraveled underneath me. Watching this woman come undone was a beautiful sight indeed. With an animalistic grunt seconds later, I was right behind her.

I pulled out and threw the condom away in the trash, then laid on my back next to her. Her eyes were closed, but her hand patted at my chest.

"That was like...so good," she breathed out. Her chest was still heaving from the exertion.

"You're out of breath? I did all the work," I teased.

She gave me the finger.

"Happy birthday!" I exclaimed and buried myself in her neck, kissing her and making her giggle.

"I can't believe the first time you told me you loved me was during sex. It doesn't count!"

"What? It so counts!" I argued. I hugged her around the waist and put my head in the crook of her neck. "I'll say it again. I love you, Roxanne Desjardins, you infuriating, complicated woman."

She squirmed in my arms but only so she could shift onto her side and look me in the eye. She reached up to push my hair out of my face. "I love you too, Michael Bennett, you patient, gentle giant," she whispered.

I groaned at my phone buzzing on the bedside table. To my surprise, there were a lot of messages from TJ.

TJ: *Hey, are you home? I didn't tell Roxie I was gonna be home late tonight so we could grab a drink for our birthday.*

TJ: *NEVER MIND! Do you always fuck chicks this loud??*

TJ: *Why is my sister's phone in the living room? And she's not here?*

TJ: *WHAT THE FUCK DUDE!*

"Love, what's wrong?" she asked me. "You look like you saw a ghost."

"Um, Rox...angel...don't freak out."

"What?"

I showed her my texts, and her face went pale.

We were so fucked.

CHAPTER TWENTY-SEVEN

ROXANNE

This was a disaster. After awesome birthday sex with my boyfriend, after he told me he loved me for the first time, this had to happen. I swear the hockey gods had it out for me. I wanted to sit Tristan down and tell him that Benny and I were together; I didn't want him to come home and hear us having sex.

Why didn't he tell me he was coming home?

"Are you sure that's why he said, 'what the fuck?' Maybe he's just annoyed having to hear you have sex?" I asked.

Benny shook his head. "Nah, I'm pretty sure he knows you're here. Your phone's in the living room."

I dropped my head into his chest and groaned. "This is so fucked. What do we do?"

He sighed but wrapped his arms around me and held me to his chest to comfort me. "I think we just have to deal with it."

The TV was on in the living room, with the volume

turned all the way up. Shit, how loud had we been? I rolled onto my back and out of bed. I went into Benny's dresser drawer to pull out a clean pair of underwear I had stored in there. Since we got back from Canada, I hadn't been sleeping in Tristan's bed. I didn't bother with a bra but threw on Benny's sweatshirt and a pair of pajama pants. He pulled on his jeans and t-shirt. We both looked nervous, like two teenagers caught in the act.

He reached out a hand to smooth down my hair and kissed me softly. "It's gonna be okay," he reassured me.

I bit my lip. "I didn't want him to find out this way."

He caressed my cheek with his thumb. "Hey. I love you, okay?"

I lifted my face up, and he met me in a gentle kiss. "I love you too."

If anyone had told me months ago that I would be standing in front of this mountain of a man and confessing my love to him, I would have laughed in their face. Probably would have thrown a drink at them too.

"I'm not afraid of your brother."

"Why not?"

He smirked. "Because you're scarier, and because I'm never going back to the way things were before. I told you: I'm always gonna fight for you, angel. For us."

Seriously, how did I hate this man for so long? How?

I wound my hair on top of my head and found a hair tie on top of the dresser to tie it back in. A messy bun was probably better than wild sex hair. I ran to the bathroom and swiped a make-up remover wipe across my face. My lipstick was smeared across my lips from when I went down on Benny. Definitely didn't need my brother to see me like that. I splashed water on my face. It wasn't perfect, but it would have to do.

Benny gripped my hand in his when I came out, and he swung open his bedroom door. I pulled away from him and went into the kitchen to grab Tristan a beer. He needed a drink to handle this conversation.

My twin brother sat on the couch and fumed.

"Here, you douche," I said and offered the beer to him. I sat on the arm of the couch next to him.

He took the beer from me, but he looked pissed. Benny stood in the kitchen, apparently unsure if he should stay there or join us in the living room. It was probably safer if he stayed several feet away from my brother.

Tristan looked between me and Benny. "What — and I cannot stress this enough — the fuck?" he asked.

"What do you want from me?" I asked and threw my hands up.

"For you to not fuck my teammates!" my brother seethed.

"This is the first one I've ever shown any interest in."

"I thought you hated his guts."

"I fucked it out of her," Benny snapped.

"BENNY! Not helping!" I sneered at him, then touched my brother's hand. "I didn't want you to find out like this. We wanted to wait until you got home to tell you in person."

Tristan stared at me like I had three heads. "How long has this been going on?"

"Not long," I said. "Since I had to go home and get shit from Lisa's."

Tristan shook his head in disgust. "I need something stronger."

He handed me back the beer and stalked into the kitchen to pour a line of shots. Benny and I shrugged at each other, not sure where we went from here. Tristan handed

Benny a shot. He shook his head, but my twin insisted. "Drink that shit, asshole. Roxie, you're doing one too."

I walked into the kitchen and took the shot glass from my brother's hand. Benny and I shared a look of annoyance, but we all knocked back our shots in unison. The alcohol burned on the way down my throat, but I shook it off. Tristan poured himself another.

"Are you mad because of the code?" I asked.

"I'm more mad you didn't tell me. You're my best friend," he exclaimed. "But, fuck, I don't want you to date a hockey player."

"Tristan, you're a hockey player," I argued.

He ran his hands through his hair in frustration. "Roxie, you know relationships with us are complicated. We're on the road all the time; we can get traded—"

I held up my hand. "I know what it's like. I grew up with it, remember?"

"Roxie, he likes the Bears," Tristan said like it was the worst thing about Benny. I laughed because it kind of was.

I gave my twin a sad smile. "I know, but what can I do?" I crossed over to my boyfriend and grabbed his face in my hands. "Look at this cute face!"

Tristan groaned, but then he narrowed his eyes at Benny. "Okay, man. You know what has to happen."

Benny walked over to my brother and held his hands out to his sides. "You want to do it now?"

Tristan stood up to his full height and studied Benny.

"Not the face. She loves this face," Benny said to my brother.

I didn't understand what was happening until Tristan clocked Benny hard in the stomach.

"Tristan! What the fuck!" I yelled.

Benny hunched over and tried to catch his breath.

When he rose to his full height, he peered down at my brother. "We good?"

"Fuck no! I just had to listen to you fuck my sister!" he snarled.

"Well, too fucking bad because I love your sister, and I don't give a fuck what you think. And quit this misogynistic 'code' bullshit! Rox can make her own choices."

My brother scrubbed a hand across his face. "Fine. You and me, big guy. We're getting a drink…or three."

"Tristan! Please don't kill my boyfriend! He's a lightweight," I begged.

Tristan hung his head. "Shit, this is serious, isn't it?"

I bit my lip. "Tristan, I love him."

Tristan closed his eyes and pinched the bridge of his nose. "Fuck, Roxie. Seriously?"

"Yes!" I cried and then punched him in the arm.

He rubbed his arm. "Ow, that hurt."

"That was the point, you douche! Don't punch my boyfriend again. Got it?"

I walked over to Benny and gave him a quick kiss. "I'm sorry."

He brushed a loose strand of hair out of my face. "It's fine. Don't wait up, okay?"

"Please don't try to keep up with my brother."

He smiled at me and caressed my cheek with his thumb. I leaned into the feeling of his hand on me. "I love you, okay? Your brother's just mad, but I'm not going anywhere. I told you, I'm not letting you go."

I nodded again, but I felt like I was going to cry. "I love you too. So much."

My twin made gagging sounds behind me, but I gave him the finger while I kissed my boyfriend goodbye. I truly hoped Benny didn't try to keep up with Tristan. Despite his size, Benny was a lightweight with drinking. I could drink him under the table, and Tristan was a thousand times worse.

"Will you ask Noah to go with you?" I asked.

He furrowed his brow. "Why?"

"So he can act as a buffer, so Tristan doesn't murder you."

Benny kissed me again. "I can take your brother."

"Love, please?" I asked.

He caressed my cheek with his thumb and kissed my forehead. "Okay. Whatever you want."

❇

I ended up tossing and turning in bed without Benny. I hadn't expected this from my brother, but from the look on Benny's face he had been waiting for this fallout. It explained why he took that punch like it was nothing. He was used to taking hits on the ice, but Benny wasn't a big fighter, and you never wanted to fight your teammate.

When I woke up the next morning and he wasn't in bed with me, I got scared, but then I tripped over him lying on the floor. "Benny?" I whispered in confusion.

He groaned and felt his head. "Shush, angel. Why are you screaming?"

"I'm not," I said even quieter. I went to my knees and brushed his sweaty hair out of his face. He looked like death, and his skin was warm to the touch. "Oh, love. Did you try to match drinks with my brother last night?"

He groaned as if in pain. "I didn't try. Your dad made me do shots."

"My dad? He's still in town? Wait, didn't I ask you to take Noah so he could be a buffer?"

He glared at me. "Do you think Noah Kennedy can say no to your dad and your brother? That dude is too nice."

I laughed. "I know! He's such a Canadian stereotype. I'm sorry. I hope my dad wasn't too hard on you."

"Angel, please," he groaned and held his head.

"How much did they grill you?"

"Rox, please stop talking and let me die here."

I kissed his forehead. "Oh, I'm so sorry, love. Come on, the bed will be more comfortable."

"No. I have to get up."

I furrowed my brow. "Why?"

"I'm supposed to go work out with your brother and dad in an hour. Your dad wants to get on the ice together."

I shook my head. "Oh, they're really punishing you. He's probably going to make you bag skate. Dad's evil like that."

He groaned, but then he grinned up at me and pulled me down into a kiss. "So worth it. You're worth it. Rox, I love you so much, I will do whatever drills your dad makes me do today. Fuck, I'd bag skate all day for you."

I kissed him back but pulled away before it could go any further. "That's the nicest thing to say to a Canadian girl. I'll make coffee for both of us."

Tristan sat at the island eating oatmeal and looking like he hadn't drunk my boyfriend under the table last night.

I flicked his ear. "You're a dick."

He grinned. "He deserved it."

I sighed and put my hands over my face. "I'm sorry you had to find out that way. I wanted to tell you on my own terms."

His eyebrows shot up. "Yeah, I *never* want to hear that again."

"I can't believe you're mad about this."

He sighed. "I feel like I'm supposed to hate all your partners, and all of your previous ones have SUUCKKKED!"

"You've never said anything before."

"Not my place. Benny's a good guy."

I poured myself and my boyfriend coffee. "You were right about him; he's not a bad guy. I wanted to tell you in person. I didn't set out for this, you know?"

He sighed. "I kind of had a feeling this was gonna happen."

"How?" I asked and gave him an annoyed look.

He glared at me. "Because every time you two would get into your fights over nothing, it looked like fucking foreplay." He made a grossed-out face and pretended to hurl.

"Then why are you mad?" I asked.

"Because I thought you hated him so much, it was never gonna happen!"

I glared at him. "Did you and Dad really grill him last night?"

Tristan smirked. "Yup!"

I cringed. "Surprised he hasn't ghosted me already."

"I don't think he could. You were sleeping in his bed."

I gave him the finger. "You're a real fucking asshole, you know that, right?"

He laughed. "Damn, you must love him."

I smiled to myself and took a sip of my coffee. "Yeah...I do. I mean fuck, Tristan, he wants me to play hockey again. He got me back on the ice, and I didn't think that would ever happen."

He cocked his head at me. "I've been trying to get you on the ice for three years."

I nodded and sipped on my coffee in contemplation. "I

know. He was pushier. You know what did it for me, though?"

"What?"

"When we were in Canada, some drunk guy tried to hit on me at the hotel bar and called me fat when I rejected him, and Benny tried to fight him. I got fucking pissed at him for it, but..."

"You liked that he wanted to protect you," my brother finished my sentence.

I gave him a dopey smile. "Yeah."

There was a knock on the door, and I glanced at Tristan, who nodded his head at me to go get it. I glared again and shouldn't have been surprised when I opened it and saw my dad behind it. He muscled his way in with his gear bag and a stick. I went back into the kitchen to return to my coffee. Tristan tried to swipe the second cup, but I slapped his hand away.

"Get out of here," I snapped.

"Glad to know I'm not the only one who has to endure that wrath," I heard from behind me.

I beamed at Benny. He took the cup I offered him and drank a sip. "Ah, thanks, angel. I needed this."

He leaned down to kiss me, and I leaned it into, pulling his face down to me by grabbing his hair. I slipped him some tongue, but mostly just to gross out my brother.

"EW!" Tristan yelled.

My dad glared at my boyfriend, and I glared back. "You"—I pointed at my dad and then at Tristan—"and you better be nice to him today. I have to get to work." I turned back to my boyfriend with an apologetic look, but he shooed me away, and I got out of there as quickly as I could.

I didn't envy my man today. Bag skating was bad enough, but it was torture when you were hungover.

CHAPTER TWENTY-EIGHT

BENNY

My legs were on fire as Alain Desjardins blew the whistle and shouted, "Again!" in his French-Canadian accent. What did I do to deserve this? Oh right, I fucked his daughter, and now he and his son were punishing me for it.

It was so worth it. S*he* was worth it.

I glanced over at TJ, and he grinned as he pumped his legs and skated down the ice. I sighed and sprinted off to follow him. Of course, Alain was making us bag skate today. I was starting to dislike Rox's dad.

I followed TJ to the blue line and back, feeling the ice beneath my skates and getting my bearings. I was no slouch during the off-season; I hit the gym every day and trained with my teammates as much as possible. I shouldn't have been struggling on the ice today, but I was hungover and felt like I was going to puke.

We skated over to the bench for a water break. Alain

skated around the rink and took shots at the goal at the other end. I gulped down my water and stared at him in disbelief.

"Damn, your dad could still play. He's still got it," I said to TJ.

TJ laughed. "Yeah, I think he only retired because Mom was afraid of him getting another concussion."

That explained a lot about why my girl was scared about playing hockey after her own concussion.

I took my helmet off and shook out my sweaty hair. "T, I'm sorry you had to hear—"

TJ held his hand up to cut me off. "Stop. I never want to hear that again." He started making a puking sound, and I punched him in the shoulder. He laughed and shrugged. "But I can't say I'm surprised."

"No?"

"You've been in love with my sister since the day you met her, but you always put your foot in your mouth and pissed her off."

I smirked and took another sip of my water. "Still kind of do."

He shook his head and gave me a funny look. "Did you call her some sort of pet name this morning?"

"Yeah, I did."

"Hmm."

I eyed him carefully. "What?"

He shrugged. "I thought she didn't like that."

"She doesn't like being called baby. She gave me the business about that. I call her angel."

TJ furrowed his brow. "Did you give her some cheesy line about her falling from heaven or some shit?"

I shook my head. "Fuck no! She crawled up from hell to annoy me, duh."

TJ burst out in laughter. "Holy shit. Did you say that to her?"

I gave him a look.

"Christ, Benny, how are you not dead?"

I smirked at him. "I'm good at eating—"

"EW! I don't want to know! Don't even finish that sentence!" he shrieked.

"Let's go, boys. Enough chit-chatting. I want to see you finding the back of the net!" Alain yelled at us.

TJ and I rolled our eyes and skated over to the net. TJ took a couple of practice shots and started laughing suddenly. "Dad, remember when you used to make us do this at all hours of the night until it was perfect? Then Roxie got so pissed, she wristed a shot into your car window?"

Their dad chuckled. "Roxie girl was a spitfire. Still is."

I smiled at that. My girl was a spitfire, and it was one of the reasons why I loved her. She sure made things interesting.

Alain worked us hard all morning, and I knew part of it was to grind my gears about dating his daughter. It pissed me off because where the fuck had he been all this time? Suddenly he was overprotective of his daughter when he hadn't tried to be a part of her life in years? I was angry for her.

I was stewing towards the end of the session, and this guy was getting under my skin. I ended up getting up in his face. "Man, what's your problem with me? I'm not good enough for your daughter?" I barked at him.

He laughed. "Nope. No one's good enough for my little girl."

"You don't get to decide who she dates. She's a grown-ass woman."

He smirked at me. "Are you done?"

"No, I'm not. Fuck the both of you for training me like a dog today!"

Rox's parents, not supporting who she was, had shadows of my parents, and it pissed me off. I cooled down after I hit the showers, but I was glad I drove myself here because TJ and his dad were gone by the time I got out. I checked my phone and saw some texts from Rox. That put a smile on my face.

ROX: *I'm sorry you have to endure my family today.*

I smiled and texted her back.

ME: *Got to defend my girl. What's your day like today?*
ROX: *Not that bad, why?*
ME: *I'm bringing you lunch.*

We practiced in the suburbs, so I took the turnpike back to Philly and to the arena where Rox's office was located. First, I stopped at the sandwich place she liked and got her a cheesesteak while I got a boring salad because I needed to stick to my training diet. She'd probably get mad at me about the cheesesteak because she was trying to train too, but I knew she'd want it. I strode in and smiled at the receptionist.

"Oh, hi, Benny. How's the off-season going?" Cindy asked.

I ran a hand through my hair. "Not bad. I had a tough training session today. Rox around?"

Cindy smiled at me. I wasn't sure if people in the front office knew we were dating, especially since we had only recently become official. Although, once we started this physical thing, I knew I was hers. It just took some convincing on her part.

I stopped short when I saw TJ hanging outside of Rox's office, chatting up the blonde girl who sat outside her office. The blonde rolled her eyes at TJ; he was lying on the flirting real thick. He looked up when he saw me and smirked.

"Dad! You can't harass my boyfriend when you haven't talked to me in years. Will you two get out of here?" she yelled at them. I stopped there, frozen, when Alain walked out of her office and TJ followed him.

Alain gave me a nod, and then he and TJ walked out. I walked inside and saw Rox with her head in her hands. She looked up at the sound of me entering and gave me a tired smile.

"Hey," she said.

"Did you chew your dad out because of me?" I asked.

She growled in frustration. I liked this protective side of her when it came to me. "He was just giving you a hard time. He likes you."

I scrunched up my face in confusion. "He likes me so much he had me doing lines all day?"

"Oh, you poor baby. He likes that you got in his face and stood up for me and our relationship. He said it made him realize you're serious about me."

"Seriously?" I huffed.

"He likes it when a man stands up for his woman," she said and rolled her eyes. "He's trying to make amends with me, but thank you for what you said to him. You're not wrong."

"What about your mom?" I asked.

She shrugged and looked at her phone. "She left me a voicemail yesterday."

"Oh?"

She nodded. "When I talked with my dad, he said she wants to mend our relationship, but I'm not sure I want to call her back."

That made me sad for her, but with the way my parents

were, I understood her reasons. I handed over her cheesesteak and started shaking up my salad. I pulled the chair closer to her desk and sat across from her.

I reached across the desk and squeezed her hand. "Whatever you decide, I'm here for you."

She nodded but then stood up and shut her office door. I raised an eyebrow at that.

She laughed. "So no one will bother me and ask me a million questions while we have lunch. Look, I'm even going to turn off my monitor; the emails can wait."

I dug into my salad and watched her devour her sandwich. "Your dad's something else."

She laughed. "Tell me about it. I hated having him as a coach in peewee."

"I'm proud of you for getting back on the ice. Have you decided on joining a league yet?"

She frowned but shoved her sandwich in her mouth, so she didn't have to answer. I knew when to press my girl, so I changed the subject instead. "Is your dad sticking around?"

She nodded but seemed annoyed still. "He wants to spend time with us."

"That's good, right?"

She nodded, but she seemed conflicted.

I knew it wasn't my fight with my parents, but I doubted my parents would ever come around with my sister. That bummed me out, but we were better off without them. Maybe it didn't have to be the same for Rox. Maybe she could have the relationship she wanted with her parents. I wanted that for her, but I'd support whatever decision she made.

She smiled. "Thanks for coming to see me. I always miss your face when I'm at work."

"I miss you too," I said. "When the season starts, it's gonna be hard being away from you."

She frowned. "I know, but it'll be okay. We have to try, right?"

I reached across her desk and grabbed her hand. "Rox, we spent so many years hating each other; I don't want to go back to that. It was miserable."

"Do you think we moved too fast?"

I shook my head. "Nah. As your brother pointed out to me today, I probably had feelings for you for years."

She glanced at the clock. "Shit, I have a meeting in like twenty minutes that I'm not prepared for."

I threw our trash in the garbage and leaned over her desk to kiss her. "Have a good rest of your day. What do you want for dinner?"

She wrinkled her nose. "You don't have to cook for me all the time, you know."

"I want to do it now because once my season starts, it will be sparse."

She shrugged. "Whatever you want, love."

She walked over to the door and opened it again. I stood in the doorway of her office and bent down again to kiss her goodbye. Loving this woman was the best feeling in the world. I never imagined a life where Roxanne Desjardins spent most of her time kissing me instead of staring daggers at me. It was a pleasant change of pace, and I never wanted to go back to the way things were before.

CHAPTER TWENTY-NINE

ROXANNE

I walked into the condo after work to find my dad and my boyfriend laughing over dinner. Tristan was nowhere in sight. I looked around the room in confusion and shrugged off my blazer. The conversation seemed civil, so I was suspicious.

"Roxie girl!" my dad called. "Glad you found a partner who can cook."

I glared. "Why? I'm a superb cook."

Benny grinned at me. "That's true. We like cooking together. She's an excellent cooking partner."

"Where's Tristan?" I asked.

Benny cocked his head next door. "He went to hang with Noah for a while since Dinah's at a work conference."

I nodded in understanding and went to the stove to make myself a plate. My brother and Noah had the biggest bromance on the Bulldogs. Poor Dinah; she probably got to see my annoying brother all the time.

Benny and my dad had the hockey game on. I took my

plate into the living room and sat down next to Benny. I sighed and shared a look with my dad. "Ugh, can't Boston let someone else try for once?"

Benny smirked. "NOPE! We're winners, baby!"

I gave him the finger, and he laughed and pulled me to his side. I kissed his temple and smoothed down his hair. "You need a haircut," I said to him.

He waved me off. "Yeah, yeah, I'll get to it."

I glanced over at my dad, and he smiled at me. "What?" I asked.

"You look really happy is all," he said, and then he looked at Benny. "You better treat her right."

"He does," I said.

My dad stared down at Benny. "I mean it."

"Dad, he's a saint. I'm the asshole in this relationship."

I felt Benny's shoulders shake as he held in his laughter. I cut a glare at him, and he placated me with a kiss on my temple. It wasn't a lie, though. Even when I thought he hated me, I think it was always me that started it. Maybe he was right in thinking I got off on it.

I ate my dinner while the three of us watched game three of the final series together. Dad and Benny hadn't waited for me to get home. I stayed a little late at work tonight and told Benny to start dinner without me. I hadn't expected to find my dad here when I got home.

The game hadn't started until eight, which meant it was past my bedtime by the time it was supposed to be over. It ended up going into a second overtime, and I couldn't keep my eyes open. I yawned and leaned into Benny's chest.

"Why don't you go to bed?" he suggested.

I closed my eyes but shook my head. "No. Must watch hockey."

"Come on, you have work in the morning. I'll tell you the score when I come in."

"Ugh, fine!" I said. I went to wash my face and do all my nighttime stuff before I crawled into bed. Benny placed the covers over me and kissed me. "Goodnight, angel."

"Don't let my dad chirp you too much."

He smiled. "I think he likes me now. Turns out all I needed to do was feed you Desjardins and you stop hating me. Although, he tried to tell me I should sleep on the couch until we move you in to your apartment."

"Seriously?" I groaned and rolled my eyes.

He laughed. "Yeah. I told him you were a grown-ass adult who could make her own decisions."

"Aw, love. It's so sexy when you stand up to my dad. And to my brother."

He smiled at me. "Go to bed. I'll come in when the game's over."

"I can't wait to move into my apartment so these cock blocks are gone."

"Me too."

"I'm going to fuck you on every surface of my apartment."

"Jesus, Rox. Please don't say shit like that when I have to go watch the rest of the game with your dad."

I laughed evilly and turned on my side. He shut off the light and went back into the living room. I couldn't wait until I had my own place. It had been great when Tristan was in Russia, but now that he was back, I needed to get out of here. I was moving into my new apartment in a couple of days, so it wouldn't be too long until I had Benny all to myself again.

❄

"Dad, it's fine!" I insisted and started unpacking the box for the kitchen.

I was finally moving into my new apartment, and already my dad complained it was too small.

Okay, do you want to pay my rent?

I wasn't even gonna make that joke because he might have thought I was being serious. Dad had been frugal with his money when he was a player, so I knew he could pay for my rent, but I didn't want my rent to be paid by 'daddy.' I was an independent woman, damn it!

I was glad I was finally getting my own space. Especially since last night we thought we'd had quiet sex with Benny's hand over my mouth, but apparently not, judging by my brother's annoyed looks over his coffee this morning. Oops! It was safe to say my six-foot-four boyfriend would be over here way more than I would be over there.

Benny and Tristan were currently putting together my bed, which Benny and I had to go to IKEA to buy. That had been a nightmare. I had to get so much furniture and then pack it all up to bring it over here. I never had to do that before. Benny and I got into a huge argument in the middle of IKEA because he wanted to buy my furniture for me. Ugh, that man! I loved him so much, but he didn't need to buy me things. I know it was because he made so much more money than me and he wanted to help, but I didn't need him to do that.

Noah and my dad were still bringing in some of my boxes. There was a ton to unpack, and I was already exhausted. That was with four ridiculously ripped men helping me get everything in and put together. Dinah had offered me her meathead brothers, but I didn't think we needed them. I was still debating if I should have declined or not.

"I think it's too small. What's the neighborhood like?" Dad asked again.

I unpacked a beer glass and put it in the cabinet. "It's fine. Aaron Riley's wife used to live here. Tristan, please help!" I cried.

"Dad, she's fine," he grunted from the other room.

I gestured with my hands to my twin. "See? I'm good. Don't worry about me."

Dad scowled. "I worry about your safety."

"Dad!" I screeched. "I carry pepper spray. My six-foot-four massive boyfriend will be over here all the time. I'm fine."

I think that made it worse because he grumbled under his breath, but he let the argument drop. Thankfully, Noah asked him some hockey questions to distract him. I mouthed 'thank you' at Noah, and he smiled at me from over my dad's shoulder. Everyone needed a Noah in their life.

When I got my stuff from Lisa's, I realized how little I actually had. Most of the stuff that was mine in the apartment was clothes, books, and my hockey gear. I didn't have any glass or cookware. That hadn't clicked into place until Benny and I went to buy furniture, and I had to buy all that other stuff. Getting your own place was a lot of work. Today was about getting the big stuff like my furniture in. I'd unpack everything else later.

I ordered a pizza to thank the guys for helping me out. Luckily, they didn't care about having to eat off paper plates.

Dad was flying back to St. Catharines in the morning, so I hugged him tightly goodbye. It had been good spending time with him for the past couple of days. He wanted me to call my mom back, but I wasn't ready to talk to her yet. I wasn't sure I ever would be.

"I want you to be happy, Roxie," he said.

"Dad, I am happy."

"I love you, kiddo. I know I should have been more supportive. I should have—"

"Dad, it's fine."

"Will you talk to your mother?"

I chewed on my lip. Her voicemail still sat on my phone, unanswered. "I'll think about it."

He gave me a big hug, wrapping me in his bear-like embrace, and I had to admit I missed my dad's hugs. I hadn't realized until he came to visit how much I had missed him. I wasn't sure mom would ever accept my bisexuality, though. Despite his urging that we bury the hatchet, I didn't want to call her back.

I hugged him one last time, and then he left. Not before he told Benny again that he better treat me right. Noah and my brother got the hint to get out as soon as my dad left. Even though Tristan made a gagging motion behind Benny's back. Dick. One day that boy was going to meet a nice girl and love her the way I loved Benny. I hoped. I worried my brother was going to end up sad and lonely if he kept sleeping his way through all of Philly.

I slumped down on my couch with a sigh, and Benny came out of my bedroom. I drank the rest of my beer and felt the couch sink next to me with Benny's weight. I leaned into him, and he wrapped an arm around me.

"Mmm. Thanks for helping me today," I said.

He kissed the top of my head. "Of course."

"I'm so glad I have my own place now."

"It's small, but it's good you have a place for yourself."

I ran a hand down his chest and fingered his belt. I leaned back on the couch and pulled him down with me.

He smiled and kissed me deeply. "You want to know the best part?" I asked.

"What's that?" he asked into my ear, pausing for the briefest of moments from kissing my neck.

"You don't have to cover my moans with your hand tonight."

He grinned. "It was kind of fun, though."

I rubbed the front of his pants. "Yeah? You enjoy restraining me?"

"Maybe..." he trailed off and had a wicked grin on his face.

"C'mere you, and kiss me like you mean it," I ordered.

He frowned. "I thought I was in charge."

I gripped him through his jeans. "It's cute that you think that, but we both know I own this dick."

I yelped when he tossed me over his shoulder and took me to my bed. I loved this man.

CHAPTER THIRTY

BENNY

I stirred in Roxanne's bed at the sound of a buzzing phone. I turned towards her side of the bed and mumbled, "Rox, turn off your alarm."

I patted the bed and opened my eyes to discover she wasn't there. That was odd. It was Sunday morning, and she wasn't an early riser on the weekends. Especially since me, TJ, Noah, and her dad had moved her into her new apartment last night. After everyone left, naturally, we proceeded to christen her apartment. On her bed, the couch, the kitchen table, the shower, and even the kitchen counter. It had been exhausting but worth it. Waking up, I felt like I was floating on cloud nine.

The buzzing continued, and I realized it was my phone. I glanced at the caller ID and noticed it was my agent, Steve.

I grumbled into the phone when I answered it.

"Hello to you, too," he said with a chuckle.

I sat up in bed, ran a hand down my face, and wiped the

sleep from my eyes. "Sorry, man, I was still asleep. What's up?"

"Okay, so remember how you asked me to tell the Bulldogs if they wanted to trade you, you'd want to go to Boston?"

"Yeah...but I just wanted to give them my wishlist. I want to stay in Philly," I said.

"Right. I told them you were committed to staying here and being on the team through your contract."

"Okay...so why are you calling me?"

"Well, you know free agency is about to start, and people are looking into everything. There's a report going around that you requested a trade."

"What?"

"Relax, man, it's all speculation, but I wanted to give you the heads up..."

I stopped listening to Steve because I remembered a conversation I had with Riley that I brushed off. He said Rox would go ballistic if she found out I asked for a trade. Especially after I told her I wanted to stay in Philly for her.

FUCK!

I heard the front door slam, and then the bedroom door opened with another angry slam. Rox walked in with a look that could strike me dead.

"Look, man, I have to go," I told my agent in a rush and hung up on him. I threw my phone down on the bed at the same time Rox started throwing my clothes at my head. "Angel."

"You fucking lied to me. I can't believe I trusted you!" she screeched and started pacing back and forth.

There was a wildfire in her eyes but not the sexy kind I loved. More like the old Rox, where she looked at me with complete disgust. Like one wrong move and she would stab me in the throat. A stone dropped into my stomach at her looking at me that way.

I slid out of bed and walked over to her. I grabbed her arms, but she pushed me away. "Roxanne, it's not what you think," I said.

She glared at me. "You lied right to my face."

"Will you let me explain?" I asked, exasperated.

"Did you or did you not ask for a trade to Boston?" she seethed.

"Well, kinda, but—"

"GET OUT!" she screamed, but I saw the tears welling in her eyes. It broke my heart to know that I caused her this pain.

"Let me explain. It's not—"

"GET OUT! I never want to see you again!" she screamed and turned away from me.

I started pulling on my clothes, but I stood there in the doorway, staring at her. She sank down on the bed with her back to me, and I saw her shoulders shaking, so I knew she was crying.

"Rox, please," I begged.

"Just go!" she snapped at me, but she didn't turn around.

I turned to walk out of the room, but then I stopped.

I wasn't letting this woman go that easily. I wouldn't let this misunderstanding break us up. I told her I would never let her go and never stop fighting for her. If I left now, I would let her down. I would be going back against my word, and I never did that.

I stomped across the room and bent down onto my knees in front of her. "Rox, come on. Talk to me."

She shook her head. "I told you to go!"

I slid my hands into her hair and kissed her hard. She

didn't kiss me back, so I knew I had to do a lot of groveling. "Angel, please..." I begged.

Her tears fell down her face, and I wiped them away with my thumbs. My heart ached that I had caused her to feel this way. She still wouldn't look at me, so I moved to sit next to her and pulled her into my chest. She didn't pull away this time as I wrapped my arm around her back and stroked her hair. The sound of her sobs in my chest felt like a stab to my heart.

"Roxanne, let's talk about this."

"No!" she snapped.

"Angel, look at me," I urged, but she shook her head and continued to sob into my chest. Fuck, maybe I *was* an asshole. "Roxanne, I'm not going to leave. Not by choice."

"I thought you loved me," she sobbed into my chest. "Why does everyone either cheat on me or leave me? Am I so unworthy of love?"

I rubbed comforting circles on her back. "Angel, my contract isn't no-trade. If the team wants to trade me they will."

"Okay, but why did you ask for a trade?"

"I didn't. Well, not really. I just wanted the option to go to Boston *if* they traded me. If I have to leave Philly, I want to be near my family."

She pulled away from me and wiped the tears from her eyes. "Oh. Oh, God. I'm an asshole, aren't I?"

"No, you're not. You have a right to be upset. I should have at least told you instead of catching you off guard."

She wiped her face again. "I'm sorry for overreacting."

I brought her hand up to my lips and kissed her tattoo. "I want to stay here. I want to be with you, and I will do everything in my power to do that, but..."

"What?"

"Your brother was right; this job can be tough on relationships. One minute, I'm lacing up my skates, and the next, I'm on a plane to a different city. I can't control that, so if we're gonna do this, understand it will be hard. This relationship will essentially be long-distance for half the year, and that's with me living in the same city as you."

"This will be hard," she agreed.

She looked up at me with tear-stained eyes. I cupped her face and kissed her. "I love you. You know that, right? I love you so much, and I hate that I made you cry. It's breaking my heart, but you let me know now if you can't do this," I said.

"What?" she asked, and her face fell into disbelief.

"Rox, I'm serious. If you can't handle the hockey girlfriend life, maybe we shouldn't have started this."

"I love you. I don't want you to leave me. I didn't expect to find love so soon or with someone I hated."

"To be clear, I don't think you hated me. You loved fighting with me. You got off on it."

That got a laugh out of her. "That's not true."

"Bullshit! You always looked at me like you weren't sure if you wanted to punch me or suck my dick."

That got me a playful punch in the shoulder. "I changed my mind. Go to Boston, you ass," she said with a smile cutting through her tear-stained face.

I smiled back at her and pulled her into my lap. I rubbed her back soothingly while she leaned into me. "Do you want me to go talk to the GM? To make my case that I want to stay here?" I asked.

She shook her head. "No. Whatever happens, happens. I'm sorry I overreacted. Tristan always tells me I self-sabotage all my relationships."

Huh. That was interesting.

"Not this one. I'm not letting you go. I told you, I'll always fight for you. For *us*. We're not breaking up, Roxanne."

"You're too good a man. I don't deserve you, not after all the torment I put you through over the years. I'm such a bitch."

She looked up at me, her pale face stained with tears, and it wrenched something inside me. I caressed her face. "I don't care because I love you. You're so worthy of my love. Don't make yourself think you don't deserve what I can give you."

I kissed her hard on the mouth, sighing when she melted into the kiss and opened her mouth to my tongue. My hands went into her hair, wrapping that luscious dark mass around my wrist.

"I'm sorry," I blurted out when I pulled away. "I hate seeing you cry because of something I did. It gutted me to see you like that. I'm sorry. Forgive me?"

"I'm the one who should apologize, not you. Let me make it up to you."

I smirked at her. "Oh, no one's stopping you."

"Asshole."

"Your asshole."

"Damn right."

"C'mere," I ordered huskily. I pulled her into another searing kiss and showed her just how sorry I was.

If I had walked out today when she asked, it would have been the end of us. But Rox was my end game, even if she didn't know it yet.

CHAPTER THIRTY-ONE

ROXANNE

I was exhausted. After all the moving and all the lovemaking and then fighting with Benny, I wanted to sleep for the rest of the day. He seemed to want to do that too, but reluctantly, he got out of bed and started getting dressed.

"You got somewhere to be?" I asked.

"Unfortunately. Riley and I were gonna get some ice time in."

I rolled my eyes at him. "Do you ever quit? Can't you enjoy your off-season?"

He smiled at me. "Yeah, I could, but I gotta keep training. Plus, I think Riley needs to get out of his condo."

I raised an eyebrow. "Are things bad with him and Fi?"

Benny shook his head. "No, they're great. She just gets into her moods when she's in the middle of revising. So he knows to give her space."

"That's... Wow, Aaron Riley with a wife, I never thought I would see the day."

"Did you ever think the two of us would get together either?" he asked with a grin.

I shook my head with a laugh. Definitely not. "Fuck no! I hated you for years. YEARS!"

He sat on my bed while he pulled on his shoes and tied them. "I thought we went over this. You loved fighting with me."

He ducked when I threw a pillow at his head. "I did not!"

He leaned down and gave me a quick kiss. "You're literally getting off on arguing with me about it right now."

I grumbled at him. Damn this man for being right.

"Do you want to come?" he asked.

I shook my head. "I'm exhausted, and I need to finish unpacking."

He kissed my forehead. "I'll see you later, okay?"

"Love?"

"Yeah, angel?"

I chewed on my lip. "Is your family gonna hate me now?"

He furrowed his brow. "Why would they hate you?"

"For keeping you in Philly. That's why you asked for a trade to Boston, right?"

He leaned down and kissed me again. "I didn't ask for a trade, remember? I just told the team if they wanted to trade me, I wanted to go to Boston."

"I know how important your family is to you; it's one of the reasons I love you. But I don't want them to hate me if I keep you here."

"No, angel, my family's not gonna hate you. They'll nag you about us getting married and having lots of babies, though."

I made a face, and he laughed. I was glad we were on the same page about that.

"You know why I didn't hide out in Boston while you were living in my condo?"

I shook my head.

"My grandfather told me to come back to Philly and woo you. So did my sister. And my sister-in-law. And my grandmother."

"What?"

He grimaced. "Apparently, my entire family had a pool on when we would finally get together."

I gave him a sly grin. "You've talked about me with your family?"

"Yeah, about how you crawled up from hell to annoy me."

"Jerk!"

"You love me."

I grinned at him. "I do."

He ran a hand through his hair and smoothed it down. "Truth be told, my grandfather told me not to ask for a trade. I'm sure I'll get an earful about that."

"I'm sorry for being a raging bitch about this, but I'm glad you fought for me today and made me listen. I don't deserve you."

He shook his head. "No, Rox, you deserve everything I can give you. I told you, I'll never stop fighting for you, and that wasn't a lie. I love you, angel, so much."

"I love you too. But get out of here before Riley asks if I chained you to the bed."

He waggled his eyebrows at me. "I wouldn't be opposed to that if you wanted to try it out later."

I laughed. "Get out of here, ya horndog!"

He gave me a cheeky grin, and I kissed him goodbye.

Michael Bennett was such a good person, and I didn't understand why he put up with my asshole behavior. The way he fought for me and for our relationship made me love him even more. I had to be prepared for the possibility that he could get traded to a different city, though. That was one reason why I'd never been interested in dating a hockey player—their lives were too unpredictable. But now I was in too deep with Benny. When I thought about it, if he got traded, the idea of going with him wherever he went didn't scare me.

Eventually, I crawled out of bed, showered, and worked on unpacking the rest of my things. I was interrupted by a knock on the door and was surprised when I opened it to reveal my twin brother behind it with a six-pack of beer in his hand.

"Um, hi?" I asked.

"You weren't responding to my texts," he said and muscled his way into my apartment.

I locked the door behind him, then walked back into the kitchen and looked at my phone sitting on the kitchen table. I hadn't heard the texts over the music I had been playing.

He popped open two beers and put them in glasses before handing me one of them. "I came to make sure you were okay," he said.

"About..." I trailed off, still lost at what he was talking about.

He stared at me. "I knew how you'd react to the report about Benny."

"Oh!"

Tristan furrowed his brow. "You seem okay about this. I thought you would have tossed him out and sabotaged this relationship."

I sighed and took a swig of my beer. "I tried. He wouldn't let me."

My brother tipped back his head with a laugh. "Damn, Benny's too good for you."

"I know! I don't think I deserve him," I admitted.

"Shit, I came over here thinking you were freaking out and needed me."

"I do need you. You're my brother and best friend," I said with a smile. We clinked beer glasses and took a drink at the same time.

"Except you pretty much ghosted me while I was at Worlds," he teased.

I frowned. "Sorry. I was busy."

"Busy with my roommate's tongue in your mouth?"

I hit him in the chest. "Don't be an ass. I was busy with his dick in my mouth."

"Ew! File that under shit I never needed to know."

I cackled. "What's going on with you?" I asked.

He eyed me cautiously and crossed to sit in the chair at the table. I followed him and sat across from him. My brother wasn't a sensitive guy. He was a funny guy who liked to party, and even though I joked he didn't have feelings, I could tell when he was hurting.

"What do you mean, what's going on with me?" he asked.

I looked at him over my beer glass. "Tristan, I can tell when something's bothering you. Is this about Taylor?"

Taylor was this girl he had been seeing casually. He wanted it to be casual, but she wanted a relationship. He let her go but then realized it was a mistake. He had called me about it and had been a complete wreck. The only relationship my brother had that lasted longer than a few months had been in high school with my friend Natalie. She really did a number on him.

"She's done with me," he admitted sadly.

"Oh, bud, I'm sorry. What happened?"

He shrugged. "I messed up. I thought I didn't want a relationship, but it was nice having someone give a shit about TJ the person and not TJ the hockey player. Maybe I don't want to be a bachelor for life?"

I smirked at him but let him continue.

"Then, seeing you with Benny...man, he loves you. Watching him get up into Dad's face and defend you sealed the deal on that. If you two can find happiness, maybe I can too."

"Aw, Tristan! You actually have feelings!"

He glared at me. "Of course, I have fucking feelings. I just don't announce it to the world like you do."

"So, did you talk to her?"

He nodded but had a grimace on his face. "Yeah, but she has a boyfriend now, and she said she's happy."

I reached across the table to squeeze his hand. "I'm sorry. You'll find someone."

He shrugged and took another sip of his beer. "There might be someone, but I'm not sure she's interested."

My eyebrow quirked up. "Oh? Who?"

He shook his head. "I'm not telling."

"Mean!"

He laughed. "You know, I wish you would have told me you applied for the job with the team. I would have helped you. I wouldn't have told Benny he could move in."

"Why did you?" I asked.

He shrugged. "I don't know."

I raised my eyebrow. I knew exactly why he had asked. Despite his party-boy behavior, my brother had some demons to work out, and he didn't like to be alone with his thoughts.

I took a sip of my beer and waited for him to tell me.

He sighed. "I don't like being alone."

"Duh! I know that."

He glared at me but changed the subject. "So, you and dad talked, right?"

I nodded. "He wants to make amends..." I trailed off when something dawned on me. "Tristan, are you the reason Dad came around?"

He picked at the label on his beer. "I hope so. I tried to talk some sense into both of them. They're from a different generation, Roxie. I know it doesn't excuse how they reacted, but I tried to help them get that it doesn't matter who you date, you're still you."

I felt my eyes getting misty, but this time it was happy tears. "Oh, dude," I whispered.

My brother sighed. "Oh, come on, Roxie, don't do that."

I wiped my eyes. "I can't help it." I looked at my phone, where the voicemail from my mom blinked back at me. I still hadn't listened to it, half afraid of what it would say. "She left me a message."

"Who?"

"Mom."

"Yeah? What'd it say?"

I shrugged. "I haven't listened to it yet. I usually just delete anything from her."

"Maybe you should listen to this one? Maybe Mom changed?"

"I'm afraid she'll think me being with Benny means I'm straight."

Tristan cleared his throat. "Then explain it to her.

Speaking of which, this thing with Benny...it's serious, right? I know the big doof loves you, but..."

"Yeah, it is. He would have left when I told him to this morning if it wasn't."

"I want you to be happy. I wish you didn't do it with one of my teammates, but he's a good guy. Don't break his heart."

"Shouldn't you be saying, 'if he hurts you, I'll kill him'?" I asked with a laugh.

Tristan gave me an exasperated look. "Please, if he hurt you, you'd kill him. Why do you need me to say shit like that?"

"He bought me new skates..." I trailed off.

Tristan cringed. "Yeah, that sucks that you gotta break them in."

"I know! But he did it because I was complaining about how shitty my boots were getting, and I was putting it off."

"He did it because he thinks you can play in the PHF."

I shook my head. "I don't want to play professionally; I just want to do it for funzies. I really miss it."

"You should play pro, dude!"

I wrinkled my nose. "They don't make any money."

"Okay, true, but you should be out there with the other players of your caliber."

"Have you been talking to Benny about this?" I asked and glared at him. My dad had mentioned something to me, too. I swear all three of them were ganging up on me about it.

Tristan smirked. "Maybe. I can't believe he got you back on the ice. Fuck, Rox, you might marry that man."

I scrunched up my face. "No, we aren't the marriage type."

Tristan rolled his eyes. "Yeah, it's why you're fucking perfect for each other."

I stuck out my tongue at him, and he kicked my foot. I had been wrapped up in Benny for so long that I forgot how much I missed my twin brother. Moving here on a whim was the best decision I ever made.

Tristan left a little while later because he was supposed to do weight training with Noah. I busied myself with unpacking until the voicemail nagged at me to listen to it.

I slumped down on my couch and pressed play.

My mom's voice came out of the device. *"Hey, Roxie girl, happy birthday. I know you don't want to hear from me, and you have every right to be angry with me. I deserve it. I should have listened to you when you told me about your bisexuality. I still don't understand it, but...your father and I want you to be happy. That's all I've ever wanted. Call me back, please?"*

I stared down at my phone in my hand and debated what to do. Dad had been pressuring me to talk to my mom, and now she was trying to make amends. Before I talked myself out of it, I dialed her number and pressed my phone to my ear.

"Roxie!" my mom's cheery voice rang through my ear.

"Hey, Mom," I mumbled.

There was a beat of silence.

"I'm sorry," she said.

"You should be."

She laughed. "Okay, I deserve that. I'm...I don't understand this bi or pan thing, but I shouldn't have reacted that way."

"Mom, it's been years. I have nothing to say to you."

"I know, sweetheart. But I want...I'm just sorry."

"Okay."

We were silent for a couple seconds, but it felt like minutes had passed. I wasn't sure what to say to her. I was still angry at how she'd treated me, and I didn't think I'd be quick to forgive her. It had been three years since I last talked to her, and that had ended in a massive fight. We had a full-on screaming match, and I told her to go to hell and never speak to me again. Another example of how I held grudges and was an asshole without letting people apologize. I wasn't sure either of us could come back from that.

"Do you forgive me?" she asked.

"I don't know. It really hurt, Mom. And now..."

"What?"

I sighed. "I'm dating someone new, but I don't want you to think that means I'm straight. He might be my person, but that doesn't change who I am."

"Okay, I get that. Tristan explained that to me."

He did? My brother said nothing of the sort to me. Tristan pretended he didn't care about anyone sometimes, but it was all a facade.

"Why the change now?" I asked.

"I've been trying to get in contact with you since we got into that fight after your concussion. I was so scared of losing my child, and you wouldn't talk to me! Why do you think I still reach out in the hopes one day you'd pick up?"

Okay, she had a point there. She might have reacted poorly when I came out, but I also stormed out and never came back. That was another rash Roxanne Desjardins move. When she came to see me at the hospital the night of my spill on the ice, I told her I never wanted to see her again. Screamed it at her. The pain of her being biphobic had been too raw back then. It still felt too raw now. I had iced her out because I didn't want to hear any more biphobic rhetoric from her. But maybe it wasn't just her fault. Maybe it was mine, too.

I ran a hand through my hair. "Mom, if you seriously want to make up for everything, you need to understand how hurtful and biphobic you were. I'm always gonna be bisexual; it's a part of my identity. You have to understand that it doesn't matter what gender my partner is, I'm still bi. I think I can forgive you, but it's gonna take me some time."

"I should have tried harder. I should have told you I didn't understand it. I still don't, but Tristan told me it's not for me to understand, only for me to accept that's who you are. Your father and I just want you both to find the love we have. That's all we ever wanted for both of you kids."

"Okay."

"And...I missed my girl. I know we haven't always seen eye-to-eye, but Roxie, you're my daughter. I've only ever wanted the best for you. I shouldn't have dismissed you like that."

I picked at a thread on my jeans. I wanted to forgive my mom, but I was still unsure. Her reaction to my identity was a punch to the gut, but now she seemed willing to accept who I was. Maybe Tristan was right; maybe Mom had changed.

"Is this because of Tristan?" I asked.

She sighed. "Yes, your brother put a lot of things into perspective for us. Helped both of us see that nothing about you would ever change."

This sorta explained why Tristan constantly told me our parents would come around and that maybe I should reach out to them. He was being a little sneak and trying to be the family mediator!

"Now tell me about the guy," she changed the subject.

I cringed. "He's a hockey player."

"Roxie, no! Being a WAG is so hard."

I laughed. "Mom, you were a WAG!"

She laughed with me. "It's so hard with them being away all the time. Then when they get hurt, you can't take the pain away from them, no matter how much you want to. But tell me about him."

So I did. I talked to my mom for the first time in years and told her all about Benny and our whirlwind romance. It was so odd.

I still had apprehension about forgiving my mom, but if she was willing to work at it with me, I was willing to try it too. Our relationship had never been perfect, and it would take a lot to rebuild it, but I would try if she would. It was never too late to say sorry; I knew that better than anyone.

CHAPTER THIRTY-TWO

BENNY

I watched Riley flying across the ice, doing laps. When I got traded to the Bulldogs from the Colorado Blizzard, I wasn't sure what it was going to mean. I didn't even know if the team was going to re-sign me. I spent a year in limbo, and Riley helped me out of my funk. Then the team turned around and signed me to a five-year contract.

Riley skated over to the bench and sprayed ice on me with a cheeky grin. "Dick!" I exclaimed, but I grinned, too.

He poked at my stick with his. "What's with all the rainbow tape? You didn't use to use it all the time," he pointed out.

I liked the diversity stuff we did in the league, even though I still saw a lot of toxic masculinity and racism in hockey. Rox's worries about the media's perception of me if I had fought that guy in Canada weren't unfounded. I was a brown guy who played hockey and was constantly scrutinized by the media in a predominately white sport. I'd seen my fair share of racist shit in the game over the years.

Last season, some douche playing for San Jose called me a Mexican slur, and nothing fucking happened. No fine, not even a penalty, so I knew the league still had a long way to go. It wasn't just race stuff, either. Some guys might sneer at you on the ice using a gay slur too. In my case, sometimes it was a gay *and* racist slur. I wanted to be a part of the culture change. Maybe that was part of the reason I wrapped the top of my stick with rainbow tape.

Riley nudged me. "Well?"

"You know my sister's gay," I said.

"Yeah, but you usually only use the rainbow tape when we're asked to," he argued back.

"Rox is bisexual."

"Oh. Right. So you gonna use that tape from now on?"

"Why not?" I asked.

We skated to center ice and started doing shooting drills. Riley wanted to focus on what we were doing wrong and what he could do to help defend the net. Wouldn't have been surprised if he made me watch video after we were done today. The guy was obsessed with stats and going back to watch as much video as possible. He'd probably be an excellent coach after he retired. If G wasn't already the captain, he would have been next in line. He already had the "A" on his jersey.

"So how pissed was Rox about the Boston reports?" Riley asked when he blocked my shot into the net.

I sighed. "Don't remind me. We almost broke up because of it."

"Dude, I TOLD you she would be pissed."

"I put it out there that if they were thinking of trading me, I wanted to go to Boston, but I want to stay here."

Riley laughed at me again. "You're a dumbass."

"I know. I should have listened to you. I almost lost her today." I shot the puck past him into the net.

He shook his head at me. "Come on. You here to run drills with me, or what?"

He took off with the puck before I gave him an answer.

I pumped my legs and followed behind him, trying to bat the puck away from him. We scrummed together until our ice time was almost up.

I took off my helmet and ran a hand through my sweaty hair.

"Are you growing out your flow?" Riley asked.

I laughed. "Nah, just been lazy."

"Too busy with a certain dark-haired woman?"

I smirked. "Exactly." I picked my phone up off the ledge of the bench and cringed at all the texts from my sister.

LILIANA: *Abuelo told you NOT to ask for a trade!*

LILIANA: *MICHAEL! Answer me!*

"What's wrong?" Riley asked.

I sighed. "My sister must have seen the reports. I think I need to sort this shit out."

Riley patted me on the back. "Good luck with that one, man."

"I'll deal with it later."

After hitting the showers, I headed back to my condo. I flopped back on my bed and pulled out my phone. I didn't think a text message would be good enough for my sister, so I was going to have to make this a phone call. I sighed and dialed the familiar number.

"MICHAEL!" she screeched into my ear.

"Liliana, calm down," I said.

"You can't jeopardize your career like this." she was still in screech mode.

"I know."

"Then what the fuck, man?"

I sighed. "I asked them to consider Boston if they wanted to trade me."

"MICHAEL!"

"But I don't want to go," I admitted.

She was quiet for a moment. "Okay..." she trailed off and calmed down a little. "Why not?"

"It was before...um...so I kind of have a new girlfriend?"

"Oh, really?"

I could almost see the smirk on my sister's face, even though she was a thousand miles away in Boston.

"Yeah, you would like her. She doesn't take my bullshit, and she yells at me just as much as you do."

Liliana laughed. "Holy shit, did you start dating who I think you did?"

"Yes," I said through gritted teeth.

"Knew it! Yes! I won the pool!"

"You are all a bunch of jerks."

Liliana cackled in my ear. "When do I finally get to meet the famous Roxanne Desjardins?"

I sighed. "I'm not trying to drive her away."

"Hush, you love us, and so will she. Abuelo will be so happy."

"You all need to mind ya business."

"You *are* our business, baby brother. She didn't toss you on your ass when she found out you were trying to leave her?"

I groaned. "She tried, but I made her listen to me, and we worked through it. I don't want to lose her."

"Holy shit, that's so mature. I think you're in a real, healthy, adult relationship now. You love this woman, don't you?"

"Yeah, Lil, I really do."

She made a cooing 'aw' sound. "So what are you gonna do?"

"I don't know," I admitted and fingered a loose thread on my comforter. "Probably call Steve, see if there is anything we need to do, but if they trade me, there's nothing I can do. Rox and I talked about it this morning."

"But you're good, right?"

"Definitely," I said, and I beamed with happiness.

"Then why are you calling me?"

I laughed. "So you would stop freaking out over text messages. I've been training with Riley all afternoon."

"I'm happy for you," Liliana told me, and her voice got soft like she was getting all emotional. Cool, more tears from the women I loved today. "You sound really happy, and I hope you and Roxanne make this work."

"Aw, Liliana! Are you crying?" I asked.

"SHUT UP!" she screeched at me.

"Love ya, sis."

"Love you too, ass wipe." My sister cackled on the other end. "I should warn you, though. Abuelo's mad that you wanted to ruin your career in Philly for him."

I sighed.

My sister sighed on her end too. "I know you want to take care of them. Since Mom and Dad are the way they are, our grandparents are important to you. They're important to me too."

"I want them to be proud of me. I want to make sure they're taken care of."

"They're proud of you. You're a good man, and that's because of Abuelo. He taught you that."

"I want to be worthy of them. They're the best people I

know. Supported me when I needed it and you when you came out."

"They're so proud of you. I'm proud of you, too. Don't forget that."

I talked with my sister for a bit longer. She filled me in on what the kids were up to, and then eventually, she handed the phone off to my grandparents separately so they could get mad at me for asking for a trade.

"You figure things out with your woman?" Abuelo asked.

"Yeah, I did," I admitted.

The old man chuckled. "Told you."

"You were right. I just needed to show her who I was."

"I'm so happy for you, mijo. I can't wait to meet her."

I smiled to myself at that. "She'd love you."

Eventually, I hung up with my family. They had always been supportive, and even though I was estranged from my parents, I knew my grandparents would always be supportive of what I did. It was nice to have them, to have a family that cared about you.

I laid back on my bed and scrolled through my phone. I hadn't seen any texts from Rox today, but I figured she was busy unpacking the rest of her boxes. I should go help her finish up. I scrolled through Instagram and landed on a photo TJ had posted of him and Rox drinking beers and clinking glasses. His caption read, 'When you're a twin, you're never alone because you have a built-in best friend... or a colossal pain in your ass.'

I dropped the phone on the bed beside me and closed my eyes in contentment. I was so tired, I ended up passing out for a few hours.

When I woke up, I heard the front door open and the

sound of TJ's hyena-like laughter. I glanced up when I saw Rox standing in the doorway of my bedroom.

"Tired?" she asked as she walked across the room and over to the bed.

"C'mere you," I said and smiled when she slipped into the bed beside me and curled around my side. I wrapped my arm around her back and hugged her. "I missed you."

She laughed into my chest. "Oh no, what did I do to you? It's only been a few hours."

I kissed the top of her head. "Still missed you."

She glanced up at me. "Missed you too," she admitted.

"Ew, get a room!" TJ teased as he passed my room and went into his own.

Rox gave him the finger.

"You think he'll get over it?" I asked.

She nodded. "He's just teasing you."

"Dick."

She laughed. "Totally! Hey, guess what?"

"What, angel?"

"I talked to my mom today."

She was biting her lip, so I wasn't sure how I was supposed to react. "That's...good?"

She nodded. "I think so. She apologized for her reaction. She still doesn't understand bisexuality, but she wants to repair our relationship."

I squeezed her towards me. "Hey, that's great!"

She sighed.

"Not great?" I asked and furrowed my brow in confusion.

She shook her head. "No, it's weird, but if my parents want to make up for everything, I'm willing to forgive them. All I ever wanted was for them to accept me."

I pulled her wrist to my lips and kissed her maple leaf tattoo. "I accept you. All of you, always."

"I love you," she said.

I leaned my forehead against hers. "I love you too."

"Benny, I'm a difficult person. You know that, right?"

I cupped her face. "I enjoy a challenge. I'm not going anywhere."

She kissed me fiercely in response. "Promise?" she asked when she pulled away.

"I'm always gonna fight for you, bad girl. Always."

Her smile could have lit up the whole room, but then she kissed me again, and everything else melted away.

EPILOGUE

8 MONTHS LATER
ROXANNE

I was wrapping rainbow tape on my stick when my teammate Kelly nudged my elbow.

"What?" I snapped.

Yeah, it was Beer League, but I still didn't like to be bothered when I was going through my pre-game rituals. I ended up joining this team because Dinah's brother Eddie was the captain, and when I had gotten my fourth tattoo last summer in his shop, we got to talking about it. Tonight was the final game of our season, and I was ready to bring it home.

Kelly laughed and showed me her phone. "That's your man, right?" she asked.

On the screen was a video from the Bulldogs game where Benny was getting interviewed during warm-ups. The Bulldogs were at home tonight for the first game in the first round of the playoffs. I was so proud of them, but unfortunately, I had my own game to win tonight, so I couldn't cheer on my love.

I watched the video and saw the interviewer point to the rainbow tape on Benny's stick.

"Why use that tape all the time?" the reporter asked.

Benny ran his hand through his freshly cut dark hair. "My sister's gay and my partner's bisexual, so I felt like it was one way I could let the two women I love the most in the world know I support them. That I support the LGBT+ community and want to be a good ally."

"Is diversity an important thing for you in hockey?"

"Of course. I want kids like me to see themselves not only out here on the ice but as fans too. Hockey should be for everyone, but we still have a lot of work to do in that regard. There needs to be a culture change."

"Thanks, Benny. Good luck in the game," the reporter said, and then Benny skated away.

I smiled while I finished taping my stick and laced up my skates. Benny was getting tired of being asked about the tape on his stick all the time, but the media liked to ask the same questions about guys who spoke out all the time. It always made me proud to hear his answer.

"Yeah, that's him," I said with a grin.

"Damn, he's FIIINE. How did you land him?" Kelly asked.

I laughed. "Funny story: we used to hate each other."

Allison, our goaltender, threw a towel in our direction. "Enough chit-chat, ladies. We have a game to win!"

"You got it!" I cheered and pulled my jersey over my head. "You know, if it wasn't for that insufferable man, I wouldn't be playing with you guys right now."

They both laughed.

"I think I owe that man a beer," Kelly said.

I laughed and shook my head at her. I finished taping up my stick and prepared to get out on the ice.

Playing on this team was everything I wanted. Yeah, the ice surface could suck, and sometimes half your team mysteriously disappeared, but playing this game I loved again was all I wanted. Benny had been nagging me about PHF free agency, but playing for fun took the pressure off my shoulders. If we won tonight, we would win the championship.

I skated onto the ice and started doing my stretches while Kelly and Eddie took some laps around our zone. I took some practice shots at Allison and did my own laps before the game started.

When the game started, I took the opening face-off at puck drop. I carried the puck up the left side of the offensive zone. The lumbering defenseman on the opposing team was after me, so I flicked the shot back to Eddie, but he couldn't complete it, and it got turned over in the neutral zone. I raced down the ice, trying to get the puck out of our zone and out of Allison's crease. Adrenaline pumped through my veins, and even though my legs were on fire, I loved being back on the ice.

During the change-up, I hobbled onto the bench exhausted and took a gulp of water. I had probably two minutes before I needed to be back on the ice. You played a lot of ice time in Beer League, especially when half your bench disappeared.

This game was cutthroat since it was for the championship, which was really just bragging rights, but I didn't care. It meant a championship!

Because of the lack of a bench, we skated hard all night long. My chest was heavy, and I felt like I was going to pass out. During a turnover, I got possession of the puck, and I skated down the ice on the breakaway. I took the shot with no hesitation. I didn't see if the goal made it in until my teammates were skating back on the ice and hugging me.

"We did it!" Eddie cheered, and he patted me on the back. Kelly and Allison dive-bombed me with hugs. I couldn't believe that shot went in!

Afterward, in the locker room, Kelly tossed me a beer. "Shotgun that shit, Hockey Girl!" she ordered.

I did as she asked while my teammates cheered me on.

"Bar?" Allison asked.

"Eileen's?" I asked hopefully. I was planning on catching up with Benny there tonight anyway.

"Where else?" Kelly teased.

"It is THE hockey bar in Philly. I need to shower first, though," I said.

I took a quick shower and told them I'd meet them over at the bar. Eileen's had become a major hot spot for me since I moved here. The owners Marc and Hal were ex-Bulldogs, and they both reminded me of my dad. Especially Marc, since he was French-Canadian like Dad.

When I exited the locker room after my shower, I came face-to-face with my parents standing in the lobby waiting for me. Dad was beaming, and my mom was holding a glass vase with cherry blossom branches arranged neatly together. It surprised me to see them because I didn't know they were coming to my game.

"Mom? Dad?"

Instead of an answer, Dad pulled me into that big bear hug of his. "Roxie girl, that goal!"

"Hon, let her breathe," Mom said.

Dad laughed and let me go.

"Here, for you," Mom said to me and handed me the vase of flowers.

I touched a petal and realized they were real. Cherry

blossoms were hard to find and expensive, but Mom was trying because she knew they were my favorite.

It had almost been a year since I moved to Philadelphia, but in that time, I had been working on mending my relationship with my parents. My relationship with Dad went back to normal, like nothing had happened. I was still me, I just happened to be bi. With Mom, we still had our moments, but she was trying, and I appreciated the effort.

"Thanks, Mom," I said. "But what are you doing here?"

Dad shook his head. "Wanted to see you play."

"You should play for the PHF!" Mom exclaimed.

I shook my head. "Nah. I like beer league."

Dad frowned. "We'll talk about that later."

I rolled my eyes. All the men in my life were making it their goal to convince me I should play professionally. If the PHF ever got a Philly team, maybe I'd consider it.

"Have you seen Benny today?" Mom asked.

I shook my head. "Nah, I left work before he got to the arena. We're gonna meet up at Eileen's."

"I could use a drink," Dad said.

I shook my keys at him. "I can drive you over unless you got a rental car."

Dad took my gear bag and hefted it over his large shoulder. "Nope, we'll ride with you. We can talk about all those dropped passes you made in the first period."

"Hon!" Mom scolded.

I shook my head. Of course, my father, a Stanley Cup winner, wanted to break down all my mistakes in my game. Even though I scored the game-winning goal.

I let Dad talk while we got into my little Honda Civic and drove over to the bar. The rink I played at was on the other side of Philly, which was a pain since the team always went to Eileen's after a game.

When we got to the bar, my parents sat at the bar and struck up a conversation with Halvard Holmstrom. Despite being the owner, Hal was hands-on at the bar. I think he just liked to talk hockey with all the fans and players who frequented his bar.

I found my teammates in our usual booth in the back. Eddie Mezzanetti gave me a hug. "Let me grab you a beer."

I grimaced. "Sorry, my parents surprised me, so I'm gonna hang with them."

He waved me off. "I get it, but let me buy you a beer first for scoring that game-winning goal."

I smiled. "Okay."

I introduced Eddie to my parents while he bought me a beer, and eventually, he wandered off back to the team.

"Are you in town long?" I asked my parents while I watched the Bulldogs game on the TV above the bar.

"The weekend," Mom said.

I nodded. "Okay, let's do dinner tomorrow?"

Dad nodded. "We can go over what you need to work on next season."

"Don't listen to your father. You looked good on the ice," Mom said.

"Thanks, Mom," I said and tipped more beer into my mouth.

Dad would be the annoying hockey coach now that I was playing again. I understood why Tristan complained about his pointers now.

"But..." she said and trailed off.

I narrowed my eyes. "But what?"

"You should play professionally!" Dad said.

I shook my head at him.

I hung with my parents at the bar, watching the rest of

the game and the post-game interviews. I beamed while watching Benny doing his post-game interview.

A little while later, I saw Dinah and Fi enter the bar with a couple of the other WAGs. I knew it wouldn't be long before the team showed up. I wanted to be in my bed, but Benny had been on the road all week, and I wanted to see him. I was willing to lose sleep if that meant I got to see him.

When I saw him enter the bar a little while later, I jumped up from my seat. His dark brown eyes honed in on me, and he smiled when I ran over and jumped into his arms.

"Missed you," I whispered into his ear as I nuzzled into his neck.

He laughed and held onto my hips tightly. "I missed you so much, Rox."

"You're here!" I cheered happily.

He pushed my hair out of my face. "I raced out of the locker room as soon as I could. I heard you won."

I nodded. "I got the game-winning goal."

He gently put me back down on the ground. "I wished I could have seen it, angel."

"S'okay. Did you know my parents came to see my game?"

He nodded, but he was being shifty. There was something he wasn't telling me. "Yeah, they wanted to surprise you."

"We're gonna do dinner with them tomorrow."

He smiled big at me. He then eyed my parents, who gave him a thumbs up. What was that about?

"Love?" I asked.

He looked back at me, and I noticed Benny looked nervous. What did he have to be nervous about?

"Can't wait. But I really want you tangled up in my sheets right now," he said with a grin.

"Your place or mine?" I asked.

Benny frowned at my question. "I want to show you something. Will you ride with me?"

"But my car's here."

"Okay, follow me then?"

I nodded, but I was still suspicious, especially when I looked back and saw my parents give Benny a look of encouragement.

What was going on? Shit, was he proposing? I didn't want to get married, and neither did he. Right? No, he wouldn't do that. He would talk to me about it first. Wouldn't he?

I shook my thoughts away and climbed into my car. I followed Benny's SUV out of the parking lot. At first, I thought we were heading back to his place since we were going to Old City, but then we took a different turn. When he parked, I went around the block to find a parking spot elsewhere. He must have jogged to find me because he was waiting on the sidewalk outside for me when I got out of my car. He took my hand in his, and we walked up to a condo building and went into the lobby.

I didn't know what was going on. Maybe this was one of the other guys' places and we were going over for drinks? That didn't make sense if he said he wanted to show me something.

I should have been suspicious when the front desk concierge waved to Benny like he knew him. He pushed the elevator button, and we went up to the fourth floor. I followed him to a door before I finally made him stop.

"Okay, what's going on?" I asked.

He produced a key and opened the door. He opened it

to a mostly empty but new-looking condo. We walked into the hall with a kitchen to our left that had granite countertops and Sub-Zero appliances. There was a lot of open space, which I assumed was the living area, and there was a little balcony outside in front of us. I walked further into the room and noticed there was a small staircase. Benny nodded at me, and I walked up to find a bedroom with an en-suite bath. His bed was set up in the bedroom, as well as his dresser, but not much else.

I looked at him in confusion.

"What do you think?" he asked.

"Nice, but I'm confused? Why's your bed here?"

He crossed the room to me and put his hands on my hips. "Because I bought this place."

"Oh! Oh, that's good. You shouldn't still have a roommate."

"See, that's where you're wrong. I would very much like to have a roommate."

I raised an eyebrow. "Okay..." I trailed off, still not sure what he was trying to say to me.

"One to share my bed with. Maybe a Lily-white Canadian girl with sexy tattoos and a dirty mouth."

I gaped at him. "Wait...are you asking me to move in with you?"

"Angel, we aren't marriage people, but I love you, and I think you're my forever."

"What?" I asked in surprise.

"I know it's hard with me being on the road all the time. But I want you here when I get home and there in the morning when I wake up. I want to build my life with you as my partner."

"This is...unexpected."

"What do you say, Rox? Will you move in with me?" he

asked. I nodded and swiped at my eyes. He pulled me into his chest. "Aw, don't cry."

"I'm sorry!"

He looked down at me and kissed the top of my head. "What do you say?"

"Yes! Yes, I want to share my life with you too. But my lease isn't up for another couple of months."

"I know, but that gives us time to merge our stuff and make this place ours."

I laughed into his chest. "You're such a soft boy."

"You love it."

"I do..." I trailed off and eyed up his neatly made-up bed.

He had been on the road all week, so I didn't know when he had time to do all this. I wondered if his sister had something to do with this. She had harped on us about settling down at Christmas. Of course, she meant marriage and babies, and it got his entire family started in on us. Maybe our moving in together would placate her for a few years.

"When did you have time to do all this?" I asked.

"Doesn't matter," he muttered as he cupped my face.

"Oh my God—my mother helped you!" I exclaimed.

He laughed. "Busted. And your dad."

"That's why they're in town."

"And to see you."

I breathed a sigh of relief. "Shit, I thought you were gonna propose, and then I was gonna say no!"

He shook his head. "Nope. I know we're on the same page about that. We don't need to get married to prove our love for each other. But I want to live with you and annoy you every day for as long as you let me."

I grinned. "I thought I was the annoying one?"

"Will you just kiss me already?"

Before I could protest, he bent his head to mine and captured my lips in a searing, passionate kiss.

"We're gonna christen the bed, right?" I asked when we came up for air.

He lifted me up into his arms and kissed me senseless. I took that as a FUCK YES!

I never thought that I would have found love with this man, never in a million years, but now that I had, I never wanted to let him go. I didn't deserve Michael Bennett, but he sure did everything in his power to prove to me he would fight for me. Always.

***

ACKNOWLEDGMENTS

Whew! I can't believe this book is finally out! I know Benny and Rox's story has been one that has long been awaited, so I hope you all love their story as much as I do. I've been pretty open about the fact that they are my favorite couple for a lot of reasons. I loved writing this big burly hockey player who is really just a soft boy and writing a truly ASSHOLE of a heroine. Hi, guess why I love her so much?

I love Rox. When I put on dark lipstick, I feel like I am channeling her. I wish I could have come to terms with my own sexuality as soon as she did. But it's okay, because she prodded me to come out and feel okay within my own bisexuality. Because of that, this story is probably my most personal to date. Which makes it so much scarier to release to the world.

I have a lot of people to thank for helping bring this book to fruition.

First my soul sisters for letting me constantly annoy them in the group chat on a daily basis. And for telling me that they liked the cover and didn't think it screamed St. Paddy's Day like my partner thought. LOL.

My beta team, Becky, Chris, Jim, you all helped me so much with this book, like you have with the other ones. Also shoutout to Kat Obie who helped immensely with the hockey player stuff and fixing some of the errors in the book. Your insider knowledge as a hockey player were so helpful!

I also want to thank Melissa Cruz from Salt and Sage for sensitivity reading this piece. I appreciate your thoughtful comments to help me get Benny right. I hope I did him justice.

Thanks again to my editor Charlie Knight for working on this one too. I'm glad you loved Benny and Rox as much as I do, and I can't wait to give you more of the Bulldogs series!

And to you dear reader, for taking another chance on me and reading this book. I hope you are enjoying this series. There are more coming soon, I promise!

ALSO BY DANICA FLYNN

PHILADELPHIA BULLDOGS

Take The Shot

Score Her Heart

Against The Boards

MACGREGOR BROTHERS BREWING COMPANY

Accidentally In Love

ABOUT THE AUTHOR

Danica Flynn is a marketer by day, and a writer by nights and weekends. AKA she doesn't sleep! She is a rabid hockey fan of both The Philadelphia Flyers and the Metropolitan Riveters. When not writing, she can be found hanging with her partner, playing video games, and reading a ton of books.

CPSIA information can be obtained
at www.ICGtesting.com
Printed in the USA
BVHW041841120222
628675BV00010B/22